CONQUERED BY THE VIKING

ASHE BARKER

Published by Stormy Night Publications and Design, LLC.
www.StormyNightPublications.com

Cover design by Korey Mae Johnson
www.koreymaejohnson.com

Images by Period Images and Dreamstime/Vian1980

1st Print Edition. February 2018

ISBN-13: 978-1985704794

ISBN-10: 198570479X

FOR AUDIENCES 18+ ONLY

This book is intended for adults only. Spanking and other sexual activities represented in this book are fantasies only, intended for adults.

CHAPTER ONE

The girl straightened, rubbed her aching back with her grimy palm. She flung the shovel aside, then fell to her knees, weeping. The mound of soft earth mocked her, a permanent memorial to all she had lost. All that had been savagely ripped from her by the bastard Norsemen as they rampaged through her land, taking what they wanted and trampling the rest.

Her father, murdered. Her two older brothers, taken as slaves. Her mother, raped and left for dead.

Merewyn herself had only escaped their vile attentions because her mother, Ronat, had chosen that day to replenish her supplies of herbal remedies. Skilled in the art of healing and herbal potions, Ronat had declared herself in need of the horehound required to prepare a linctus to relieve the coughing that often beset Merewyn's father during the winter months. Perhaps a little marjoram might also be found, and if she was lucky a few sprigs of rosemary and sage too. Ronat had clambered up to the top of the cliffs in search of the elusive plants and had spotted the dreaded dragon ships as they swept in from the sea. She had run back to their cottage and had bid her daughter to flee, to hide in the forest and not return until all was quiet.

Merewyn did as she was told. Terror lent her the speed she needed to escape. She ran as hard and as far as she could through the thickly wooded terrain. She ran until her sides burned and her legs collapsed under her and she could run no further. Then, she climbed.

For two days Merewyn had crouched in the fork of an ancient oak, her ears attuned to the slightest sound that might indicate she had been discovered. The occasional scream reached her, sometimes a guttural cry of pain or terror, or the triumphant roars of their attackers as the Viking warriors pillaged and robbed and burnt the Celtic homesteads scattered along the Northumbrian coastline. Throughout it all Merewyn cowered in the tree, dreading the heavy tread of leather boots, the clash of those great iron swords against the trunk of her refuge.

The Vikings didn't find her. Eventually the forest fell silent, yet still Merewyn waited. Another full night and half the next day she huddled in her hiding place, too terrified to return to her home. Only the dread prospect of a third night without food or shelter forced her from the tree. Slowly, cautiously, her heart leaping at every whisper in the branches above her, every rustle in the undergrowth beneath her feet, she made her way home.

She emerged from the woodland into the clearing that had been her family's small farm to find nothing but smoking ruins. Their cottage was destroyed, the thatch roof gone, the walls charred and crumbling. Her father and brothers had harvested their crops not more than a sennight before, their precious food safely stored to see them through the winter. The barn, what remained of it, now stood empty and ruined. The Nordic invaders had not even taken their grain and hay, they had simply scattered it and trampled the supplies into the dirt.

Merewyn had combed the smouldering wreckage in search of her family. She quickly found her father's body, his throat cut, but there was no sign of her mother or brothers. At seventeen summers Merewyn was the youngest. Her twin brothers, Nyle and Bowdyn, were twenty. Tall, strapping young men both, Nyle was soon to be wed to Deva, a lass from a neighbouring farmstead. Merewyn had looked forward to having a sister at last.

Now, they were gone. She did not know if they lived still or had died in the attack. Lost, bewildered, Merewyn had wandered aimlessly through the debris searching for any remnant of her former life, anything left undamaged by the Vikings. She found nothing.

It was only when she ventured behind the barn in search of stray livestock that might have miraculously eluded the Norsemen's vicious axes that she discovered her mother lying battered among the rubble.

But, Ronat lived. Merewyn knelt beside the prone form, dribbled water from the stream onto her mother's parched lips and cleansed the wounds on her face and body as best she could. At last, driven by a purpose, Merewyn fashioned a crude shelter from what remained of their cottage and dragged Ronat into the protection it offered. She tended her, and over the coming days and weeks her mother regained some of her strength. When Ronat regained consciousness she was able to tell the story, or those bits of it that she could recall. Merewyn learned that Nyle and Bowdyn had been led in chains, along with other healthy young men and women, to the dragon ships. They would be made slaves, forced to toil for the Viking conquerors. The old, the sick, the very young—they were slaughtered and left behind.

Ronat refused to say what had happened to her, just that the Vikings had caught her as she attempted to flee. Merewyn did not press the matter. She was thankful that anyone was left alive.

Soon, Ronat was able to sit up, and under her direction Merewyn managed to salvage enough food to sustain them in the immediate aftermath of the raid. As Ronat regained her strength, the pair of them worked to restore what they could. Their first, and grimmest, task was to bury Merewyn's father. Next, they repaired the cottage as best they could, gathered straw and twigs to re-thatch the roof, and Merewyn scoured the forest for any of their livestock that might remain. She found two goats and half a dozen chickens. It was a start.

They fashioned pens from the debris, and Merewyn could have whooped for joy when she collected her first two eggs. The goats were less productive since neither had any milk, but they might yield meat should times become seriously hard over the winter.

As Ronat and Merewyn ventured further afield in search of what aid might be found, they learned that no one in the vicinity had fared any better than they. Neighbouring farms were laid waste like theirs, crops stolen or destroyed. All who had survived were hungry and wretched. Two women living alone would be easy prey for the greedy or the plain desperate. Ronat insisted they be ready to defend what was theirs, meagre though it was. During those first dire weeks they took it in turn to sleep, and kept a shovel or scythe to hand in case of unwelcome intruders.

Four months passed, the most miserable, fearful winter Merewyn had ever known. She and Ronat mourned those they had lost as they battled to survive. As the snow started they huddled shivering around the flickering flames of their paltry fire, fuelled by the few lumps of wood or sticks they could collect. They lived off eggs until the hens ceased to lay, then they made do with nuts and what berries remained on the trees and bushes. They foraged the woods for anything edible, and made soup from nettles. Eventually they slaughtered their goats. Mostly, they went hungry.

It was not until the spring, when the snow melted and the first shoots of new growth started to prick the frigid earth, that Merewyn realised that her mother was pregnant. Ronat still refused to speak of the Vikings, would not discuss her condition or how it came about. Merewyn had been brought up on a farm, had lived among livestock her entire life so she understood the basic facts of life. She also understood that in a few more months they would have another mouth to feed, somehow.

It was midsummer when Ronat went into labour. They had been tending their crop of turnips, daring to hope that, along with the carrots and beans they had managed to plant and the wheat that now swayed in the gentle breeze, they might have sufficient food to take them through the next winter. Ronat suddenly dropped her rake and clutched at her distended belly. Liquid dribbled from between her legs onto the earth at her feet. Merewyn helped her mother back to the cottage and eased her onto the pallet they shared. There was no aid to be had, no wise women on the neighbouring farms experienced in birthing who would come to assist. It was just Merewyn, and she did her best.

Her best turned out to be good enough, though only just. After two days of labour, Merewyn's tiny brother slithered into the world. Ronat insisted that he be named Connell, after her dead husband. For herself, she had survived the birth, but the experience had drained what remained of her strength. Broken, haggard, Ronat was barely able to crawl from the pallet, unable to do anything apart from feed the squalling infant.

Merewyn returned to the fields. She worked alone, dragging what sustenance she could from the unrelenting earth to provide food for what remained of her family. She toiled from sunrise until darkness fell. Then she slept, exhausted from her labours.

Ronat did what she could to help her daughter, but her health was broken. Reduced to just pottering about the cottage, she never recovered her former vitality and almost four months after the birth of her baby son, she succumbed to a fever. She died in Merewyn's arms.

Once again, Merewyn dug a grave, but this time she did it alone. Now, her mother lay in the cold earth beside her father. Merewyn wept at the graveside, tears of bitter frustration and abject fear for what the future might hold. She knew herself to be truly alone in the world, apart from the tiny scrap of humanity who even now whimpered on the ground at her side, demanding to be fed.

Merewyn gathered Connell to her and staggered to her feet. She eased back the threadbare shawl that enveloped him and mustered a tearful smile. The baby gazed back at her, his blue eyes a permanent reminder of his Nordic heritage. It was a detail Merewyn chose to ignore. Whatever his origins this tiny child was her blood, the last link to her mother. There was no one else.

"Do not be afraid, little man. I shall take care of you. Of us. We *will* survive."

Merewyn turned, left the graves behind. She made her weary way back to the cottage. She had work to do.

• • • • • • •

One year later…

Her eyes hurt. Her ears ached. Even the ends of her hair pained her. Every movement was agony, her joints stiff and sore. Merewyn forced her eyelids apart.

Rain battered the thatch above her, the steady drip somewhere to her left a sure sign that the roof was leaking again. It would require fixing, but not now. Not today, when it took all the strength she had just to lift her shoulders from the mattress.

Merewyn rolled onto her side and reached for the cot that stood beside her pallet. Connell was awake, his miserable, hungry cries stirring her to action.

She was ill, the malady creeping up on her over recent days. First her throat became sore, and her head ached. She was hot, then so cold her teeth chattered, then she was drenched with sweat again. She could not eat, and she could barely get to her feet. She had managed to prepare some warm milk and a little honey for Connell the previous evening, before collapsing onto her bed. She had slept fitfully, tossing and turning, her throat afire with every swallow. Now in the cold light of a stormy autumn morn, she could no longer stand unaided.

But she must, for Connell could not tend himself. If she did not feed him the baby would starve. It was that simple. Merewyn struggled to sit up, then shoved her feet out from under the rough wool blanket. There was a little bread still, she thought, if she could just reach the jar in which it was stored. That and some of the broth she made a few days ago would have to suffice to pacify Connell's hunger. Perhaps by tomorrow she would feel well enough to venture outside, maybe forage for mushrooms or blackberries.

Clutching the blanket around herself, she made her unsteady way across the one-roomed cottage, hanging on to what sticks of furniture graced their sparse home. She reached the cold slab by the door where an earthenware pot stood. With dismay, she peered into the depths of the jar and found it empty.

No bread. And she knew she'd used the last of the honey yesterday. Connell whined, his plaintive cries causing her head to throb. In desperation Merewyn lifted the lids on each of the storage barrels lining the walls. All stood empty, waiting for her to regain sufficient strength to go out to the barn to bring in more grain to be ground into flour. A hessian sack yielded one solitary carrot, but that was it.

Connell hated carrots.

Merewyn groaned. There was nothing else for it. She had to go out. Wild brambles sprouted from the crevices on the cliffs, and she knew them to be laden with ripe fruit. She could take the empty jar and collect enough to satisfy Connell for a day or two. The walk there, usually just a few minutes, would probably take an hour in this foul weather and feeling as ill as she did, especially as she would have to carry Connell on her back. The child was just starting to walk but was not yet able to manage the rough terrain beyond their cottage. Merewyn looked longingly back to her rumpled bed. She swayed on her feet, but couldn't weaken.

"Please, do not cry so. I shall find something for you to

eat. We must go up the meadow and…" She could not complete her attempt to comfort the child as she collapsed in a fit of hacking coughs. Bent double, Merewyn fought for breath, for the strength to carry on.

She found both, somewhere. Slowly, painfully, she pulled on her leather boots. They had been her brother's, and were too large for her. The soles leaked too, but they were the best she had. She dragged a shawl around her shoulders, then hoisted the sling she used to carry Connell. She picked up the wriggling child and managed to install him in the harness on her back, then clutched the empty jar before pulling a blanket over the pair of them.

She cracked open the door and was at once whipped by the angry, gusting wind. Sharp, stinging rain spattered against her face. It was a day for slamming the door shut, bolting it and huddling inside before a roaring hearth. She needed firewood too. Perhaps, on the way back…

Bending into the wind, Merewyn concentrated on placing one foot before the other. Her progress was slow, painfully, agonisingly slow as she climbed the gentle incline toward the cliffs. She sheltered under the trees where she could, but such respite was sparse. Mostly she was exposed to the inhospitable elements, fighting her way through the teeth of the gale. On several occasions she stumbled to her knees, but each time she managed to get to her feet. Vile though this journey was, it was preferable to collapsing out here and freezing to death.

At last she reached the sandy cliff path. To her right brambles covered the rocks, tumbling over the large boulders. The ripe fruit glittered, dark and juicy and plentiful. She would soon fill her jar.

Merewyn offered up thanks as she plucked at the plump berries, passing several to Connell to satisfy his immediate needs. The rest she dropped into her pot until the vessel was filled to the rim. Soaked to the skin now, but satisfied with a job well done, she tucked the jar under her blanket and straightened her aching back. Unless she was mistaken, the wind was dropping. Perhaps the worst of the weather was past. Merewyn gazed out across the choppy North Sea, and her breath caught in her throat.

A dragon ship lay on its side, perhaps half a mile out to sea. The mast was broken, the crimson sail tattered and flapping in the waves. The proud serpent that graced the prow was almost fully submerged. Despite the sorry state of the Viking longship, and the absence of any sign of life aboard, Merewyn still retreated in horror.

Vikings! Here, again! The Nordic savages had returned.

She must get back to her cottage, barricade herself and Connell inside. She had weapons, tools with which she might protect herself and her baby brother. The shovel was heavy and sturdy, her scythe was freshly sharpened.

Still clutching her precious jar, and conscious that these berries might be all the sustenance they had for the foreseeable future, Merewyn hurried downhill. The going was rough, treacherous and slippery from the recent rain. She constantly lost her footing. It was after slithering into the ditch for the third time that she opted to take a less arduous route, skirting the woods to approach her cottage from the rear. It would take longer but she lacked the strength to make the more direct journey.

"Hush, please, be silent…" she admonished Connell when he started to grizzle again. "They must not take us. We shall soon be home…"

She lurched from one tree to the next, hanging on to the wet trunks to steady herself as she staggered toward her home. She paused to wipe her hand across her brow, pushing the sodden blanket from her face. Had she not done so, she might have missed him.

The Viking lay face down, motionless, not twenty feet from her. His light blond hair was matted with blood, his woollen tunic ripped at the shoulder. He wore wool breeches, and was missing a boot.

For several moments Merewyn stood, rooted to the spot. She stared at the apparition before her, barely daring to breathe. What to do? How should she deal with this man, this threat to her meagre existence?

He did not move. Was he dead? Oh, sweet Jesu, she hoped so for that would spare her the task of killing him. She might loathe and fear the Vikings, but even so Merewyn baulked at cold-blooded murder. Still, she would do what she must. It was him or them.

She retreated behind a tree where she set her blanket on the ground, along with the jar of blackberries. Then she hauled Connell from the sling and placed him next to her things. "Be quiet and stay here. I will not be long." It was best he not witness what would happen next.

Merewyn coughed painfully as she approached the prone Norseman. Her lungs hurt, a stabbing ache under her ribs. Her head pounded, and she could barely see straight. Desperation kept her moving though, and she circled the large body, peering at the Viking for any sign of life. She could now see that the blood on his head came from a wound on his temple. A vicious-looking bruise bloomed there, and he had an ugly gash on his arm also. The man must have come from the wrecked dragon ship, and had not fared well in his encounter with the sea.

Merewyn crouched beside him, taking care to maintain a safe distance. The man lay face down so she could not see if his chest moved or not. There was nothing else for it. She managed to screw up enough courage to reach out and place the backs of her fingers close to his mouth and nose.

Breath tickled her skin. The sensation was soft, barely there, but offered the proof she needed. Dreaded. The Viking lived still, and therefore he was dangerous. Deadly.

She would have to kill him.

Merewyn had no weapon with her. She cursed herself for leaving behind the sharp knife she used for preparing vegetables. She considered smothering him with the blanket she had left behind the trees, but dismissed that notion. What if he recovered consciousness? Injured arm or not, he would easily overpower her. She might fashion some sort of noose with her shawl and attempt to strangle him, but the same objections applied. No, she needed to do something that did not rely upon her strength to succeed.

Her gaze fell on the rocks that lay strewn about them on the forest floor. If she could just manage to lift one of those, a heavy one, she could clout him on the head with it. Surely, he would not survive such an assault, not on top of his existing injuries. But she must hurry. He might regain consciousness at any moment.

She scrambled across the muddy ground to the closest rocks. She tried one, then another, but they were too large. In her weakened state she couldn't lift them. Merewyn sobbed in desperation as she moved to the next pile. Kneeling beside these, she found one that she was able to grapple into her arms. She tested the weight. It would have to do.

Merewyn got to her feet, the boulder cradled in her embrace. She turned back to the unconscious Viking and cried out in terror. His eyes were open. They were blue, she noted, irrelevantly, and they followed her as she approached him. He opened his mouth as though to speak, but no words emerged.

"I am sorry..." mouthed Merewyn as she lifted the heavy rock.

"Stop!" The shout echoed through the air, loud, urgent.

Merewyn spun, off balance. The boulder fell useless from her grasp to roll away across the ground. Another Viking emerged from the woodland, his harsh features angry. He was handsome, she thought, for a Norse savage. And very, very big. His dark blond hair hung dripping wet around his broad shoulders and his eyes were the deep cerulean blue she recognised as typically Viking. His clothing, similar to that worn by the man on the ground, was also wet. Two more equally damp Norsemen followed him from the trees.

Merewyn barely had time to take in these few details before the leader, the one who had shouted at her, charged forward to seize her around the middle. The pair of them hurtled into the undergrowth. Merewyn knew one final, jolting wave of pain and swore that every bone in her body had shattered. Then she sank into dark, blessed oblivion.

CHAPTER TWO

"Steady the mast. Swing her about. Hold on…"

Mathios yelled his instructions as his men scurried to obey. The deck heaved under their feet, the sturdy craft tossing and twisting on the turbulent waves. Built for speed and stability, the dragon ship was his pride and joy and could cope with most conditions but was wholly overwhelmed by the force of this sudden storm. Mathios knew it. They would be fortunate indeed to survive this gale.

"Look out!" He bellowed the warning, but too late. The rope securing the lower edge of the bright red sail had snapped, whipping around to hit one of his men in the middle of the back. The man toppled overboard to sink without a trace, and the now loosened sail flapped crazily in the gale.

"Grab it. Make it secure. You, and you, help me…" Mathios dived for the dangling edge of the sail only to have it snatched from his grip by a gust of wind. "Fuck! Lower the sail. We might yet save the ship."

It was a losing battle, but Mathios and his men fought it anyway because the alternative was worse. It was only when the craft tilted to the right and capsized onto her side that he ordered his men to abandon ship. "Grab what you can, anything that might float. Make for the beach."

Mathios was the last to hurl himself over the side, reluctant even now to leave his doomed ship to her fate. He grabbed at an oar as it swirled past, narrowly missing his head. It provided enough buoyancy to keep him afloat in the churning waves. The current carried him toward the shore, perhaps a mile or so distant. He twisted in the water and saw that several of his men were also managing to remain afloat. A reasonable swimmer himself, he knew that for many of his men this was a skill they had never mastered. Vikings preferred to rely on their ships. Mathios called out words of encouragement to them.

"We're not dead yet. Get ashore. It's not too far. We'll regroup on the beach."

The man closest to him, Ormarr, lifted a hand to acknowledge his words. There was nothing more Mathios could do until they were safe on dry land. He kicked hard, and turned his face toward the rocky Northumbrian coastline.

Despite the sudden violent squall that had wrecked his precious ship, the elements appeared to be on Mathios' side as he struck out for the shore. The current helped, the waves finally depositing him face down on the sandy beach. Coughing saltwater from his mouth, Mathios scrambled onto all fours to check to his left and right.

There.

He recognised the blue tunic of Olav, his cousin and second-in-command, and the green leggings worn by young Vikarr. It was the lad's first experience of seafaring and Mathios hoped he would not be too discouraged by the watery outcome this day. Sooner or later this happened to all of them; such were the vagaries of the sea.

Mathios knelt up, scanned the beach for more survivors. He called out to Olav. "Who else made it?"

"I saw Hakon. He was at my side..." Olav stood up and limped toward Mathios. "Yes, there he is. And Ormarr too."

Mathios turned to look in the direction indicated by his

cousin. Two battered figures made their way across the beach, teetering on unsteady legs. Mathios raised an arm in greeting.

"Over here. To me."

The five men hugged and clapped each other on the back, relief at their deliverance from the waves writ across all their features.

"Anyone else?" Mathios was conscious that he had sailed with fourteen men. He knew that one of them, Njal, had likely drowned when he was knocked overboard by the loose sail, but that left nine unaccounted for.

"Arne. He made it to the shore, definitely. I saw him on the beach while I was still out there." Hakon gestured with his thumb to indicate the roiling ocean at their rear. "He was heading up toward the trees."

"What the fuck for? I told everyone to meet here, on the beach." Exasperated, Mathios scanned the edge of the forest that extended right down to the shore.

"Maybe he didn't hear. Or needed a piss." Hakon shrugged as he offered the explanation. "I definitely saw him, Jarl."

"Okay. We'll need to go find him. First, we scour the beach, half a mile in each direction, check for any more survivors. Or bodies." Mathios paused, then, "Olav, take Hakon and go that way." He pointed to his left. "Ormarr, Vikarr, you're with me. We meet back here before the sun reaches the tip of that pine over yonder."

The Vikings separated into the two groups and each set off at a brisk march. Despite their ordeal, and some minor injuries, every one of them appreciated the need to locate their missing warriors quickly.

Mathios' party made the grim discovery of three bodies that had been washed up on the shore. Daichi, Vadik, Yaegar—good men, all of them. Under his breath Mathios cursed their foul luck that had led to this, then ordered that the dead men be dragged into the shelter of the trees, there to await proper burial.

Satisfied that no more survivors were to be found in this direction, Mathios called a halt to the search. "We return to meet the others. Let us hope they had better luck."

Olav's group had indeed fared better. As the other team approached, Mathios could see that their ranks were swelled to four. He recognised Ivar and Ywan, brothers who were rarely encountered apart. No doubt they had clung to the same piece of wreckage and would either sink or float together. The gods had smiled on them this day.

"We found one body," said Olav. "It was Alfgeirr."

Mathios nodded. That left just two whose fates were unknown, but he presumed them to have perished. Along with Njal, he knew that Petrekr and Saxi had died bravely, battling the elements, and the three Viking heroes would even now be approaching Valhalla in the arms of the Valkyries. He turned his attention to those still living.

"What weapons do we have?" Mathios' own sword still hung from his belt, and his dagger was firmly wedged in the back of his sodden trousers. He had taken a risk in keeping them when he leapt overboard; iron was heavy and not known for floating. But a warrior does not relinquish his weapon if he can help it.

"I have a sword, Jarl, and a dagger." Olav was the first to reply.

"And I have an axe. I lost my dagger, though." This from Ormarr.

One by one they announced what arms they possessed. Their tally was four swords, six daggers, an axe, a spear that had been washed up on the beach, and a bow but no arrows. Mathios ensured that every man had the means to defend himself before moving on to the next pressing matter.

"We must find Arne." Mathios turned to Hakon. "Where did you last see him, exactly?"

"Up there, Jarl." The man pointed to the closest trees. "He was weaving about as though he didn't know where he was or where he was going."

"Right. We'll find him. Look for any tracks…"

The men fanned out to examine the undergrowth. It wasn't long before the shout went up. "Here. The bracken has been trampled down." Olav waved the others over to where he stood peering at the ground. "Look, there's his trail. It has to be him."

It was as good a lead as any. Mathios crouched to examine the flattened grass then nodded. "This way. Follow me."

The tracks led them perhaps a quarter of a mile due west before petering out when the terrain became rockier. Mathios halted. "We need to split up. Olav, Hakon, Ivar, and Ywan, you take the path to the right. Ormarr and Vikarr, you're with me again."

Olav set off as directed, heading north. Mathios and his team continued forward.

"What was that? Did anyone else hear something?" Mathios stopped, listening, but there was only silence. Even so, he could swear by the great Thor that he heard a sound in the distance, a faint cry possibly.

His companions shook their heads. They set off again.

"There! I definitely heard something." Mathios halted again and turned to check with his men.

"Me too," agreed Ormarr. "An animal…?"

Mathios was not certain, but sensible precautions were called for. "Maybe. Have daggers to hand." A wild boar emerging suddenly from the undergrowth could be deadly. "It sounded to be coming from this direction." He led the way, scanning the forest floor in all directions before proceeding with care.

The sound reached his ears again. Mathios glanced over his shoulder. Both his companions nodded, they heard it too. The cry was almost human. He knew foxes made such a sound when mating, but that was usually at night, not in the broad light of an autumn morn, in the teeth of a gale.

Moving on instinct they picked up speed, making their way through the thickly wooded terrain at a sprint. They emerged into a clearing and Mathios could barely believe the sight that met his eyes. His missing warrior, Arne, lay on the ground. A few feet away stood a young woman, unkempt in appearance, her bedraggled, sodden clothing hanging from her thin frame. She struggled to maintain her grip on a large lump of rock that she cradled in her arms. From her stance it was clear to Mathios that she intended to drop the boulder on his fallen comrade.

"Stop!" the command rang out. Mathios had instinctively used the local Anglo-Saxon dialect. He drew his weapon from the back of his breeches, intending to enforce his order with his dagger but at the last moment the wench dropped the rock. He sheathed his knife again and took a pace forward. The girl stared at him, her eyes wide, uncomprehending, then she bent forward. Fearing that she meant to pick up her rock again, Mathios was spurred into action. He leapt forward, covering the few yards that separated them to seize her around the waist and carry the pair of them to the ground. The wench crumpled beneath him. By the time he had shoved himself up on one elbow to check her fate she was already unconscious.

"See to Arne." He rolled from the woman, a Celt by the looks of her. There was no mistaking the heat emanating from her slender body. She was shaking, her teeth chattering despite her insensible state. She was going nowhere and no longer offered any threat. Mathios saw no need to restrain her and left her where she was while he checked on the condition of his warrior.

Arne was pushing himself up onto all fours, his bloodstained hair falling over his face. He fingered his head wound and groaned.

"Did she do that?" Mathios crouched beside the man.

"No. Something hit me while I was still in the water." He looked about him. "Where are we? I don't remember…"

"You were washed up on the beach like the rest of us but for some reason you didn't stay put and wait."

"I'm not sure… I think—"

"What happened? We heard a shout…" Olav and his

men arrived at a sprint. "You found him, I see."

"Aye, and just in time by the looks of things." Mathios stood and prowled back to where the Celtic wench still lay. "She was about to brain Arne with a rock."

"Really?" Olav came to stand beside him to regard the inert form at their feet. "From the looks of her she'd have more chance of taking to the air and flying round yonder oak. Are you sure she could even lift a rock let alone make a weapon of it?"

"I'm sure," growled Mathios. "I know what I saw."

"She wasn't going to do it." This from Arne. "That might have been her plan, but she changed her mind."

Mathios eyed him warily. "You think so? That's not how it looked when we arrived."

"I saw her. I looked into her eyes. There was fear in them, and confusion. Regret too. But not murder."

"Are you sure? You were barely conscious yourself."

"I saw, Jarl. She came right up to me. The wench was standing over me when I opened my eyes. If she truly meant me harm she could have done it, but she didn't. She backed off."

Mathios allowed himself a noncommittal snort. He would reserve judgement, for now. He crouched to lay his palm on the girl's forehead. "She has a fever."

"We should finish her off now. The vicious little bitch would have killed Arne if we'd been even a few moments later." Ormarr was already drawing his dagger. "I'm happy enough to do what needs to be done."

"Put your knife away, Ormarr. Any talk of retribution may well be irrelevant. She's burning up and looks to be half dead already." Mathios peered into the inert features. The wench might be pretty enough if she was not so thin, her waist-length dark hair less matted. Sweat beaded on her forehead, her skin was pallid. Air rattled in her throat and a glance at her chest showed her breathing to be shallow and rapid. Mathios feared she was not long for this world, and despite his reservations about her malicious intent he could not avoid the conclusion that her demise would actually be a pity.

Ormarr sought to press his case. “But Jarl, I—”

“Enough.” Mathios pulled the wench into his arms and straightened. “The matter will be decided by the gods. If she lives, we shall have the truth from her. Meanwhile, we have the pressing business of seeking shelter and warmth since we find ourselves stranded on these shores for a while at least. Some food would not go amiss either.”

“There must be a settlement hereabouts. She can’t have come far in that state.” Olav could usually be relied upon for sensible comment.

“What about that cottage we spotted?” Ivar pointed back the way they had come. “It looked to be partly in ruins, but maybe it would do.”

Olav agreed. “It’s the closest place where we might make camp. There’s shelter to be had. It’ll do to start with at least.”

“You lead the way.” Mathios shifted the girl in his arms. “How far is it?”

Olav hauled Arne to his feet and supported him with an arm about his waist. “A few minutes’ walk, no more. You can lean on me, Arne, and we can—”

A shrill, plaintive cry caused them to stop in their tracks.

“What the fuck is that?” Mathios scanned the clearing. “That’s what we heard before. It sounds to be close by.”

“Behind those trees,” whispered Vikarr, his dagger already drawn.

“Go with the lad,” Mathios instructed Hakon. “Find out what’s making that noise.”

The two Vikings crept forward. Ivar and Ywan joined them. They disappeared into the dense shrubbery while the rest waited in silence.

“Thor’s fucking teeth.” The oath came from Ivar.

“What is it? What have you found?” Mathios called out, already moving to follow his men.

“Just these, Jarl.” Ivar reappeared carrying a large jar and a wet blanket. "Oh, and that…" he gestured over his shoulder with his thumb as his brother emerged from the trees.

"By Odin's balls," breathed Mathios.

Ywan walked toward them, a child of perhaps a year old cradled in his arms. The little one was squalling in earnest now, his reddened face showing his discontent and his small feet kicking within the blanket that enveloped him.

"How did that get there?" Ormarr peered suspiciously at the child. "What are we going to do with it?"

Mathios glanced at the girl in his arms. "I think it's pretty clear how he got here. It *is* a he, I assume?"

Ywan shrugged.

The gender of the child was neither here nor there. Mathios made up his mind. "Bring the baby with us. We'll decide what's to be done once we've made camp and got a fire going, and put some food in our bellies."

"There's these." Ivar offered the jar to Mathios. "It's full of blackberries."

"Share them around. Oh, and make sure he gets some." Mathios nodded at the crying child. "He sounds hungry."

•••••••

The trek to the cottage was mercifully short, though the accommodations offered at the semi-derelict farmstead were crude to say the least. From the outside the place appeared deserted, but they needed to be certain. Mathios sent three of his men off to scout the area for any signs of the inhabitants. Meanwhile he and the rest set to making themselves comfortable.

The house consisted of just one room, with an adjoining barn. The roof of the cottage was in poor repair, but it was clear that someone had attempted to render the thatch weatherproof though with limited success. The barn was in ruins, though a rough chicken coop occupied one end of it. It was clear that someone lived here. Or tried to.

The cottage was sparsely furnished, just a table, a chair, and a narrow pallet on the floor. A smaller cot stood beside the pallet, further evidence that this was the home of the wench he still carried and her baby.

Arne sank onto the solitary chair.

"Are you all right there?" Mathios asked. "You could take the bed."

"Aye, Jarl. I'll do."

Satisfied, Mathios lowered his burden onto the pallet and unlaced the rough, oversized boots on her feet. He removed the footwear, then dragged the one dry blanket up over her. She would need to be got out of the rest of her wet clothes fairly soon, but first they all needed warmth. A cursory check on the fire pit in the middle of the room showed it to be cold. It was obvious no flame had burned there for several days at least.

Mathios started issuing commands. "Find some firewood and start a blaze. Is there anything here to eat?"

Within half an hour a fire crackled in the hearth, the logs provided by Ormarr's trusty axe. A search of the cottage yielded little, though, in the way of food.

"Two eggs and a few sorry-looking carrots." Olav reported the tally. "We need to take a couple of rabbits, Jarl, and quick, while there's still daylight. Otherwise we'll all go hungry this night."

"See to it," commanded Mathios. "Food and firewood are our immediate priorities, and tending any wounds."

"I believe we have not fared too badly, considering. Even Arne's thick skull seems not to be as battered as we thought and Vikarr is binding the wound on his arm. He'll be okay after a day or two's rest." Olav gathered his damp cloak about him. "I'll take Ivar and Ywan and see what we can rustle up for our *nattmal*."

"Give the little man to me," offered Arne. "If I can't do much else I can at least see to him."

Ywan handed over the baby, clearly relieved to pass him on to someone else.

"He stinks." The Viking wrinkled his nose in distaste. "And I think he pissed on me."

"He did right," observed Olav from the door of the cottage. "You'll need to find some dry rags."

"Rags? What for?" Arne peered at the small boy as though the child himself might explain.

Olav grinned. "You need to wrap them around, to soak up whatever comes out."

"Are you sure?" Arne was far from convinced.

Olav nodded emphatically. "I am father to six. I've shared my longhouse with enough squalling infants to know how they're cared for. Admitted, my wife actually does most of that, but there are times a man just has to get his hands dirty. Your time has come, my friend. Rags, definitely."

The child's face was stained with blackberry juice, as were his small fingers. He was quiet now though, and peering at the Vikings with undisguised fascination. They returned his steady gaze with dawning horror.

"Maybe someone else should—" Arne's enthusiasm for the task had evaporated.

"Ywan, stop your whining and find some rags for Arne," instructed Mathios. "And you, make sure you don't drop him. It would be a pity to rescue the lad, just to have him perish through your ham-fistedness."

Arne appeared to be reconciled to the necessity of caring for the little boy and had already started to peel the damp clothing away from the small body. "We'll be fine," he assured his leader, already returning the child's intense gaze. "You should see to the lass."

Indeed he should, starting with making sure she, too, was dry and warm. As all his men barring Arne and the youth, Vikarr, filed out in search of their supper and the means to cook it, Mathios turned his attention to the wan figure on the pallet. He knelt beside her and peeled back the blanket. She was no longer shivering, but her skin was chilled and clammy. He needed to get her warm and dry if she was to have a realistic chance of surviving the ague that racked her frail body. There was also the matter of possible contagion.

"Until we know if this illness is infectious no one but me is to tend her."

"But Jarl, what if—"

Mathios silenced the lad with one raised hand. "If it can be spread, I've already been in close contact with her. No one else has thus far and I intend to keep it that way. The baby too. His cot must be moved away from the bed."

Vikarr nodded and scuttled over to grasp the cot and drag it across the cottage, depositing it as far from the pallet as he could. "What should I do now, Jarl?"

"See if you can coddle those eggs over the fire, then share them out. Make sure the little one has his portion too."

"What about the others?"

"Don't worry about them. Olav will bring back meat for all." Mathios had no doubt at all on that matter. Olav was the best hunter among them.

A quick survey of the room turned up little in the way of spare clothing, He had to conclude that the wench only possessed that which she stood up in. Or rather, lay down. No matter, she could sleep naked for now provided the room was warm and there was sufficient bedding.

"Vikarr, can you dry the blanket we found with the baby? Hang it close to the fire."

"Yes, Jarl." The youth leapt to do his bidding.

Mathios did not exactly lack experience in getting a female naked, but up to now the women he had undressed had all been conscious and cooperative. He would have to do his best. He started with the Celtic wench's feet. He had pulled off her boots before he covered her with the blanket, but now he peeled off her wool stockings also. Next, he shoved his arm under her and lifted her to a sitting position. From there it was relatively easy to tug her rough kirtle up and over her head. Her coarse undershirt followed, rendering the wench naked from the waist up.

Mathios could not help but cast an appreciative eye over her small but pert breasts, the slight mound of her stomach, though he sought to keep his perusal to a minimum. He was deft as he removed the one remaining garment, her soaked skirt, and flung that onto the pile of clothing beside the pallet. He settled her back on the mattress and pulled the blanket back over her. On impulse he smoothed the tangled hair back from her forehead. It was lank under his fingers, badly in need of a wash. Like all Vikings, Mathios set great store by personal cleanliness but in the case of this little Celtic wench such niceties must wait.

"There's a stream outside. Go fetch some clean water, Vikarr."

"You mean to wash her?"

"For drinking. Be quick."

The youth returned with a cup of cool water. Mathios dribbled a few drops onto the girl's parched lips. He was pleased when her mouth worked to accept the refreshment.

"You would like more?" he murmured and tilted her head forward to aid her in drinking. She took several mouthfuls, then he laid her flat again and pulled the blanket up to her chin. The awful rattling in her throat seemed to Mathios to have eased somewhat and she appeared more comfortable. The room was warm now, and she was at least dry. It was all he could do for her.

CHAPTER THREE

"Tomorrow we go back to the beach, check for any wreckage, anything we might salvage."

Mathios chewed on a piece of meat, savouring the succulent flesh. Olav had managed to fashion traps from debris he found in the barn and had caught six fine, plump rabbits for their supper. They had eaten well, and even the baby appeared pleased with the fare. Arne had insisted they chop the pieces of meat finely for him and the child now dozed on Arne's lap, the grease from his meal still daubed across his chin.

The wench had not woken up, but she slept more peacefully now that she was warm and comfortable. They had all managed to dry their wet clothing, and now sat around the table on a variety of upturned barrels dragged inside from the barn, buckets, and a crude bench fashioned from planks and two conveniently shaped rocks.

"We are to bed down in here, then, Jarl?" enquired Hakon.

"Yes. We shall be cramped but each man must make himself as comfortable as he can. At least we have shelter."

The Vikings nodded. They had slept in worse conditions.

• • • • • • •

The following morning Mathios woke to the sound of plaintive whimpering from the cot, now situated in a corner as far from the pallet as could be contrived. He shoved himself up on one elbow to see that Olav was already making his way between the sleeping warriors to reach the grizzling baby.

"Hush, lad. You'll wake everyone." Mathios watched as his cousin bent to pluck the child from the cot and bounced him in his arms. The whimpering stopped and the baby reached for Olav's stubby beard. "Ah, you like to play, do you? Later, lad. First we must find you something to eat."

"There might be more eggs. I'll check." Mathios rolled from under the fur he had dragged over himself and stretched. He was stiff, the earthen floor of the cottage offering little in the way of comfort.

"Aye, you do that. I'll just get this blaze livened up a bit." Olav held the baby close while he used his free hand to prod the smouldering embers in the fire pit. Mathios dropped a fresh log on as he passed and the flames leapt into life.

He found three eggs. Not much, but with a broth made from the carcases of yesterday's rabbits it would do to get them started on the day. By the time Mathios returned to the cottage Olav had a pot of water steaming over the hearth and the rest of his men were stirring.

The wench on the pallet remained unconscious, though she did accept a few more drops of fresh water and her skin tone appeared slightly better to Mathios.

After they had eaten their *dagmal*, the meal traditionally taken by Vikings an hour or so after rising and completing the first tasks of the day, Mathios issued his instructions.

"We go to the beach first, then return here with anything salvageable. Then you, Olav, need to hunt down our supper. Take a couple of men with you. Those staying here can make a start on the roof. I prefer not to have rainwater dribbling down my neck as I sleep."

"We are to remain here for a while, then?" enquired Ormarr, eyeing their crude surroundings with distaste.

"Unless you have better accommodations in mind." Mathios quelled his rising irritation at the man's continuous complaints. "We can make this homestead more comfortable, and there is plenty to eat if we but go out and seek it."

Ormarr was far from convinced. "What about the local population? We could be attacked at any moment."

"I suspect our reputation will protect us. A few Celtic villagers wielding pitchforks and shovels are unlikely to pick a fight with armed Viking warriors. If we leave them alone, they will keep their distance." Mathios got to his feet. "So, the beach."

• • • • • • •

"It is not beyond repair."

"No, not quite."

Ivar and Ywan circled the wreck of their dragon ship discussing the sorry state of the craft that had been washed up on the shore overnight. The mast was broken, snapped clean in two, and the bright crimson sail near enough shredded. Just two of the original twenty oars remained, and the keel sported a gaping hole.

"What will it take to fix it?" demanded Mathios. Ivar and Ywan were the most skilled boat builders among his crew; he would accept their verdict on the state of his longship.

"Timber, but there's no shortage of that." Ywan tipped his head in the direction of the forest which surrounded them. "With just one axe between us, though, the felling will take a while."

His brother was more encouraging. "There may be tools we could make use of at the farmstead. We need to have a proper look around."

Ywan flattened his lips, considering. "And we shall

require fabric to repair the sail, good woollen cloth."

"We shall find some, even if we must weave it ourselves." Mathios was determined to see the repairs completed, and his longship once more skimming across the waves. "How long will it take?"

Ywan and Ivar looked at each other and Mathios swore they affected some form of silent communication known only to them. "Four weeks, maybe five. Assuming we can find the materials we need, and the weather is kind to us."

Four weeks. Mathios tipped back his head to stare into the gloomy skies, the remnants of yesterday's storm still apparent in the various shades of grey. Already autumn was well advanced. Four weeks would see the winter fully upon them. Even if their ship was made good once more, putting to sea would be hazardous to say the least. For the time being, they were stranded on this hostile foreign shore.

Mathios thought quickly through the various implications.

"Right. It looks as though we're going to spend the winter here. We'll make the repairs to our ship in readiness for setting sail for home as soon as spring returns and conditions improve. Ywan and Ivar, you will be in charge of the repairs, with help from the rest of us as you need it. Olav, you will ensure we have supplies and that we have stores set aside to see us through the coldest months. Ormarr, you are a carpenter, so when not aiding Ywan and Ivar, you will fashion such furniture as we need to pass the winter months in comfort."

Hakon was keen to offer his contribution. "I have some skills in metalworking, Jarl. I can make the tools we need if we do not find them."

"Thank you. All must do their part to make the cottage habitable, and if possible repair the barn so we may make use of it for storage. We start now."

"Aye, Jarl." The Viking warriors murmured their assent. With no further prompting from their leader, Ywan and Ivar, aided by Ormarr, started to calculate the quantity of timber required and the likely source of it.

"I saw a stand of decent pines, maybe a mile or so from here," suggested Ormarr. "Come, I shall show you."

At last, he has ceased to moan. Mathios grinned as the three set off in search of the wood they needed. Olav was already rounding up those who would join him in hunting. He set off with Hakon and Vikarr in tow.

Mathios returned to the cottage alone. Arne, still nursing his head wound, had remained behind to keep an eye on the sick girl and the now lively little boy. He had strict instructions not to approach the pallet unless it was absolutely necessary, and to ensure the child remained at a safe distance too. The pair were seated at the table when Mathios entered and Arne was attempting to sing to the little boy.

Poor child, has he not suffered enough already? Mathios opted not to comment and instead strode over to the bed.

"Has she stirred?"

"No, Jarl. Not once."

Mathios went down on his haunches to better inspect her pallid complexion. He laid his hand on the girl's forehead. She was still overwarm, but he fancied perhaps a little cooler than yesterday. Certainly, she seemed no worse. He settled beside the pallet and lifted her to offer her a sip of water.

"Where are the others?" Arne peered at the door as though expecting the rest of their group to follow Mathios into the cottage.

"We found our ship washed up on the beach, damaged but not beyond repair. Ywan, Ivar, and Ormarr have gone in search of timber in order to start work on it."

Arne's face split in a wide smile. "So we can leave here? We are not stranded after all?"

"We are, but only for the winter. The work will take a few weeks, by which time the weather will have turned. We must resign ourselves to spending a winter on these shores, but we shall see our home again before much longer. Olav,

Hakon, and Vikarr are hunting, but we shall need to forage too as we can't live on just meat and fish until spring."

Arne shrugged. "I have no quarrel with a diet of meat and fish. We are to stay here, then? In this cottage?"

"I see no better solution."

"What about her?" Arne nodded in the direction of the pallet. "She will not welcome us, that's for sure."

Mathios paused, then, "She will have no choice. She will come to realise that we mean her no harm, we just want to share her home for a few months."

"But what if she refuses? I do not believe she would have done me real harm in the forest yesterday, but it was obvious she was far from pleased to find me there."

"If she does not cooperate she will find herself tied to that bed until March. She will see sense, eventually."

"And if she does not?"

"Then there will be consequences. I have no wish to harm the wench, but we are here to stay, and she must accept that whether she likes the idea or not."

• • • • • • •

The following three days were busy ones for the Vikings. They commenced the task of felling trees and dragged the logs to the beach, as well as completing the repairs to the thatch above their heads. All were relieved when the roof was finally made watertight. Ormarr turned his attention to the door next, which was warped and ill-fitting. He managed to alter it to exclude all but the most determined draughts. His rabbit traps set and doing their work well, Olav turned his hand to fishing from the cliffs. He managed to return with several fine cod. Meanwhile Vikarr fashioned a crude lamp from a chipped earthenware mug, which he filled with oil from the liver of Olav's cod to provide light. They were starting to make themselves comfortable.

"The lad needs milk," announced Arne, bouncing the boy on his lap as the child chuntered happily. "Where can we get a cow?"

"We could steal one," suggested Hakon. "There must be other farms in the area."

"And invite retribution from every Celtic farmer for miles about? No," insisted Mathios. "We shall trade for a cow if we need it, and for any other supplies we cannot obtain any other way. We also need grain, and the cloth for our sail."

"What if the Celts do not wish to trade with us?" asked Olav. "And what can we offer as payment?"

"They will." Mathios was confident. "No one refuses a decent trade, not even the Celts. We have rabbit skins, and could hunt for more pelts. We could trade any fish we don't need for our own use, or perhaps some fine venison. What are the chances of taking a decent stag, do you think?"

"Fair enough," conceded Olav. "We shall require arrows, but we can start to fashion those."

"Right then. The cow first…"

He paused when Vikarr caught his eye from his seat on the opposite side of the table. The youth gestured to the pallet behind him. Mathios turned.

The wench was awake. She lay motionless, her eyes open. They were a dark brown colour, he noted, and she regarded the Norsemen with an expression of pure horror.

Mathios got to his feet and approached the bed. The wench shrank away from him, clutching the blanket to her chin as she wriggled backward until she was pressed against the outer wall of the cottage. Mathios crouched beside the pallet.

"How do you feel?" He spoke in the Celtic tongue, glad that he had learnt it from the slaves in his father's longhouse.

She did not reply. Mathios reached out and laid his palm on her forehead. It felt cool to the touch, her skin no longer clammy.

"Good," he said, careful to keep his tone low. "You are much improved." He reached for the pitcher of fresh water he had insisted they kept close by and poured a little into a mug. "Here, you should drink this."

The wench continued to stare at him as though he might have sprouted an additional head. Mathios reached for her, intending to assist her as he had while she was unconscious. She whimpered and pulled the blanket higher as though she might yet hide from him.

"You have no need to be afraid, I will not harm you." He took hold of the blanket and gently but firmly tugged it from her face. The battle was an unequal one. The girl lay still, her eyes like saucers as she awaited her fate.

Mathios reached for her again and this time she offered no resistance as he slid his arm under her and raised her shoulders from the mattress. He placed the cup at her lips and tipped it slightly so she could take a few sips. Her cold fingers curled around his hand as she sought to grip the cup herself, though he did not relinquish it. When she had had enough she turned her face away and he set the cup aside.

"Do you think you could eat anything? We have fish." He beckoned to Vikarr, who brought a plate over with a portion of that day's catch upon it. "Try a little, just a few mouthfuls. You must be hungry, you have not eaten for days."

"I… I…" The wench tried to speak but her voice seemed to have deserted her.

Mathios placed the food on the pallet beside her. He considered picking up a piece of the cod and feeding it to her from his fingers. He might have done so, but when he cupped her jaw to lift her face toward him, she fell into a dead faint.

Not an ideal start. They had work to do, clearly. Mathios laid her back down, made sure the blanket was tucked in around her, and let her be.

• • • • • • •

Voices. Men, laughing, talking, their speech

incomprehensible.

Footsteps. Heavy, booted feet.

The scrape of furniture, the clash of metal. The crackle of a hearty blaze and the solid thump of a log being tossed into the flames.

Merewyn lay still, listening. Trembling. Something nagged at the edges of her consciousness, something elusive yet compelling, a reason why she must wake up. There was something she had to do, but she dare not. She quaked every time footsteps drew close to where she huddled, barely daring to breathe until they receded again. She dared not open her eyes. If she did not do so, she could pretend that the vision from before had been a dream, a vile nightmare to haunt and torment her in her illness.

Yes, that must be it, a delusion brought on by the sickness she had endured. Her home was not teeming with Viking warriors. It could not be, the prospect was too awful and completely impossible. If those murdering savages had truly returned, she would not be alive to know of it. Merewyn grasped the covers more tightly and prayed that this hallucination would soon pass.

"I know that you are awake, little Celt."

The voice was low, soft even, the words were spoken in her own tongue but in an accent she did not recognise. She clung to her blanket and her eyelids remained firmly closed.

"You will have to look at me at some time, it may as well be now."

The fires of Hades would freeze over first. Merewyn lay motionless and prayed for deliverance.

"I have food here. You must be hungry."

She was. She was famished but terror was a more powerful motivator by far.

"If you will not speak to me, there is another here who you may be more pleased to see."

He spoke a few words in the harsher-sounding tongue that she assumed was that of the Norsemen, and more footsteps approached her pallet. If it was possible to die of fear she would expire at this very moment.

"Little Celt, your baby has missed you. He needs you to wake up."

Baby? Connell? Her head cleared momentarily and she knew why she must return to the land of the living. Her tiny, helpless brother needed her, he could not survive without her. How long had she lain here, unconscious, neglecting him?

She had no choice. She prised her eyelids apart.

The man was huge, though she could not tell exactly how tall as he crouched beside her bed. She recognised him at once; he was the one who had shouted at her in the forest and flung her to the ground as though she was weightless. She had thought he would kill her there and then, but seemingly he had not bothered to do so. Yet.

He was handsome, this warrior who had invaded her home, but in a manner that terrified her. His hair was light and fell to his shoulders, and he was beardless. His jaw was strong and square, his nose straight, his cheekbones angular in a face that exuded an air of command. But it was his eyes that captivated her. They were blue, the colour of cornflowers, sharp, intelligent, assessing. He met her gaze steadily and he held it. She wanted to look away but was powerless to do so until he broke the contact by turning to address the man who stood behind him.

Merewyn glanced up now and recognised the other Viking, the one she had found lying on the ground. She had told herself she must put an end to the threat while she could, but the chance was forever lost now. He towered over her, and he held Connell in his arms.

Merewyn let out an anguished cry, a plea for mercy as she reached for the baby. She must save Connell, protect him from harm, from the menace of these lawless, marauding raiders. She tried to sit up, realising too late that she was naked beneath the blanket that covered her.

The Viking chief chuckled and signalled to his man to pass Connell to her at the same time as he reached to lift the blanket and cover her naked breasts.

"You are very lovely, little Celt, but I do not consider it wise to parade your beauty before my men."

Merewyn had no words. She hugged Connell's squirming body to her, buried her nose in his hair, breathed in the warm, wholesome smell of him. As far as she could tell he was unhurt but she would put nothing past these men.

"Your food is there." The Viking beside her spoke again, and gestured to a plate on the floor next to her. "Fish again, for we have rather a lot of it just now. And there is water too, from the stream. We will leave you to eat."

He rose to his feet, and she could see that he was as tall as the other man though perhaps not quite so brawny. Even so, he was broad shouldered and muscles bulged beneath his light green wool tunic. His sleeves were rolled back to the elbow to reveal arms that were tanned and powerful. One of them, the left, bore the scar of an earlier battle. This man was no stranger to violence and Merewyn had no doubt she would see the truth of that soon enough, when it suited him. She tightened her grip on Connell and watched as both Vikings left her to return to the table where two more of their kind sat and watched the exchange with interest.

The two Norsemen sat down and soon the conversation resumed, a low hum of voices and words she could not understand though there was no obvious menace in them. Her stomach growled and the aroma of the fish was irresistible. Merewyn reached for the plate and pulled it closer, arranging Connell so that he was seated on the pallet beside her. The Viking had given her a decent portion, easily enough for them both.

She picked up a piece of fish and offered it to Connell. He pushed it away and tried to scramble over the bed to the floor.

"No, you must stay here where you are safe." She grabbed for him at the same time as she put the morsel in her own mouth. It was delicious. She chewed, swallowed, and took another piece, all the time holding on to the wriggling child. "Eat this, Connell. It is good and we may not have food again for some time." Merewyn resolved to take what sustenance they could, there was no saying when their next meal might come. Usually she had no difficulty in persuading her baby brother to eat, he was ever hungry. But today, when it mattered, he refused the food. "Connell, please eat. And be still…"

At last her pleas seemed to have some effect. The baby settled beside her and rammed his thumb in his mouth. Despite all her efforts Merewyn was unable to coax him to try the succulent fish so she ate most of it herself, saving a portion for the child should he be hungry later. Her hunger satisfied for now, and her concerns for Connell somewhat allayed, she settled back to consider her dilemma.

She had been stripped, that much was clear. What more might they have done to her whilst she was unconscious and unable to help herself? She felt weak, her throat still hurt but not much, and her breathing was somewhat laboured. Other than that she felt no discomfort, and surely she would if… if…

And the Viking had covered her when she had inadvertently let the blanket slip. He had appeared concerned, for her modesty or her safety she was not quite sure, but it was odd, not what she had expected.

She lay down and eyed the intruders warily. They seemed unconcerned at her presence, their conversation casual. The blond chief laughed and slapped the young man next to him between the shoulder blades. The youth grinned back and said something that made his leader laugh again.

Perplexed, but not daring to let down her guard, Merewyn settled back against the mattress. She was weary suddenly, her fatigue the lingering effect of her illness. She rolled onto her side, turning her back on the men in the room and curling around the warm body of her little brother.

"We shall survive, I promise you. I will do whatever I

must, but we *shall* survive this."

CHAPTER FOUR

Connell was gone.

Merewyn shoved herself up on her elbow and viewed the empty space in the bed with dismay. She turned, careful to clutch the blanket over her naked breasts and sat up to scan the room.

Vikings were everywhere. She could not count them, but there were more than the four she had seen earlier. And no sign of the baby. Panic mounted as she peered about her. She spied Connells's cot at the other side of the cottage, but could see that it was empty.

Why have they moved Connell's bed? And what have these fiends done with my brother?

"P-please..." she whispered. No one heard her. She tried again, louder. "Where is Connell?"

The two Norsemen closest to her turned. One spoke to the other, who shrugged.

"My brother? He was here, and..."

The youth who had been laughing with the blond chief ambled over to offer her a drink of water. Merewyn shook her head and repeated her question but fared no better. It would seem that only the chief understood her language, and he was not present.

The door opened, and he entered. Merewyn was relieved, despite her abject fear of this man. At least he could speak to her and answer her questions. She started to ask again, but the words died in her throat when the Nordic leader was followed through the door by the large Viking she had almost murdered in the forest. Connell sat on the man's shoulder, his tiny fingers tangled in the Norseman's dark blond locks. The baby was snugly wrapped in a rough cloak made of furs, rabbit perhaps, and clearly looked to be enjoying himself immensely. He grinned and squealed with delight when the Viking reached up to tickle him.

"Connell!" Merewyn cried out his name, and would have run across the room to pluck her brother from the peril of these wild raiders if her legs would have supported her in such an ambitious endeavour. "Give him back to me. Please."

The chief paused, then reached to lift the baby down. He murmured something to the other Viking, then carried the boy over to her pallet and passed him to Merewyn. He crouched beside her and held out his hand to the baby. Connell grasped his finger and pulled himself to his feet, then proceeded to bounce up and down.

"You need have no fear. He is safe. We went to feed the chickens and he came with us, is all. He enjoys the task—"

"He does not!" Merewyn protested. "He is too small to be made to work. He is just a baby." She wrapped her arms around the little boy to still his jaunty dance.

"Aye, but he likes to play, almost as much as he likes to eat. Feeding the chickens is a game to him. His name is Connell, then? We had wondered…"

"Yes," she whispered, hugging her brother to her. "Connell."

"And your name?" His voice was gentle. "What are you called, little Celt?"

It would do no harm, surely, to tell him her name. "Merewyn," she murmured.

"A pretty name. I am Mathios. And this is Arne." He

pointed to the man who had carried Connell on his shoulder. "Arne has taken care of Connell, mostly, whilst you were ill. I have tended you."

"H-how long was I ill for?"

"It has been five days since we found you. Your baby was crying, fortunately, or we might not have known he was there and could have left him behind in the forest."

"Five days? It cannot be…" Merewyn was incredulous. And confused. There was no way that Connell would have survived alone for five days. Neither would she, in all probability. These Vikings had cared for her brother, that much was obvious, and probably saved his life. Hers too. But why? Why would they do such a thing when it would have been easier to just let the pair of them die?

"My clothing? Why… why did you remove it?"

His lip quirked in a manner she found singularly disconcerting. "It was wet. I had to make you warm and dry."

"But—"

"I will not insult your intelligence by seeking to suggest I did not enjoy stripping you, but be assured I did so out of necessity."

"You did not…? I mean, I am…"

"I did not touch you other than what was required in order to see to your comfort. I am no abuser of helpless women."

A lie. They were all the same, these Vikings, and her mother had paid the price.

Mathios leaned closer, the blue of his eyes darkening. "You are very tempting, little Merewyn, but you will not be harmed. I will not rape you, and neither will any of my men. That is not to say I do not desire you, but there will be no need for force. You will give me what I want, freely, when the time comes."

"Never! I will not." She backed away, broke his compelling gaze.

He smiled, an expression that caused her stomach to

clench and a peculiar warmth to spread between her thighs. Merewyn did not much care for the sensation.

"We shall see," he murmured. "For now, though, I prefer to discuss what happened on the day we found you. What do you recall of it?"

Her head ached. Both stunned and relieved at the shift in conversation, she furrowed her brow as she struggled to remember. "I was outside, on the cliffs. I saw your ship, I was scared, and…"

"Yes, I know. You found Arne in the forest. He was hurt. You picked up a rock."

Yes, she recalled it now. Vividly. She had not wanted to kill the unconscious man, but knew she had no choice. But then, when the moment arrived…

"Arne says you did not intend him harm. Is that true?"

"I… I do not know."

The Viking frowned. "You do not know?"

"I am not sure. I thought…"

"It is only because Arne spoke up for you that you are unharmed." His tone had hardened. "If we are attacked, I *will* exact retribution."

She watched him, silent, waiting. Had he brought her here, cared for her, only to enjoy the sport of killing her now?

The Viking, Mathios, regarded her and appeared to be considering his next move. Merewyn's mouth was dry.

"I trust Arne, and I am prepared to accept his version of what took place. But still we find ourselves in an awkward situation. If you saw our ship you will know that it was wrecked in the storm that day. Of fourteen men aboard just eight survived." He paused, drew in a deep breath then let it out slowly. "We can repair our ship, but it will take time, and the ship will not be seaworthy before the onset of winter. So, we are stranded here, which means you will have our company for the next few months whether you like it or not."

Merewyn shook her head, fought to quell the rising

panic. "You cannot stay here. This is my home, *our* home…"

"Sadly, we have no choice. Neither do you."

"But—"

"You have my word that we mean you no harm. We seek shelter, that is all, and a place to spend the winter since it will be impossible to sail before spring. And we have found what we seek. Here. If you give us no trouble, we will treat you and your baby well. You have already seen that we are capable of it. But I will have your promise, now, that you will not seek to obstruct our plans or to do us harm. You may not choose to make us welcome, I understand that, but you will at least be cooperative and obedient. Do I have your word?"

The very notion was absurd. "There is not the space here for so many. And, I have barely enough food…"

"We will make do. And we can provide for ourselves, and for you too. We do not intend to rob you, we will work while we are here in payment for your hospitality. We have already repaired your roof and made the door fit properly. So, do I have your word?"

"I… I am not sure. I cannot—" A thought occurred to her, an awful fate and one that had befallen those close to her. "Will you make slaves of us? Will you force Connell and me to come to your land with you when you leave?"

Mathios shook his head. "No, we will not. As soon as the weather permits us to sail we will do so and leave you here, your food stores replenished and your home in better repair than we found it. You will not have cause to regret aiding us."

"It is not aid if not given freely."

"Perhaps not, but if you do not give me your promise, you will enjoy little in the way of freedom whilst we are here. I cannot permit you to make a nuisance of yourself or to put my men in danger. If I cannot trust you, you will spend much of your time confined to this cottage, often bound, always guarded. And you will be punished for any disobedience or disrespect. I think you will find it a miserable existence, but it does not have to be like that. I am offering you something better. All I require from you is your word."

"I am not sure. I do not understand any of this. Why should I believe you?"

"Why would you not?"

There were many reasons. She had but to look at her ruined home, the graves outside, and the senseless cruelty of these Norsemen was clear enough. Vikings could not be trusted. Vikings would murder and steal and destroy as it suited them. This one, this Mathios, might seem gentle, reasonable even, but he was no different, not really. They were all thieves and worse. He might be lying to her now. Indeed, he probably was. Why, then, should she not lie to him?

"Very well, you have my promise." Merewyn blurted the words out before she had time to reconsider.

Mathios nodded. "Good. I am pleased that we understand each other. Please remember though, I will have your obedience and compliance or you will suffer the consequences. I will not tolerate defiance or disrespect. Is that clear?"

"Yes, it is clear." Merewyn held Connell close. She would do what she had to, say what she must in order to keep the pair of them safe. And if—when—a chance to escape presented itself, she would take it.

• • • • • • •

The next two days were tense but uneventful. Merewyn was still weak, and fearful of the rowdy Vikings who filled her tiny home with their din and their overwhelming presence. She spent most of the time in her bed and her strength slowly returned though she found even the slightest activity exhausting. Despite her fears she appreciated the Vikings' apparent willingness to see to

Connell's needs. They included him in their meals, and often took him with them when they went about their business beyond the cottage. Merewyn learnt that Arne had made the rabbit skin cloak for him to ensure he was protected from the chilly weather and Hakon was fashioning a tiny pair of boots.

"He is well able to walk," Mathios explained. "But he will require footwear if he is to go outside."

Merewyn pondered their generosity. She would have struggled to supply shoes for the little boy herself, but this was no reason to soften her attitude.

Mathios returned her clothes to her, now dried and ready to wear again. It galled her that she was still too weak to dress herself but she submitted to his offer of aid. He had already seen her nude body, after all. He was quick and efficient in the task, and she felt more confident now that she was no longer obliged to hide beneath the blanket whenever the Vikings were close.

They came and went. Often just one or two of her unwelcome guests remained in the cottage, the rest leaving the dwelling to be about their various tasks. She assumed the repairs to their ship would take precedence, but she could not help noticing a growing pile of firewood beside the door and the regular supply of meat. Rabbits were plentiful, fish also. She and Connell ate better than they had during his entire life and it was clear that the boy thrived on the attention lavished upon him by the Vikings. One of them, the man who appeared to be in command whenever Mathios was absent, even carved a boat from a piece of firewood and gave it to the child. It was Connell's first plaything.

By the third day after she properly regained consciousness Merewyn was feeling restless and frustrated. She now knew the names of most of the Vikings, but found it impossible to converse with any but Mathios, even had she wished to as their tongue was incomprehensible to her. Connell appeared to experience no such difficulties and had giggled happily when Olav spoke to him then produced his rabbit fur cloak. The child had yet to utter his first proper word but it would not surprise Merewyn if it were in Norse.

She sat on her pallet and tried to drag her comb though her lank hair but her locks were hopelessly matted. Her attempts to fashion a rough plait proved equally futile. Mathios watched her fruitless efforts from where he sat on an upturned barrel beside the fire pit. Only he and Vikarr were in the cottage, the rest having accompanied Olav on a fishing expedition. Merewyn gathered it was their intention to catch enough fish to be able to offer the surplus for trade.

"Would you like a bath?"

Merewyn started at the question from the Viking chief, then shook her head. "I would love one, but it is not possible. I have no tub."

"There is a bathtub in the barn. We found it there."

"Aye, but it is broken." Yet another example of the destruction wrought by the Vikings who had raided her home.

"It *was* broken. Hakon has repaired it. We have all made use of it and I can assure you it does not leak."

"You have fixed it? How?"

"I did not enquire as to the precise method but be assured Hakon did a fine job. Shall I have the tub brought in here for your use?"

"What about the water? We do not have enough…"

"There is as much water as we need in the stream. Certainly, there is sufficient for you to have a bath."

"But would it not take too long to heat the water?"

"Not really, if we bank the fire up. In any case, you are not in a hurry, are you?"

He demolished all her objections, and despite her determination to hate these Vikings who trespassed in her home, the prospect of a warm bath and clean hair was an alluring one. Why should she not take advantage of such comforts as might be offered? She well knew that her situation might change at any moment.

"Thank you. I would like a bath, if that can be arranged."

Mathios hauled the iron tub into the cottage himself, the muscles in his arms and back bulging as he set it down close to the fire pit. Next, he set Vikarr to fetching buckets of water from the stream and had him pour them into the large pot over the fire. As the water warmed, the Viking youth transferred it to the bathtub then set more on to heat. It took over an hour, but eventually the tub was over half full.

"That is enough. Thank you." Merewyn stood beside the tub and peered into the steaming water. She then looked at the two Vikings. "Am I to have no privacy in which to bathe?"

Mathios shook his head. "You are still weak. It would be unsafe for you to bathe alone. One of us should remain, though you may choose which one of us that is."

"That is not necessary." On this point, Merewyn was absolutely determined. She folded her arms across her chest and glared at the Viking chief.

Mathios narrowed his eyes. "I could insist."

"Please do not." Merewyn held his gaze for several seconds, then lowered her eyes, defeated. "Please…"

He appeared to consider her request for several moments, then, "Very well, though we will both be just outside. You will call out if you require assistance."

"I am sure I—"

"You will call out."

His tone brooked no further argument. Merewyn simply nodded.

With a sharp tilt of his head Mathios ordered the younger man from the cottage, then followed him out of the door. Merewyn was alone with her bathwater.

It took her several minutes to undress as her joints still ached from the fever and her arms were stiff. She struggled to reach the fastenings behind her back, but she was determined to manage alone. At last she was naked. Merewyn stepped gingerly into the water. It was cooling, but still warm enough to cause her to sigh in contentment as she sank into the welcoming depths.

For several minutes she lay still, absorbing the comforting heat and simply savouring the quiet peace of the moment. She could not recall when she had last enjoyed the luxury of a warm bath. Usually she and Connell made do with the stream, a bracing experience even in the summer and one she preferred to avoid entirely in the winter months.

The water cooled yet more and Merewyn became aware of the passing of time. How long had she simply lain here? Too long. She reached for the scrap of fabric Mathios had left draped over the foot of the bathtub and started to rub her legs.

She was soon exhausted. Merewyn had underestimated the extent to which her illness had sapped her strength. Every movement, each stretch of her arms, cost her dearly. She groaned in frustration as she realised that she would be quite unable to wash her hair.

Mathios had been right. She did need help. He had offered, and she had turned him away, insisting that he leave her alone. The choice now facing her was stark. She must either call him back and ask for his aid, or make do with dirty hair for at least a few more days until she was able to shift properly for herself.

Really, there was no choice at all. And maybe if she were to sit up and cover herself with her arms, then perhaps…

"Excuse me…" Merewyn wondered if Vikarr would be the one closest. Perhaps he would come. The prospect of the youth attending her bath filled her with a mixture of emotions. Vikarr was infinitely less formidable than the Viking leader, but for some perverse reason she would prefer Mathios.

She was granted her wish. Mathios was the one who stepped back through the door. He regarded her from across the tiny room, his arms folded and one blond eyebrow raised.

"I… I wonder if perhaps you could…" Merewyn fell

silent, intimidated by the amusement in his expression, not to mention the lazy, appreciative manner with which the tall Viking perused her shivering body as she huddled in the tub.

"Problem, Merewyn?" He quirked his lip, obviously enjoying the fact that he had been proved right.

"My hair. I cannot..."

"Ah, I see. You would like me to assist you?"

"Yes," she muttered. "Please."

Mathios approached the cauldron suspended over the fire pit and scooped some warm water from it into a pail. He tested the temperature with his fingers, then carried it over to the tub and knelt behind her.

"Tilt your head back," he commanded, his voice surprisingly gentle.

Merewyn obeyed, and could not prevent the soft sigh that escaped when he drenched her matted locks with the warm, clean water.

"We need soap."

"I do not have any," she confessed. "It is expensive, and..."

"We do have soap. It was among the supplies we salvaged from our ship." He rose and strode across the cottage to rummage among the several sacks and boxes which the Vikings had hauled ashore from their stricken craft. "This is made from acorns. It works well enough and has a pleasant odour."

"Thank you." She offered him a timid, grateful smile. "There are plenty of acorns hereabout. Perhaps you could teach me how to make it, and... oh, that feels pleasant."

The Viking chuckled and continued to massage the soap into her hair, working up a rich lather. "I do not know how to make soap, sadly. Olav may. He appears to be skilled in any amount of ways. I shall ask him for you."

"No, really, I do not wish to... oh!"

Mathios' deft fingers found their way to the nape of her neck and caressed her sensitive skin. As Merewyn groaned her appreciation he pressed more firmly, then extended his soothing touch across her shoulders.

"That is not my hair," Merewyn observed, though she did not move to escape his knowing fingers.

"Do you wish me to stop?" He curled his hands around both her clavicles and squeezed.

Merewyn barely managed to contain the groan of pleasure, but with almost supreme effort she did so. She sat bolt upright in the cooling water, her body stiff.

This is not right. I cannot…

"What is the matter, little Celt? Am I hurting you?"

She shook her head. *No, not yet. But you will. You are a Viking, so it is in your nature. It is as much a part of you as breathing.*

"Please, I want to get out now. The water is cold."

She leaned forward, away from his sensual touch. The Viking let her go but he was not yet finished.

"I must rinse your hair, Merewyn. Be still. It will not take long."

She managed to remain in place, tipping her head back when instructed to do so. He was gentle, thorough, and efficient, but she was not fooled. Merewyn knew his sort. She had encountered the lethal violence of Vikings before and no matter how gently he treated her now, Merewyn could not help but be terrified of him. Of all Norsemen.

At the same time her body betrayed her. Would the Viking notice the way her nipples hardened when his touch fluttered close to her breasts? Could he possibly know of the furious clenching deep in her core as he unleashed feelings she had never before experienced? He awakened something within her, something warm and enticing but deadly too. Her mother was raped by a man just like this. Her father was murdered, her brothers enslaved. Vikings were cruel and merciless savages, every last one of them, and she must never forget that. To believe anything else, to be tempted by such a devil, was foolish.

She had been ill, weakened by her fever. That was the only explanation for the ridiculous fluttering in her belly, for the languorous desire to lay back in his arms and allow him to—

"Stop. I must get out. Now. Please..." She wriggled from his grip, though in truth he did not attempt to hold on to her.

"Of course. Let me—"

"I can manage. Please, leave me."

Mathios rose to his feet and went to her bed. He returned with a blanket. "Stand up, and wrap this around you."

"J-just leave it. I shall..."

"I prefer not to get soaked myself by scooping you out of there, but if I must..."

"No, I..." She had no choice but to stand up, though she pressed one arm tight across her chest and used the other in an ineffectual attempt to conceal the dark curls at the apex of her thighs.

The Viking ignored her bid for modesty and simply draped the blanket about her shoulders then lifted her from the tub as though she was weightless. He set her down on her bed, smiled at her, then summoned Vikarr to assist him in dragging the tub from the cottage.

• • • • • • •

Merewyn was in a quandary. Since her bath she could barely bring herself to look at Mathios, and on every occasion that she inadvertently did so she flushed as red as a berry. He, meanwhile, appeared quite unmoved by the intimate encounter, seemed not to have noticed her inexplicable response to his touch. If he was aware that she found it hard to catch her breath when he was near, he gave no sign of it. Which was just as well, Merewyn thought. He might mistake her natural wariness of him for... something else.

It was vital that *she* did not become similarly confused. He was a handsome man, she would acknowledge that much, and he was without fail pleasant to her. The same was true of the rest of the Norsemen, their leader's influence no doubt. Even so, she must never forget that everything could alter in a heartbeat. These men were dangerous, unpredictable, the murderers of her family. It was impossible to feel anything other than hatred for them, yet with every day that passed Merewyn found it harder to reconcile the inhuman monsters she remembered with the generous, good-natured, and considerate men who now shared her home. And with one in particular…

A couple of days after the bathing incident that had so unnerved her, Mathios again dragged the tub into the cottage and instructed Vikarr to fill it with warm water.

"But, I do not need to bathe again so soon," Merewyn protested.

Mathios grinned at her. "If you say so, little Celt. This is for me."

"You? But I thought you preferred to bathe in the barn." Surely, he could not intend to undress, in here, whilst she looked on.

"Why would I prefer a cold, draughty barn when I can take my bath here, beside the fire? You may avert your gaze, little one, if you find the matter disconcerting."

"Disconcerting? Why should I find it so? I am not in the least interested, and… and…"

"Then there is no problem. Vikarr, how are you doing with the water?"

Merewyn could but perch on a stool and watch as the two men worked to fill the tub. When Mathios considered it ready he instructed the youth to make himself useful chopping firewood, and without so much as a glance in Merewyn's direction he started to undress.

His back was to her, so he could not see that she was staring. In truth, Merewyn was mesmerised by the sight of the tall, powerful Viking disrobing before her very eyes. Horrified and fascinated in equal measure, she watched in stunned wonder as he pulled the loose woollen tunic over his head and dropped it on the floor. The muscles in his back were sharply defined, she noted, and they rippled under the skin as he moved. His shoulders, compelling enough when concealed by his garments, were nothing short of awesome when unclothed.

He bent forward to unfasten the ties of his trousers, and Merewyn seriously considered averting her eyes when he peeled them down over his slim hips to deposit them on the floor also. But she did not. Instead, she stared, open-mouthed. The Viking's bare buttocks were strangely beautiful, as was the rest of his physique. He was large, his brute strength no illusion. He could snap her in two if he chose to. She was right to fear him.

And quite, quite wrong to desire him.

"If you can manage to stop gawping, perhaps you could pass me the soap. It is in the sack over there, by the door." Mathios flung the words over his shoulder as he stepped into the tub.

"I am not gawping," spluttered Merewyn. "I was just… just…"

"The soap, if you please." He grinned at her as she shot across the room to do his bidding. "I do not suppose you might agree to wash my back for me?"

Merewyn shook her head so hard she was convinced her brains were rattling. Or would be if she had any left. She stared at the expanse of bronzed skin, taut across the planes and hollows of his muscled body, and knew she could not touch him.

Dared not touch him.

She flung the soap into the tub and retreated back to her pallet, determined to ignore the naked man who seemed to fill both her cottage and her consciousness.

Mathios bathed quickly. He was efficient, as ever, and soon called for her to pass him a dry blanket. Merewyn sprang into action, relieved that this ordeal was almost over.

"Since the tub is here, and the water is still hot, you might as well make use of it." His smile was pleasant enough, deceptively so in Merewyn's opinion.

"No, I do not think so. As I said, I bathed just the other day, and—"

"Merewyn, I would advise that you do not irritate me by wasting perfectly good hot water. It is still clean, as you can see."

It was, surprisingly so. It occurred to Merewyn to wonder just how recent Mathios' last bath had been as there was certainly not the grime of several days to be seen floating in the bathwater. She would not put it past him to take his bath out in the barn, then deliberately repeat the task indoors just to… to… disconcert her. Yes, that had been the word he used. And it had worked. She was most definitely disconcerted.

"Really, I am tired. If you do not mind I would prefer…"

"Merewyn, you will do as you are told. Did I not make that quite clear to you?"

"Yes, but—"

"Please do not waste time dithering and let your bathwater cool."

Merewyn closed her eyes in frustration, but despite her protests the attraction of another warm bath was powerful. And the Viking chief had already seen her nude body on several occasions so perhaps one more might not be especially significant.

"Very well. I suppose you will insist upon remaining here whilst I bathe."

The Viking's response was to grin at her, that sensual, lopsided smile that never failed to turn her insides to a quivering mush. Merewyn was baffled by her reaction to him. She hated the man, she was quite certain of that, yet still he fascinated her.

"Do you require my aid to undress?"

Merewyn shook her head. "No, I can manage."

Perhaps she could have managed, given time. Merewyn successfully removed her shoes and woollen stockings, and her woven belt, but her joints were still stiff and aching from her illness and she struggled with the rest. Clad now in just his trousers, Mathios stepped forward to assist her in unfastening her kirtle and pulling it over her head, to be followed by her undershirt. She stood before him, naked, and this time resisted the temptation to cover herself with her arms.

The Viking took his time in looking her up and down, his undisguised appreciation apparent in his azure eyes. Merewyn wished he would hurry up and look his fill. She knew her body to be too thin, too angular to be of real interest, but she had no idea how long he had been at sea and lacking female company. Despite his promise not to harm her, she had little faith in Viking powers of restraint.

He smiled and offered her his hand. "May I assist you? We would not wish to have you slip."

Grateful that his perusal seemed to be at an end, she accepted his aid and stepped into the warm water. As soon as she sank down into it she started to relax as the comforting heat again enveloped and soothed her. She lay back, her feet propped on the bottom rim and her shoulders resting against the opposite end. Mathios busied himself in pouring more warm water from the cauldron into the bucket, and he placed that beside the tub.

"Is there enough soap? We have plenty more."

Merewyn fished about in the water and finally retrieved a slender sliver of soap. "It seems to have almost all gone."

He produced another cake of the stuff from a rough box that had been dragged up from the beach a day or two earlier. Merewyn wondered what other delights might be contained within it and resolved to take a look at the first opportunity. Meanwhile she took the offered soap and started to work a lather on her lower legs.

She was conscious that the Viking watched her as she washed her arms, her shoulders, her stomach and lower back. She hesitated over rubbing soap into her breasts, but finally settled for kneeling up and turning her back to him in order to complete her ablutions.

"I shall wash your back. And naturally I shall help you

with your hair."

"That is quite all right. I can manage."

"No one can manage to wash their own back," he argued, approaching the tub. "Lean forward."

"But—"

He leaned down to murmur in her ear. "Obedience, Merewyn. Remember?"

She gulped, and did as she was told.

His fingers were gentle, his hands firm but efficient as he applied the soap then worked it into a lather. Next, he cupped his hands to dribble water down her spine. It was strangely erotic and Merewyn let out a contented sigh. It was so long since anyone had tended to her in such a manner, not since she was little and her mother used to care for her, though this felt very different.

"Put your head back, I shall wash your hair now."

"My hair?"

"Yes. Lie back and let your head drop back over the edge of the tub." He moved the bucket of warm water into place behind her and Merewyn realised what it was for. The clean water would be used to rinse away the dirt and grease in her waist-length locks. She remembered how pleasant it had felt when he had washed her hair before even though in doing as he instructed she would thrust her breasts up and out of the water.

"Do as I say, little Celt."

His voice had hardened, the shift almost imperceptible but enough to impel Merewyn to obedience. She tilted her head back for his ministrations, acutely conscious of the cooling air that now caressed her naked breasts. Her nipples swelled and hardened in the draught. Merewyn prayed that he might not notice, though she knew he would.

This Viking missed nothing.

He poured the clean water over her hair, lifting the long tresses to dunk them in the water before applying the soap. He massaged the lather into her scalp, his fingers working large, firm circles on her sensitised flesh. Despite the embarrassing state of her nipples, not to mention the peculiar clenching at her core that she was quite unable to control, Merewyn was mortified when she let out an involuntary moan.

"I am sorry, I did not mean—"

"It is not a problem. Please, relax, make such sounds as you wish."

"I would not wish you to think that I… I…"

"That you are enjoying this?"

"Yes."

"I know that you are, but we need not dwell upon that fact if you prefer not to."

"Thank you," she whispered.

"And this? Do you like this also?" He shifted his fingers to the nape of her neck just as he had done before, and proceeded to caress the delicate skin there.

Merewyn opted not to respond, though her nipples tightened even more and heat furled at her core.

She should have protested when his fingers once again crept over her shoulders, kneading and squeezing until she believed she might expire with the sheer pleasure of it. Her muscles stretched and loosened, the stress of recent days falling away. There was something almost magical in his touch, a knowing, practised ease. He seemed to understand her body's needs better than she did.

Merewyn lay still as he continued his exploration, his clever fingers moving lower, across her chest to find her puckered nipples.

She gasped, tried to find the words to beg him to stop but this time they would not come. He rolled the pebbled nubs between his fingers and thumbs, his touch gentle but firming as she writhed in the water. He squeezed, almost to the point of pain, then relaxed his grip and circled the sensitive peaks with his fingertips.

"Does this feel good, little Celt?"

Merewyn closed her eyes and nodded. Heat furled within her belly, spreading and blooming. She ached, deep down, between her thighs in that secret place that only she knew of. She fought the urge to reach down, as she did occasionally in the warm privacy of her bed, to seek out that exact spot where pleasure was to be found.

It was as though he was somehow privy to her most secret thoughts, her most intimate yearnings. His right hand ceased to tease and tantalise her nipple and instead he reached down into the water, between her legs to find that precise place. He was unerring, it was as though he knew exactly what would arouse her and drive her wild with desire. His fingers parted her folds and settled on the small nub that lay concealed there.

He rubbed. He flicked it with his fingertip. He slid his digits on either side and traced the outline, then he explored lower, found the entrance to her body and dipped the tip of one finger inside.

Never, when she had touched herself, had she felt like this. Not even remotely. Utterly wanton in her response, Merewyn bucked in his embrace. She lifted her arm from the water to drape it back and around his neck as though to anchor herself. He murmured something in her ear, incomprehensible words in his native tongue. She did not understand but her arousal built and bloomed anyway. It was as though her body were no longer her own but his to control. He stroked her again, caressed that sensitive bundle of nerves until she could bear it no more.

"Please..." Her voice was ragged, her breath shallow. "Please do not..."

"Do you wish me to stop, little Celt?"

Yes. No. She could find no words, so merely hung on as her inner muscles contracted and clenched.

Mathios placed his thumb over her pleasure bud at the same time as he plunged his fingers into her cunny. It was too much. Her senses were totally overwhelmed, her body weightless, floating as white light exploded behind her eyes. She shook with the power of her body's response. Wave after wave of carnal pleasure washed though her, starting at her core where his fingers still worked their sorcery and flowing right out to the ends of her fingers and toes.

The assault on her senses seemed to continue for ages, though she supposed it was over almost as quickly as it began. As her shudders subsided she lay limp in his arms, the bathwater rolling up and down in the tub from her thrashing. Her legs were spread wide, her feet dangling over the sides of the bath. She had no recollection of moving but knew she must have done so, must have opened her thighs to allow him access. And now, now that he had pleasured her, he would expect his own gratification.

Any residual pleasure fled. Merewyn cringed. What had she done? How had she allowed this to happen? He would take what he wanted and she would be powerless to resist.

"Thank you. That was beautiful." His deep timbre rumbled from somewhere behind her, close to her ear.

"I beg your pardon?" She twisted her neck to look into his eyes. They were warm, sensual. She should have found his proximity threatening, but she did not.

"Your response was beautiful. Quite exquisite. I thank you for allowing me to share it."

"I do not understand…"

"Do you not? You will. Do you feel better now?"

"I am not sure how I feel. What happened? What did you do? I have never…"

Mathios chuckled. "We should finish washing your hair while the water remains warm."

Stunned, Merewyn could only watch as he carried the bucket of now cloudy water to the door and flung the contents outside. He returned, refilled the pail with clean, hot water from the pot and proceeded to rinse the lather from her hair. Then he found the comb that she had discarded on her pallet and used it to bring her long tresses into order, his strokes firm yet gentle as he teased out the knots and gnarls before laying each smooth lock over her shoulder.

Merewyn remained still as he worked, not sure what

would happen next. Worse, she was no longer entirely certain what she *wanted* to have happen. This Viking was not at all what she expected.

"Did your husband not bring you similar joy when you shared his bed?"

"I have no husband," retorted Merewyn. Why on earth would he imagine she did?

"I realise that, else why would you and the little one be here alone? What happened to your family, Merewyn?"

Any softening in her attitude evaporated. He and his kind were responsible for the deaths of her family, for her brothers' abduction and enslavement. Vikings were the reason she and Connell were obliged to eke out a joyless, harsh living, alone and friendless in this barren place.

"They died. Or left." Her tone was clipped, her answers curt. She hoped he would not press her for more as he was certain to find her response disrespectful and he had already warned her of the consequences of such foolishness.

"I see."

Merewyn sincerely doubted that. Vikings only saw what was in their interest, what suited them. But this one seemed willing to let the matter drop, and she was glad of it.

Mathios knelt behind her as he combed her hair. When he completed the task he got to his feet. Merewyn watched, wary, as he moved over to her bed. But the Viking merely picked up a blanket and returned to the tub.

"Wrap this around yourself and sit by the fire." He offered her his hand to assist her from the rapidly cooling water, then wrapped the blanket around her shoulders. He smiled at her as he tossed more logs on the flickering flames.

Merewyn, confused and bewildered, huddled in the warmth as Mathios and Vikarr hauled the bathtub out of the cottage.

CHAPTER FIVE

With each passing day Merewyn gained in strength. She still tired easily but was no longer confined to her pallet and took to rising early, with the Vikings, and taking her breakfast with them. Their cheerful conversation echoed around her. She struggled to understand most of it, but had picked up a few words of their tongue. She knew that they referred to the morning meal as *dagmal*, and that it was eaten all together before they dispersed for their various tasks. There was little in the way of vegetables or grain so their morning fare usually consisted of eggs and whatever meat had been left over from the previous evening.

It would do. Their bellies were full, a luxury Merewyn could barely remember.

As her health returned Merewyn found her inactivity galling. By common but unspoken consent she took over the task of preparing the food that the Vikings provided each day. She was not without cooking skills though she had had little cause to employ them in recent months. Her mother had been a skilled cook, adept in creating delicate flavours to enhance their fare using the herbs and spices she collected from the surrounding countryside. Merewyn still possessed the chest Ronat had used to store her collection of herbs. It was one of the few mementos of her family to escape the destructive fury of the Vikings and she treasured it greatly though she had had little use for the contents of late. Now, she examined the herbs and selected those that could still be used. For the most part these were roots, and dried substances that did not spoil so quickly as fresh ingredients. The rest she discarded. She would replenish her supplies when the spring arrived and the various plants were again available in the meadows.

In Merewyn's hands Olav's abundant rabbits found their way into stews, flavoured with rosemary and perhaps a little sage. Merewyn foraged for what she could find to add to the pot: dandelions, nettles, the small green apples that littered the meadow. Fish she would bake with marjoram. The Vikings appreciated her efforts though they bemoaned the lack of milk to make butter and cheese.

"Where might we acquire a cow?" asked Mathios as they shared the *dagmal* one morning.

"Old Alfred might have a heifer to spare. He has a farmstead perhaps five miles inland." Merewyn recalled that the elderly farmer had been a friend of her father and they had occasionally purchased livestock from him. Old Alfred's beasts were healthy and he was known to be fair in his dealings, though whether he would wish to trade with Vikings she could not be certain. She hoped so, since dairy products would greatly enhance their diet and now that she was not constantly occupied in caring for Connell she would have the time to churn butter and make cheese. She recalled her mother had a recipe for cheese that used honey and ginger. Perhaps she might acquire those ingredients too since the Vikings seemed amenable to trading. Sadly, the local population may prove less willing.

"You can take us there?" Mathios regarded her with interest.

"Yes, but Alfred may not wish to trade with you. Or he may not have an animal he is prepared to sell." There were few in this land who had not suffered at the hands of the

Vikings in recent years and Merewyn feared the memories might still be too raw to permit the prospect of peaceful commerce to flourish.

"He will trade with us," affirmed Mathios. "One way or another. We go next week. By then you will be sufficiently recovered to undertake the walk."

Merewyn did not answer. *One way or another.* What did that mean?

If Alfred did not agree to trade willingly with the Vikings, would he be forced to do so? Or worse still, his livestock stolen? If so, she would be complicit in the robbery since she would have led the Vikings to Alfred's door. What if they threatened the old man's family, or worse? He had three daughters and several grandchildren. There were menfolk at the farmstead, as far as she knew, but they would be no match for these Vikings.

Why had she not kept her mouth shut? She'd had no need to tell them of Alfred and his herd of fine heifers. This was all her fault. She could not permit it to happen.

The men left to be about the day's tasks, leaving Merewyn alone. Mathios no longer insisted that one of his warriors remain with her, though he admonished her to rest if she felt fatigued and she was usually willing enough to do so as her strength soon ebbed. She was racked with guilt as she cleared away the remnants of their morning meal and cleaned the platters. There must be some way she could alert Alfred to the danger.

Her musings were cut short by the reappearance of a triumphant Olav, a young boar dangling across his shoulders. He dumped the carcase on the table and said something indecipherable to Merewyn. His delight in the kill was writ across his smiling features.

She just stared at the animal. Had she not been preoccupied with other concerns Merewyn would certainly share his enthusiasm for a decent leg of pork. She could cook it well enough, but unfortunately she had no knowledge of butchering. Luckily it seemed Olav did, and with Vikarr's assistance he set about slicing the carcase into convenient cuts of meat, some to be consumed in the coming days, the rest to be preserved in salt and stored for the winter. Merewyn ran hither and thither with pails of brine and between them they succeeded in reducing the beast to manageable portions. They would enjoy a fine meal of pork and chestnuts this evening.

Olav and Vikarr left to continue with whatever tasks awaited them outside. Left to herself, Merewyn placed one of the legs of pork on a spit and set it over the fire to roast. When it was tender, a couple of hours later, she sliced it into her pot with some chestnuts and a few leeks she had managed to find in her meagre kitchen garden. She opened her mother's medicine chest to select the correct herbs needed to enhance the flavour.

It was then that she saw it.

The crinkled mandrake root lay at the bottom of the casket, unused but perfectly preserved. An idea began to form.

Could she? Would it work?

Mandrake was renowned for its narcotic effect. Once imbibed it would induce sleep, for several hours at least. It would require care, naturally, to achieve the correct dosage but the herb was tasteless, so could easily be concealed in food. She glanced at the pot where the succulent pork simmered. The meat would be devoured in no time by the ravenous Norsemen. In recent days they had become accustomed to her adding flavoursome herbs to their meals and would have no suspicions. They would slumber for hours after eating the meat, ample time for her and Connell to make their escape and seek shelter with a neighbour. Not Alfred, of course not, but surely someone would take them in. She had only to remain hidden until the spring, when the Norsemen would leave and she would be able to return to her home. Or what might be left of it by then.

No matter. The Norsemen could do their worst. She had survived their destruction before and would do so again.

And this way she could not be coerced into betraying her defenceless neighbours. She could find a way to warn them, in which case they might be able to make ready and withstand any attack. Vikings dealt in stealth and speed, but without the element of surprise they were less lethal.

The plan crystallised in her mind. Merewyn took the root and sought to remember what her mother had told her about the correct dosage. Too much, and the Vikings might never wake up but that was not her intention. She had realised on that first day in the forest that she did not have the stomach for murder. She would do what she had to in order to secure her own safety and Connell's and that of her neighbours, but she would not resort to killing. That would make her no better than the Vikings.

Ronat had always admonished her to apply great care when seeking to heal with herbal remedies. It was too easy to do harm, and that must be avoided. Not all ailments could be cured, but it was often possible to provide relief, and the mandrake was particularly efficacious. When judiciously applied it would induce sleep, or dull pain. Women such as her mother trod a delicate path between being revered as a wise and good healer and being reviled as a witch. It was an unforgiving career and too many dead patients would soon get a healer condemned to a fiery end. Ronat had been a good teacher and Merewyn possessed many of her mother's skills. She had little doubt that she could employ the mandrake to subdue her unwelcome visitors long enough to affect her escape.

Merewyn quelled her misgivings at such an act. Her mother would never normally have countenanced such use of her potions, but Merewyn set aside those objections. If she were here now, surely Ronat would applaud her actions. The need was dire and urgent, the circumstances extreme. She had no choice but to use such methods as were available to her.

Merewyn worked quickly. She peeled and grated the root, and took care to add copious amounts of water to the pot to ensure the mandrake potion was well diluted when she added it to the stew. She set aside a little of the unadulterated pork for herself and for Connell. She would need to conjure up an excuse for taking their meal separately; a feigned attack of sudden fatigue would probably do the trick.

Her preparations made, Merewyn sat at the table to await the Vikings' return.

• • • • • • •

It was a cheerful group who trooped into the cottage just before nightfall. Word of Olav's success in taking the boar had got around and all were looking forward to their evening meal. Connell occupied his usual perch on Arne's shoulders, and Merewyn rushed to lift him down. She sought to settle him in his cot but unfortunately, the little boy did not appreciate his banishment to the corner and set up an insistent wailing.

"Hush. You will get your food soon enough," Merewyn admonished him as she gave the cauldron a final stir. Connell continued to complain loudly but she could not attend to him yet.

She did not even need to ask them to sit. The Vikings jostled and shoved each other as they crowded around the table, settling themselves on upturned barrels and makeshift benches as she worked quickly to fill their platters. Vikarr was first, slurping his meal down with gusto. Then Ormarr and Olav. Vikarr was already asking for more even before the rest of his colleagues had been served.

Ivar gave the youth a hard nudge with his elbow and muttered something that caused the others to laugh. Merewyn scurried about, continuing to dole out the pork until all the plates were full. Then she provided Vikarr with his second helping, though she was careful to make it a modest portion. She set her ladle down and regarded the assembled Norsemen with no small degree of anxiety.

Her breath congealed in her throat.

"No!" Merewyn leapt forward to dash the piece of pork from Arne's hand. While she had been preoccupied in serving out their food, the large Viking must have plucked Connell from his bed and settled the child on his knee intending to share his meal.

All eyes turned to her. Connell set up his wailing again at the abrupt loss of his food. Mathios lifted one eyebrow and regarded her with surprise.

"Is something amiss, Merewyn?" The Viking chief chewed thoughtfully as he waited for her answer.

"N-no," she stammered. "I merely intended that Connell would eat with me this evening, that is all."

"He seems content where he is," observed Mathios, "or he will be once he gets something to eat. Arne…?" He gestured to the warrior to continue feeding the child.

Merewyn watched in horror as Arne selected another piece of succulent pork and offered it to the baby. Connell took it in his chubby fist and started to shove it into his mouth.

"No!" She rushed around the table to grab the morsel before the eager and hungry baby could take a bite from it. "That… that piece is too big. He may choke. Please, allow me to take him. I will cut his meat more finely and you may all get on with your meal."

Mathios cocked his head to one side as he regarded her. "I am sure Arne does not mind. And the child has had no trouble eating up to now. Leave him be, Merewyn and get your own food. I see you do not have a platter."

"No, I am tired." A note of desperation had crept into her voice. "I thought to eat mine on my pallet, and Connell also needs to sleep now. Please, may I take him?"

Arne looked from her to his leader and back, clearly unsure what was happening. Connell set to wailing again. Mathios' expression hardened, his gaze was suspicious now. He furrowed his brow.

"No, leave the boy where he is. Go and help yourself

from the pot and we shall make room for you here." He shifted on the bench to create a space for her. "Arne, give the lad some of this delicious pork before our ears start to bleed."

He spoke in the English tongue but Arne took his meaning even so. Another piece of pork was selected and offered. Merewyn sprang forward to dash the entire platter to the floor, at the same moment that Vikarr toppled from his perch on a barrel.

"What the…" Mathios crouched over the youth who lay face down on the floor. He spoke to him in the Norse tongue. The lad's only response was a gentle snore.

Mathios straightened and glared at Merewyn. "What have you done? What is in this food?"

"Nothing. I mean, just a few herbs, and—"

"Yet you do not eat it, and neither will to you allow the child to do so…" He paused to swipe his hand across his brow and she saw him stagger. The drug was starting to work. She glanced around the table and was relieved to see that the rest were similarly affected. Several of the Vikings swayed in their seats. Ywan had already slumped forward to rest his head on his arms. Just a few more moments…

"The food is poisoned." Mathios' tone was accusing, his expression furious. "Is it not?" Despite the effects of the drug he was able to grasp her arm and drag her in front of him. "Tell me…"

Merewyn quaked before his anger. It never occurred to her to lie to him. "N-not poisoned. Merely a sleeping draught…"

"Why?" he demanded. "Why would you do this?"

"I… I was hoping to escape. While you were sleeping." She tried to wrestle her arm free but he was stronger and held her with ease.

"How long will the effects last? Is the dose fatal?"

She shook her head vehemently. "No, not fatal. Just enough to induce a deep sleep."

"How long?" he repeated, his voice a low growl now.

Merewyn shook, her terror almost palpable in the face of his fury. She had meant to hide in her bed, stay out of their way until they all succumbed to the soporific effects of the mandrake but her plan was unravelling fast. They would surely kill her for this.

"How long?" he demanded.

"A few hours, no more." She jumped as Ivar rolled from his seat to join Vikarr on the floor.

Mathios lurched toward her, his tall frame swaying as he fought to hang onto his senses. "You will be tied to your bed…"

Arne got to his feet, still holding Connell. He laid his hand on the chief's arm and spoke quietly to him. Mathios listened, nodded, and relinquished Merewyn's arm. "Arne has not eaten… He will…" Mathios finally succumbed to the effects of her drug and crumpled to the floor.

A stony-faced Arne stepped around his fallen chief and grasped her by the elbow. He tugged her across the cottage and shoved her down onto her pallet then set Connell beside her. Next, he produced a kerchief from within his tunic. He did not speak as he pushed Merewyn onto her stomach and pulled her hands into the small of her back where he secured them tightly with the kerchief. He allowed her to roll onto her side, then plucked the baby up again and started to walk away.

"No, wait, please…"

Arne paused and looked back at her over his shoulder. He spoke briefly to her, his tone curt. She did not understand the Nordic phrase, but his meaning was clear enough. She was to wait.

By now the rest of the Vikings were in various states of slumber, either on the floor or slumped over the table. Arne checked each in turn, then placed Connell in his cot. The large Viking spent the next few minutes hauling the cauldron containing the drugged pork from the fire and dragging it across the floor to the door. He left, to return a few minutes later, the cauldron now empty.

As Merewyn watched from her pallet, Arne roasted a few pieces of rabbit meat on a spit, a meal for himself and Connell. He did not offer anything to Merewyn. It seemed she was to go hungry.

CHAPTER SIX

His head ached. His senses were strangely dulled; a peculiar lethargy assailed every bone and muscle in his body.

Mathios rolled onto his back and sought to recall where he was. Eventually he was forced to resort to prising his eyelids apart in order to survey his surroundings and settle that pressing question. He managed to focus on the rough beams that supported the roof of the shelter, but this was not his longhouse. There were none of the familiar scents that pervaded his home—the aroma of baking bread or the smell of madder boiling over the fire to make dye. His stepmother's cheerful chatter was absent also. Instead he was surrounded by silence, broken only by the occasional snuffle or snore. He turned his head to the right. Vikarr lay sound asleep not a foot from him. To his left he spied Ivar, just starting to stir.

By Odin's blood… Mathios shoved himself up on one elbow and immediately regretted his impetuous move when the contents of his stomach threatened to spill. He groaned and lay back down, waited until the unfamiliar room ceased its spinning.

"You are awake, Jarl?"

He recognised Arne's voice and risked opening his eyes

again. The warrior stood at his feet, his arms folded over his wide chest.

"What the fuck happened? I feel like shite."

"You were drugged. And the rest, too." Arne waved his hand to indicate the room at large. Mathios ventured another look. Olav lay on his side, just beyond Ivar, and Ormarr sat slumped over the table. "How…?" he began, though the events of the previous evening were already coming back to him. Assuming it *was* the previous evening… "How long have we been asleep?" he demanded.

"Twelve hours. You are the first to regain consciousness, Jarl, though I believe Olav may be stirring. And Ivar."

"Where is she?" Mathios sat up. He remembered perfectly now, and he had matters to settle with the duplicitous Celtic wench.

"On her pallet. I bound her as you commanded and she has remained there the entire night."

"Help me up." Mathios held out his hand and his warrior hauled him to his feet. He staggered slightly but managed to hold his balance. Across the room the one he sought huddled on her pallet, her deep brown eyes wide with apprehension as she stared up at him. She would do well to fear him. And she could fucking well wait.

He made the rounds of his sleeping men, crouching by each in turn to satisfy himself that they were as well as might be hoped in the circumstances. Olav's eyelids flickered and his cousin peered up at him.

"I believe I may have been crushed by a horse. The beast actually stamped on my head, I swear…"

Mathios chuckled. Olav would live. The rest too, probably, though he was concerned about Vikarr. He recalled that the youth ate two helpings of the drugged pork, and his smaller frame would render him more susceptible to the effects of the narcotic.

"Watch him closely," he instructed Arne. Satisfied there was nothing he could do for his men apart from wait for them to wake up, he turned his attention to the girl.

Merewyn shrank away from him as he approached. Her features were pale in the thin morning light that entered through the open door to the dwelling and she looked to have been weeping. No doubt her sorrow arose from the fact that her idiotic plan had failed.

He stood at the foot of the bed and glared at the terrified wench. Her hands were bound behind her, which had the effect of pushing her pert breasts out. He could discern the outline of her nipples beneath the thin fabric of her tunic. On another day he would have appreciated the sight more. Now it merely added to his disappointment in her. He had genuinely liked the girl. He had come to an understanding with her, or so he thought. He had trusted her, so her betrayal cut deep.

Her lips moved, she mouthed something. He frowned, not quite able to…

I am sorry…

She repeated the soundless apology and this time he understood her words.

"Are you? Are you really sorry, Merewyn?" He deliberately softened his tone and he crouched to better see her features. "I can assure you, you will be much, much sorrier by the time I am done with you."

Her face paled even more. Mathios marvelled that that was even possible. He narrowed his eyes and asked the question uppermost in his mind.

"Why? Why did you do it?"

She swallowed, hard, and remained silent.

"I asked you a question. Do not make me force you to answer."

"I am sorry," she repeated.

"So I understand. Why did you poison our meal, Merewyn?"

"It was not poison… It was just a sleeping draught. I meant you no harm."

"You say the food was harmless, yet you would not eat it, nor would you allow your baby to take any." He paused, held her gaze. "I do not believe you, Merewyn. Your lies will only make matters worse for you."

"How might they be worse?" Her voice shook, she was close to tears. "I know you will kill me."

"You know this? How?"

"It… it is what you do."

"In truth, I have not yet decided what I intend to do to you, though you may be sure you will not like it. But I have more questions first." He waited, assessing her pallid face, the tears already forming behind her eyes. She would soon be weeping again, and in his experience a sobbing female was difficult to get any sense out of. "Calm yourself, girl. I am not about to hurt you. Not yet, at least."

She gulped, seemed to be fighting for control though tears had started to flow. Mathios moved around the bed to crouch beside her, and reached out to wipe away the tears with the pads of his thumbs. He deliberately gentled his voice.

"Tell me why you did it, Merewyn."

His softer tone seemed to work. "I… I wanted to escape. I thought that if I had a few hours' start you would not be able to find me."

Mathios was incredulous. Her scheme was utter madness. "Where would you have gone? It is almost winter. You would not be able to survive out in the open, Connell even less so."

"I would have run to a neighbour's home. I do not know which one, nor even which farmsteads are still occupied. But I would have found somewhere…"

"A desperate act, Merewyn, and a dangerous one. What if you found not friends but enemies? You are vulnerable, defenceless. There are those who would harm a woman alone…"

"Yes. They are called Vikings."

The accusation, and the bitterness in her retort, galled him more than he might have expected. "We have not harmed you, or even threatened to. You have been fed, protected, cared for. Your child, too. Why would you believe we mean you harm?"

"It is the Viking way."

"What do you know of the Viking way?"

"I know that you raid, that you attack without warning. That is what you planned for Alfred, is it not?"

"Alfred?"

"The man who has cows for trade."

"Ah, that Alfred. We would barter with this Alfred for a good dairy cow, that is all. We discussed our plans, you heard us. Why would you think otherwise?"

"You said… you said you would make him trade with you, one way or another."

"Yes, I said that. So?"

"So that was why I had to escape, so that you could not force me to lead you to him."

"What the fuck are you talking about?" Mathios' patience was wearing thin. "We wish to purchase a cow from him. Why would he take that amiss? He could refuse to trade with us if he wished, though that would surprise me."

"No! You mean to force him to let you have the cow. You would rob him, hurt his family, burn his home."

"We would do no such thing. I merely meant that we would offer him enough in exchange for his beast that he could not refuse. All have their price, Merewyn, even this Alfred you seek to protect."

"You… you would not have harmed him?"

Mathios shook his head. "No, we would not." He decided to explain more fully in order to convince her. "Had we been in a position to leave these shores anytime we choose to, we might have behaved as you describe. It is, as you say, our way. But we are stuck here, we have no way of leaving for several months at least. We cannot afford to provoke the local populace. We are but eight men and whilst we might be victorious in a short, brutal fight, we would be defeated in a sustained campaign. It would not make sense for us to start a war. It suits us to have peace prevail for as long as we are stranded here. We must seek to live quietly alongside Alfred and the rest, and by trading we can make our stay more comfortable. That is all we planned."

"I… I do not believe you. You are lying."

He smiled, though without humour. "I am glad you raised that matter. I have not lied to you, ever, but you cannot make the same claim."

"What do you mean?"

"You promised to cooperate, to cause me no problems. You promised me obedience and respect. In return, I guaranteed your safety. You broke your word."

"I was… I thought…"

"I know what you thought, and you were wrong. I meant what I said. You would not have been hurt, nor would anyone else, had you just done as you were told."

"I… what do you mean to do to me?"

"We shall come to that. First, you will tell me how you knew of the drug you used. Where did you obtain it?"

"M-my mother. She was a healer and she taught me her skills."

"It was she, I assume, who taught you to use herbs to flavour food."

"Yes."

"It is a pity you did not confine your culinary efforts to just that. I recall you mentioned mandrake?"

"Yes," she whispered.

"Do you have any still?"

"A little. But I swear I will never—"

"Where is it?"

"You have my word…"

"Must I tear this place apart to find it?"

She shook her head. "My herbs are in a box, in the corner where the broom and the scythe are kept. It… it is concealed beneath some sacking."

Mathios called to Olav. "Go look in the corner behind the broomstick. You are seeking a box. Bring it to me." He spoke in Norse but knew the wench understood his instruction to his man. A few minutes later Olav passed him a small wooden chest fastened with a metal hasp. It was not locked. Mathios took the box and flicked open the lid.

The aroma of marjoram and rosemary tickled his nostrils, and sage too if he was not mistaken. To the best of his knowledge those were harmless but he knew little of such things. He did not even know which plant was which.

He placed the box on the pallet beside Merewyn. "Show me the mandrake."

"It is there, at the bottom. The root…"

It appeared innocuous to Mathios, but he now knew better. He took the tuber and rolled it in his palm. "Is this all you have?"

"Yes. I swear it."

Mathios was unconvinced. "You have given your word before." He gripped her jaw with his free hand, forcing her to meet his gaze. Her fearful whimper afforded him less pleasure than he imagined it would. He relaxed his grip. "Very well. But this will be destroyed. All of it. You will have no need of herbs and potions in the future."

"But—"

"Be silent, wench, and consider yourself fortunate that I do not force you to eat this root yourself."

"That would be a lethal dose," she gasped.

"Indeed? I must take your word for that. No matter. It goes on the fire. Olav…?"

"No! Please, allow me to keep the box."

"The box? Why? What is its significance?"

"It belonged to my mother. It is one of the few things of hers which remain. Please…"

Mathios dropped the mandrake back into the casket and handed the whole lot to Olav. "Burn this."

The girl let out an anguished moan then lay down, weeping, her back to him. Mathios left her for a few moments while he oversaw the destruction of the herbs. He returned to the pallet and knelt beside it.

"Merewyn, look at me."

"I hate you," she sobbed. "You are vile, and a brute, and—"

"Turn over and look at me," he commanded. "Now."

She obeyed. Her eyes were reddened from crying, her expression one of despair rather than hatred, though he considered it a near run thing.

He placed her mother's box on the pallet.

Her eyes widened. "But I thought… Why?"

"I, too, have a mother and I would wish to be able to look her in the eye when I return home. You may keep the box."

"Th-thank you," she stammered.

"Your actions were foolish. Had you succeeded, you would have endangered yourself, and your baby, as well as putting me to the considerable bother of seeking you out. For we would have pursued you, and be assured, Merewyn, we would have found you wherever you tried to hide."

"I do not—"

"Be silent. You will be punished for your actions, but I choose not to administer your chastisement until you are fully recovered from your illness. Until then, you will be confined to this bed."

"What… what do you mean to do with me?"

"You will be whipped. I expect the lesson will be a memorable one."

"Whipped? No, please…"

"The matter is decided. You would do well to resign yourself to your punishment since there is nothing you can do or say to change it. You made a mistake, and you must pay for it. I sincerely hope you will not repeat this madness and I am prepared to do what I can to ensure that outcome." He paused to allow his words to sink in. "Now, since I am not a cruel or unreasonable man and I am aware you have been restrained here all night, I will allow you the opportunity to visit the privy. Turn around and I shall free your wrists."

Her hands trembled as he untied the kerchief. The prospect of a whipping clearly unnerved her. That was good, it suggested that when the time came the lesson would be well-learned.

• • • • • • •

The days crept past. Merewyn's wrists and ankles were bound, though Mathios allowed her to have her hands in front so she was a little more comfortable. She lay on her pallet, largely ignored by the Vikings unless one of them was instructed to escort her to the privy. Those occasions were humiliating. On the second day she protested, only to be forced to endure hours of needing to relieve herself before she was finally taken from the cottage to the place close to the edge of the woods where such functions were performed. Hakon was her companion on that occasion. He stationed himself a few feet from her whilst she completed what was necessary then led her back in silence. She had not complained since.

Arne usually brought her food, and she ate alone on her pallet. Connell took his meals with the Vikings, passed from one to the other while Merewyn could only watch from her place on the outside, excluded from the rest.

Despite the lonely monotony of her existence, time seemed to fly. Each day brought her punishment closer and Merewyn could think of little else. She became convinced she would not survive the whipping. No one had laid a hand on her since she was a child, and even then her mother's approach to discipline was not harsh. What would be Connell's fate if she died, or was injured and unable to work to support them both? Despite the loathing for the Vikings, which she told herself was undimmed, she was confused by her conflicted emotions. Mathios was angry with her and she understood why. Worse, he was disappointed in her, and that hurt. She should not care what he thought of her, but she did anyway. She feared the Viking chief, but perversely she also wished to please him.

She was ready to beg, to plead for her life, if Mathios would only listen, but he could not listen if he was not there. He would leave the cottage soon after first light and not return until it was time for the *nattmal* or evening meal. On the third day of her incarceration he left the cottage accompanied by Hakon, Ormarr, and Vikarr and did not return at nightfall. Olav was now in charge, and he did not appear concerned at the absence of his chief.

Mathios and the others returned the following afternoon, in high spirits as they were now in possession of a fine heifer, a goat, and more chickens, as well as sufficient grain to feed their livestock through the coming winter. Merewyn had to assume they had located Alfred's farmstead without her assistance.

She had expected the chief to make himself scarce again but he did not. Instead, he conferred with Olav. They both glanced in her direction several times so she presumed she was the subject of their discussion. Sure enough, Mathios approached her pallet, his expression stern and set.

"Olav informs me that you have not coughed this day." He laid his hand on her forehead. "There is no trace of the fever left. How do you feel?"

She could lie. She could claim a headache or other residual malady but that would merely prolong the agony of this waiting and ultimately anger him more if he should discover her deception. "I… I believe I am well," she whispered.

He drew a dagger and sliced though the rope binding her hands and feet. "It is time. Come with me."

CHAPTER SEVEN

He deliberately kept his expression stern and unyielding as Merewyn scrambled to her feet and followed him to the door of the dwelling. Her meek compliance was encouraging. Mathios picked up his cloak from the chair where he had left it and slung it around his shoulders. He picked up another, Vikarr's, and tossed it to the girl.

"It is chilly outside. You will need that. And some shoes."

She looked down at her feet, bare but for a pair of well-worn stockings. She rushed back to the pallet and retrieved her footwear from beside it then returned to present herself before him.

So far, so good.

"Where are we going?"

Ah, questions at last. "The barn."

"Oh. But, it is in ruins. Why…?"

"Come." He was not about to debate his plans with her. Mathios strode through the door without a backward glance, and started to march around the cottage to where the barn stood at the rear. The girl was correct of course, the barn had been derelict when they arrived. But no longer. He would not have gone to the trouble and expense of purchasing a cow had he nowhere to safely house the beast. In the weeks since he and his men had arrived here they had made substantial repairs to the cottage and outbuildings. The barn now sported a roof that was intact and reasonably weatherproof, stalls for livestock, as well as space for storing the grain they had acquired. The repairs were not complete, but the building would suit his purpose now.

Mathios reached the door and pulled it open. Merewyn trotted behind him, her expression one of amazement.

"It is mended."

"Yes, mostly. Inside, please." He gestured for her to pass him.

Inside, the roof of the barn was supported by three central poles arranged at equal intervals down its length. It was divided into two halves. The portion closest to the outer door now housed the cow who regarded them solemnly as she chewed on her straw. The goat skipped about in the pen alongside. Her shrill bleating grated on Mathios' ears. He was not fond of goats but had agreed to the purchase as he was assured the milk would be good for Connell. Mathios strode past both animals and expected Merewyn to follow.

She did not disappoint him.

The far end of the barn offered storage. A half dozen or so bundles of hay were stacked at one end along with a few sacks of grain. The rest of the space was open. A bucket stood by the pole in the middle, just as he had instructed.

Mathios turned to the bewildered girl. "You will remove your clothes."

"What?" She took a step back, away from him. "No, I will not. Surely—"

He injected a steeliness into his tone and fixed her with a look that would quell the most hardened of his warriors. "You will do as I say. I require you to be naked for this."

"But—"

"We can accomplish what must be done with just you and me present but if need be I can invite others of my men to lend their aid. Do you require my men to join us in here and strip you in readiness for your switching, or will you do it yourself?"

She gaped at him, her pretty mouth forming a startled moue as she weighed her options.

"Well, Merewyn, shall I summon Hakon or Ormarr to assist us?"

She shook her head and started to remove the cloak.

Satisfied that his instructions were to be carried out, Mathios strode past Merewyn intending to check the contents of the pail. He had asked Olav to ensure that a bundle of fine switches be prepared in his absence, all stripped smooth to make sure no sharp twigs remained. Once ready they were to be left in a bucket of water to ensure they remained fresh and supple. No sooner had he moved from his position between her and the door than Merewyn seized her chance. The wench turned on her heel and she fled.

Fuck! He cursed under his breath and went after her.

Of course, her ill-fated efforts gained her nothing. Mathios reached her in a few strides. He caught her about the waist and carried her the rest of the way to the door, then he pressed her against the heavy oaken portal as she wriggled and fought to escape him. Mathios allowed her to resist him for a few moments, enjoying the feel of her slim body squirming against his, but they had work to do. Using one hand, he caught her wrists and pinned them above her head. He turned her around so that she faced him, only to have her attempt to bring her knee up and deliver what would have been a singularly painful blow. He tightened his grip on her wrists and leaned in close.

Still she struggled, her panic mounting. This had to stop.

He leaned in so his mouth was close to her ear, then he kept his voice low and even when he spoke to her. "Merewyn, calm down. You do yourself no good by fighting me."

"I cannot… You… you…"

"Hush, and listen to me."

"Let me go. Please, I am sorry, I will never—"

"Merewyn, look at me. And listen." His tone was implacable but not harsh. Mathios used his free hand to cup her chin and force her gaze up to meet his. "There, that is better, Now, are you ready to hear what I have to say?"

"I cannot…" Her expression was one of pure terror.

Mathios decided a fresh tack was required. He released her wrists and gathered her close in his arms. He stroked large, slow circles on her back and held her against his chest until she stopped shaking. Only then did he attempt to reason with her again.

"You can do this. You have earned this switching, and you will accept it. You are not a child, you are a woman grown and I know you can conquer your fear and get through this. It will soon be over."

"But, I have never…"

He smiled at her. "Now that surprises me, but there must be a first time for everything. Let us hope you do not give me cause to repeat this lesson then."

"I will not, I swear. There is no need to… to…"

"Ah, but there is. You need to understand the consequences of disobedience and I am confident that a smarting bottom will prove most instructive in that regard. You will remember what I am about to do to you, and perhaps be deterred from contemplating similar foolishness in the future."

She was weeping in earnest now, though her frantic struggles of earlier were reduced to occasional shudders. Sensing she had ceased to fight him, he stepped back to lay his hands on her slim shoulders. She looked up and met his gaze.

"This will hurt. It is intended to. What you did was dangerous, both for us and for you. It must not happen again, or anything remotely similar and I intend to punish you now to ensure that is the case. But once we have finished here, it is done with. This unpleasantness will be in the past, we need not speak of it again."

"But, you will hurt me…"

"Yes. I will. Though I will not harm you. I have never sought to do you harm and that has not changed, even now."

Her brow furrowed, she appeared perplexed by his promises. "How will I not be harmed? You said you would take a switch to me."

He grinned. "I suspect it will require more than one switch to properly make my point, but I will take care not to injure you. Nor will I force you to endure more than you can bear. Your punishment *will* end, when I am satisfied you are truly contrite and have learnt your lesson. You *will* walk away from it."

"You do not mean to kill me?" Her beautiful brown eyes were wide, her expression hopeful now, though still perhaps a little disbelieving.

He smiled, and on impulse leaned down to kiss her forehead. "No, I do not. I have never said that I intended that."

"I thought… I thought…"

"You were wrong. So, now that we are clear what is to happen here, are you ready? Can we continue? The sooner you submit to this, the sooner we can return to the cottage and enjoy our evening meal."

"Do you swear not to beat me to death?"

He smiled again. "Yes, I swear it."

"Then, I will try."

He nodded his approval. "You will have marks, but they will fade. There will be no scars, no blood." He paused, then, "Do you trust me, Merewyn?"

She blinked, appeared to be considering his question. At last she managed to reply. "I want to trust you, Viking."

"Then I shall settle for that." He stepped away, removing his hands from her shoulders. "You were about to remove your clothing, I believe."

He took her hand and led her back to the far end of the barn. She allowed him to return her to the spot where she had stood before her ill-judged attempt to flee, her gaze apprehensive but no longer panicking. Mathios leaned against the central pole, his arms folded as he watched her.

"Please do not keep me waiting, girl."

"N-no… I am sorry."

Her stockings and threadbare shoes went first, then the cloak. Her fingers shook as she fumbled with the fastenings on her woollen tunic and apron but soon they also lay in a heap on the floor. The loose cotton undershirt was the last garment to be removed. She stood before him, naked and shivering.

He took his time in perusing the vision of loveliness now revealed. He had seen her body before, of course, but on those occasions she was either unconscious, or partially concealed in her bath. His view now was unrestricted and he meant to enjoy it. Her nipples were stiff and hard, no doubt due to the chilly temperature in the barn. They reminded him of deep pink berries and tipped her pert little breasts beautifully. He imagined closing his lips around one of those sweet buds and sucking. Hard. Would she squeal, he wondered? Or maybe she would arch her back and beg for more.

Her body was slender, perhaps too much so, but not lacking in curves where it mattered. Her hips flared, her waist dipped seductively, her stomach was softly rounded. He ached to explore the feminine contours, to acquaint himself with every slope and swell, but now was not the time. Even so, he savoured this opportunity to scrutinise his captive Celt and reaffirmed his previous conclusion. She was truly perfect. He wanted to lay his hands on her, to take his time in caressing and arousing her, to taste and feel and sample every lush curve, every delicious hollow, but he must wait. He had more pressing business to attend to.

He swung the cloak from his own shoulders and tossed it on top of the heap of her clothing then stepped away from the post. "You will come over here and place your hands on the pole. I require you to lean forward and bend over, to lift your bottom up high for me."

She hissed in a breath and remained rooted to the spot.

"Merewyn, you will obey. At once." He gestured toward the post. "Move."

She could not have shifted more slowly had her feet been made of lead, but eventually she stood before the post. Tentatively she reached out and rested her palms on it.

"Lean forward," he commanded. "You know what is required."

She made what could at best be described as a token effort. Merewyn bent at the waist but just sufficient to rest her forehead on the pole. She gripped the timber hard with her hands, her knuckles whitening under the strain.

"You can do better than that, girl. My offer to summon Ormarr and Hakon to lend their assistance remains open."

She emitted a little sob as she leaned properly forward, her rounded buttocks now raised and presented for his attention. Still Mathios was not satisfied. He gently laid his hand between her shoulder blades and pressed her upper body until she sank lower.

"Hold on to the post, hug it if you wish, and spread your legs for balance." He stood back in order to properly assess her position. "Yes, that will do. I have no wish to tie you to the post as that would be less comfortable for you, but I will do so if need be. I require you to remain still, in that exact position, until I tell you that you may move. Is that quite clear?"

"Y-yes, yes, I understand."

"Then you may tell me when you are ready for me to start."

She closed her eyes and flattened her lips against her teeth. Mathios selected a switch from the bucket where several had been prepared and left to soak for his use. He examined the slender branch and was satisfied it would meet his requirements admirably. Olav had done well. He shook the droplets of water from the smooth branch and cast an appreciative glance over Merewyn's upturned, clenching buttocks as he did so. His little Celt really did have the most delightful arse, made for spanking.

"Merewyn? Are you ready?"

She managed a swift nod and tightened her death-like grip on the post.

The first stroke was relatively light, but still she let out a sharp hiss and went up on her toes. He had known she would. Mathios allowed her a few seconds to regather her senses before he laid the next stripe across her other cheek. Two pretty, crimson streaks now adorned her creamy flesh.

The next half dozen or so were delivered in rapid succession. Merewyn jerked and cried out with each one, but she held her position perfectly. He was proud of her resilience. Now it was time to become serious.

Mathios applied more weight as he continued to strike her perfect, peachy arse with the switch. The branch became frayed so he discarded it and selected a fresh one. Merewyn groaned, she was sobbing now, her cries more shrill as each spank fell. Red wheals crisscrossed her buttocks and he paused to lay his palm over them. The flesh was already starting to swell, he felt the heat rising from her punished skin. He curled his fingers to press harder and she cried out.

"Please, do not..."

"I will touch you as I see fit during your punishment. Your body is mine, to do with as I please."

There was no further protest from Merewyn. He caressed her bottom, his touch gentle. He continued until she stopped wriggling and remained motionless under his hand. It did not escape his notice either that her pretty cunny glistened with her juices. He had no doubt at all that he was hurting her, but her arousal was undeniable. Such were the vagaries of feminine sensuality, and Mathios for one had no complaints.

He resumed his stance to continue the switching. Merewyn stiffened but did not shift.

The next few spanks were hard and sharp. She screamed with each one and panted between the strokes. Her pussy swelled, her juices pooled and dampened her inner thighs, her bottom glowed a beautiful bright red. Mathios required yet another fresh switch in order to continue.

By the time he had ruined the fourth switch Merewyn's cries had become hoarse, her voice cracking under the strain. She no longer clenched her bottom in anticipation of each stroke. She had ceased to fight the agony of her punishment. Rather she relaxed, allowed the pain to flow through her body and surrendered fully to his discipline.

It was enough. Mathios dropped the switch and did not reach for a replacement.

"We are done here. You may stand up."

Slowly, painfully, Merewyn straightened though she still clung to the post like a long-lost lover. She wept, her thin shoulders jerking with her sobs. Her bottom and upper thighs were a glorious tapestry of reds, purples, pinks, though the skin was not broken. He had taken care, as he had promised. The wheals were livid and angry-looking in the immediate aftermath of her punishment though Mathios knew the worst of the sting would soon dissipate. He turned and strode away.

"Do not leave me. Please… please stay."

Her voice was ragged, her plea one from the heart. Mathios grabbed his cloak from the ground and was back at her side in two strides. He draped the cloak over her shoulders.

"I am going nowhere. I just went to get you this. You are cold…"

"No, I am not, I…" Despite her words she clasped the cloak around her and started to sink to her knees. Mathios caught her and swung her into his arms. He carried her to where the hay was stacked at the end of the barn and laid down on it, still holding Merewyn. She settled against his chest and clung to him, her fingers clutching the front of his tunic. "I thought you were going to leave me here. I did not want to be alone."

"No," he murmured. "I would not do that. I have

punished you and you took it well. Now we are done, and I will take care of you."

"I am sorry. So sorry…"

"I know."

"You do not. I need to explain…"

"I accept your apology, for the mandrake."

"It is not that. Or, not only that…"

"Oh? What then?"

"I disappointed you. I did. Did I not?"

"Yes… perhaps." He was guarded now, reluctant to examine his own peculiar discomfort at this admission but he would not lie to her.

"I wish I had not done that. I… I want you to like me."

"I do like you." He could be honest about that, at least.

"How can you? After what I did. After… that." She gestured toward the now abandoned post, the tattered branches strewn at its base, the bucket that still contained several fresh switches.

"It is over now, I said that. And I do like you. I am proud of you."

"Proud?" She raised her ravaged face to peer up at him. "Why? What have I done to make you proud of me?"

He shrugged. "There are many reasons. I am proud of the way you accepted your punishment just now. You were scared, I know, but you managed to find courage and fortitude. I am proud of the way you have survived here, alone, taking care of your baby. Even when you were ill, you went out to seek food for him, did you not?"

"Yes, but…"

"It has been hard, but you did not weaken. You managed to survive."

"I do weaken. Sometimes."

"But even so you must have found the strength to continue, since here you are."

"I suppose that is true…" She turned to him and snuggled closer.

Mathios held her, understanding and relishing the

intimacy that bloomed between them. A spanking, especially on the bare, was a deeply personal experience for both participants, quite visceral really. It was usual afterwards for the recipient to cling to her master, to express contrition, to seek forgiveness. And it was his responsibility to provide what she sought.

"Mathios? Is that your given name?"

"It is."

"May I call you by it? Your men do not."

"To them I am Jarl. It means leader in our tongue. You may use that, or my name if you wish."

"I will use your name. Thank you." She was silent for a few moments, then, "Your men, they are angry with me also."

"They have cause to be, but they will accept your apology if it is honestly given. They know that you have paid for your mistake." He chuckled. "They will have heard you, you may be certain of that."

She groaned. "How can I say I am sorry? No one but you understands my language."

"I will help you. It will be all right."

"Thank you."

He kissed her hair. "You are most welcome, little Celt. Are you ready to go back now?"

She did not respond.

He tipped up her chin with his fingers. "Merewyn?"

"Do we have to return at once?"

"You do not wish to leave here? You are sore and it hurts to move, perhaps?"

"No. At least, not just that. I feel… unsettled."

"Unsettled?" He waited for her to expand on her statement.

"I feel that there remains something unfinished between us. I am tense, my stomach churns. I feel… I feel…"

"Remember the bathtub?" he prompted. "Is it like that?"

"Yes," she whispered. "But that would be perverse. I cannot seek pleasure, not when… when… You brought me here to punish me, not to—"

"You have been punished," he reminded her. "If you now desire to be pleasured you have only to request it."

"I cannot." She breathed the words, barely audible. "It would be wrong. You are a stranger, not my husband, nor even my betrothed."

"I am a man who can make you feel good, if you but ask me."

She fell silent, the only sound her soft breathing against his tunic. Mathios knew well the value of patience. So he waited. And was rewarded.

"Mathios? Sir?"

"Yes, Merewyn?"

"Please make me feel good again."

CHAPTER EIGHT

What on earth had possessed her? Merewyn could barely comprehend what she had done. The instant the words were out she knew she should recall them, swallow them again as though she had not spoken. But she did not.

Instead she allowed this fierce Viking chief to tilt her face up to meet his kiss.

Mathios' tongue pressed against the seam of her lips and Merewyn opened her mouth. His tongue speared inside to tangle with hers. They performed a strange and intimate dance, one of tasting and caressing and sucking until she was breathless, the air catching in her throat. At last he lifted his head to break the kiss, and peeled the cloak away from her shoulders.

Before, she had been mortified by the weight of his scrutiny. Now, Merewyn relished it. She lacked experience but was convinced she discerned approval in his heated cerulean gaze as he bared her breasts again.

"So pretty…" he murmured before lowering his head to take her engorged nipple between his lips. He squeezed it, then scraped his teeth against the turgid bud. She writhed in his arms, loving the sensations he evoked yet she was vulnerable too. He could hurt her. He had said he would not do her harm, but he so easily could. He was a Viking, and they were dangerous.

"Please…" She uttered the word, unsure what came next. Did she want him to stop or continue? Her body took the decision for her. She arched her back and thrust her breast up against his mouth.

Mathios increased the pressure. He sucked her sensitive tip at the same time as he pinched the other between his thumb and forefinger. It hurt, and it felt so good she could have wept with the delight of it. Merewyn's senses were in chaos, her responses a bewildering fusion of need and fear.

Impelled to touch him, she reached for Mathios. She clung to his shoulder, tunnelled her fingers through his hair. It was silky, softer than she had imagined. She closed her eyes and allowed her senses to reach out, to accept whatever he offered.

Mathios released her nipple and Merewyn experienced a sharp pang of disappointment. She opened her mouth to plead with him, to beg him to please not stop, to never stop, but the words died in her throat when he traced a path of kisses down her stomach. He paused at her belly to lick and to press open-mouth kisses against her flesh. It felt sublime. She tingled between her thighs. He moved on, further, deeper, edging toward that place he had touched before. It was her most secret place, the spot where pleasure lurked, where desire and arousal might be unleashed. He knew of it, had found it with ease as though he knew her intimately, knew all her private yearnings.

Mathios shifted from under her and Merewyn winced as her punished bottom pressed against the hay. The discomfort was short-lived, or irrelevant. Mathios opened the cloak fully and spread it out beneath her, He placed his hands on her knees and gently pushed them outward, spreading her thighs. Merewyn gazed up at him. She knew what he would do, how he would touch her now and she wanted it more than she could recall wanting anything before. She needed his touch more than she needed her next breath.

He smiled, then lowered his gaze to peruse that most private place. She was embarrassed, the flush crept up her face from her chest. She felt the mortifying heat of it, but could not, would not stop now.

She wanted him. Wanted this.

He slid his fingers through her slick folds, then smiled at her. "So wet, my Celt. I think you like to be spanked."

She shook her head. Surely such a notion was impossible.

"It hurts, I know, but after..." He stroked her quivering cunny.

She cried out in sheer delight, thrust her hips up toward his questing hand. He slid one long finger inside her and she moaned in surprised pleasure. This was a new sensation, one she had not experienced before in the secluded privacy of her pallet. He drove his finger in and out, slow at first, then harder, faster. Merewyn revelled in the unfamiliar sensation, her inner muscles contracting around him.

"So tight," he murmured, "and so hot."

"Please, that feels so good. I want... I want..." She had no idea what she might want but surely this Viking did. His mastery of her senses had been unerring thus far.

"I know," he replied. "Soon. But first..."

He shoved both hands under her bottom to cup each tender cheek. She was sore, it hurt. She cried out but he just chuckled. "A reminder of who is master here. Do you not agree, little Celt?"

"Yes," she breathed, loving the raw sensuality of the moment. "Yes, please."

He lifted her bottom from the hay and used his thumbs to part her inner lips. Then, as she watched in utter incredulity, he lowered his mouth to her cunny and he started to lick.

Oh, sweet Jesus and all the saints! Her breath left her body in a whoosh. Merewyn gasped, fighting for air. She was flying, weightless. He drove his tongue into that place where his finger had been just moments before, swirled it around as she moaned in delight. The pad of his thumb found her pleasure bud and stroked there, and Merewyn wondered if she might expire from the sheer joy of it. Was it too much for her heart to bear? Surely no one, no one ever before, had felt as she did now. Her senses reeled, her body was no longer hers.

This was beyond heavenly. This was paradise on earth.

The climax rushed at her, spiralling from deep within her core. Her inner muscles clenched and spasmed, she could see the stars although she was sure her eyes were closed and she let out a shriek of surprised joy. Mathios continued to stroke and lick and drive his tongue in and out of her cunny, drawing the sensation out, forcing her to experience the tumultuous release again and again until she was fully spent.

At last it was over. She lay limp, draped over the cloak like a damp rag.

Mathios gazed down at her, propped up on one elbow. Merewyn managed a self-conscious smile.

"Do you feel more settled now? After that?"

She took a moment to recollect his meaning, then she nodded, though she remained uncertain. He saw it. Did he miss nothing?

"Tell me what you want, Merewyn."

She cast aside any remaining vestiges of modesty or caution. "I want you," she whispered. "I want you inside me."

"Then you shall have what you want, little Celt."

He knelt up and unfastened the leather belt at his waist. He set that aside, and the dagger slotted into the back, then tugged his tunic over his head. Merewyn watched, open-mouthed. She recalled seeing her brothers similarly unclothed on those occasions they used the bathtub, or on days when the sun was especially hot, but her siblings bore no resemblance to the man before her now. Mathios was quite simply magnificent. His shoulders were wide, but she had known that. She really should have been prepared for the chiselled bulge of muscle and sinew, honed by a life spent at sea, or practising the arts of war and conquest, but the reality before her still caused her to catch her breath. It was not only his torso that drew her attention. His upper arms also were contoured with hard muscle. He oozed power and strength and masculine vitality, qualities that should terrify her but instead she found herself intrigued and irresistibly drawn to him. Her gaze fell on the scar that marred his lower left arm and she wondered what had happened to cause it. Perhaps she might ask him… later.

He got to his feet and for a few moments towered over her. He leaned down to loosen his leather boots, kicked those off, then unfastened his wool trousers. In the next instant he was naked.

"Oh." Merewyn could only stare at his cock. She had never seen a naked male before, had but the dimmest idea of what to expect and it was not this. Most definitely not this.

Mathios watched her intently as he fisted his erection and drew his hand back and forth. A bead of clear moisture formed on the smooth pink head. Without thinking Merewyn reached out to swipe it away with her finger. Mathios laughed. "Soon, my Celt, you will learn to clean me with your tongue."

"Oh," she repeated, utterly at a loss for more words to better express her wonder.

Perhaps he knew what she wanted to say. He grinned and knelt before her. As before, he parted her legs and shifted so his hips were between hers. He positioned the crown of his huge cock at her entrance and Merewyn stifled an urge to giggle. This was just ridiculous. He would not fit within her. It was impossible and he would see that soon enough. She was genuinely disappointed, had hoped… imagined… But no, the reality was plain enough.

Mathios shifted again, pressing forward this time. Seemingly he had not perceived the obvious difficulty. She opened her mouth to explain, then let out a startled yelp when a sudden, white-hot bolt of pain snaked through her nether regions. She lay utterly still, not daring to move in case it happened again.

Mathios, too, was motionless. She peered up at him, her gaze swimming with tears. His expression was one of puzzled disbelief. His eyes narrowed, his jaw clenched as though he fought some inner battle.

The discomfort subsided. Merewyn started to relax. She dared a slight shift of her right leg, found it to be bearable so experimented with the left. That went well also. Seemingly she had survived whatever disaster had beset them.

"I… I believe I am all right. You may stop now."

"Stop?"

"Yes. It is safe to do so. I am uninjured."

"I do not wish to stop. There are a number of things I would like to do at this moment, but to stop fucking you is not one of them."

"Oh." They were back to that, it appeared.

"Do you want me to stop?" His expression was pained.

"No. But I thought… I mean, it hurts and… You are too large, clearly."

"No, I am not. The pain has passed. It is over now."

"But I saw you. You are much too…big."

He shifted within her, just a little but sufficient to cause her inner channel to clench around his wide cock. "Am I hurting you now? Still?"

"Well, no, but—"

"Merewyn, it is painfully obvious that you do not know what the fuck you are talking about."

"But—"

"I am not too big, and I will not hurt you again."

"Do you promise?"

"Yes," he ground out. "I fucking promise."

Despite the stirrings of pleasure brought about by his cock lodged deep within her, Merewyn shrank at his harsh tone, his bitter words. "You are angry with me. I do not understand…"

He groaned and lowered his forehead to rest against hers, his weight supported on his arms. "I am sorry. I should not have sworn at you. I was surprised, that is all. I had not expected you to be a virgin."

Merewyn was equally astonished. Was it not obvious that she would be a virgin, since she had no husband? "Why would you think otherwise?"

"You have a baby. Or I thought you did. Evidently you do not."

"A baby? You mean Connell?"

"Of course I mean Connell."

"He is my brother."

Mathios closed his eyes and muttered a few words in his own tongue. Merewyn suspected it was something obscene but did not choose to seek further clarification as she had a more pressing concern occupying her mind.

The initial sensation of discomfort in her cunny had wholly transformed to one of pleasurable fullness. She wished Mathios would do something, anything, to assuage her growing urge to squeeze and clench and wrap her legs around his waist and…

He withdrew his cock, waited a moment, poised at her entrance, then he plunged back inside her, deep and hard. It felt wonderful. Merewyn reached for his shoulders, lifted her legs to hook her ankles together in the small of his back and she hung on.

Mathios treated her to several short, sharp thrusts, then he reverted to the long, deep strokes he had started with. Merewyn loved all of it. He adjusted his angle a little, and now each inward stroke seemed to heighten her pleasure, create a growing swell of intensity, ready to engulf her.

Surely she could not achieve such a feat again. She was spent, utterly exhausted. Except, it would seem she was not. Mathios seemed to know what to do, exactly how to drive his huge cock into her body to elicit the desired response. In moments her cunny was again convulsing and her head spinning, her senses whirling as she soared toward another powerful release. Her body convulsed at the same moment his cock lurched within her and he swore again in his native tongue. The wet heat of his semen filled her channel moments before he rolled to his side, bringing her with him.

They lay like that for several minutes, his cock still buried within her. Mathios was the first to move, withdrawing his now softening erection and rolling onto his back. Merewyn shuffled away from him, suddenly self-conscious and afraid of his anger though she was at a loss to comprehend where he had gained his misconceptions from. Surely she had never said anything to give him to understand Connell was her son. Why would she do that?

"Oh, no, you don't," he growled. "Get back over here. Now."

She shuffled back and found herself pulled up hard against his side, his arm around her.

"That's better. And since we have the more urgent matter out of the way, at least for now, I'd be delighted to listen to your explanation."

"Explanation?"

"Yes. How did you end up here, alone, just you and your baby brother? What happened to the rest of your family, Merewyn?"

She drew in a long, deep breath and held it. She could not readily account for her reluctance to tell this Viking of the atrocities committed by others of his race. Certainly, she no longer harboured the fear that he and his men would consider acting in similar fashion. Even were it not for their need of her cottage for the duration of their stay here, these Norsemen did not exhibit the same blood-lust she and her family had encountered before. They had offered her and Connell no violence, apart from the switching and that did seem different somehow though she could not entirely reconcile the puzzle. On the contrary, they had shown kindness, generosity even, which rendered her own actions even more incomprehensible.

Neither was she seeking sympathy since she knew Vikings to be without compassion. Although, again, Mathios and his warriors did not fit that mould. They could have abandoned her and Connell in the forest, left them to die while the Vikings moved into their dwelling. But they did not. They brought them home and cared for them, even though they had nothing to gain from doing so.

"Merewyn," prompted Mathios. "I asked you a question."

"They… they died. Or left." That much was the truth.

"Those graves in the meadow in front of your dwelling? They are members of your family?"

She nodded. "My parents."

"When did they die? The graves appear to be fairly recent."

"My father died a little over two years ago. My mother died just last autumn, when Connell was four months old. Since then it has just been the two of us. Until you came."

Mathios was silent for several minutes as though considering her reply. At last he spoke. "The baby, he does not resemble you. He has blue eyes and fair hair."

"He… he is my half-brother. We have the same mother."

"So, your mother remarried following your father's death?"

Merewyn hesitated, but did not dare to lie to him. "She did not remarry. She was… raped."

Mathios swore under his breath but did not appear unduly surprised at the shocking revelation. "Go on."

"I… that is it. She became pregnant, but never fully recovered from the birth."

"Tell me about the rape. How did that come about? Who attacked her?"

"Please, must we speak of this? It is painful, and—"

He shifted so he leaned over her then swept the tangled hair from her face with his hand. His tone was gentle, but implacable. "I insist. Tell me what happened. All of it. We will not leave this barn until I am satisfied I have the full story. And if I have to spank you again to encourage your cooperation, I shall do so. I believe that would be effective, though I might also be put to the trouble of fucking you afterwards." He grinned. "Ah, well, I daresay I shall prevail…"

She frowned, perplexed. She had never encountered a man like this, one who could threaten, cajole, and promise her ecstasy all in the same breath.

"You would not…"

"Do you care to lie across my lap, Merewyn, and we shall see?"

"No," she whispered. "I do not want you to spank me again. At least…"

"At least, not just yet?"

At her weak nod he continued. "Then I suggest you start to answer my questions."

She had no choice. Merewyn drew a long, fortifying breath, and she started. "It was Vikings. They… they were here, two years ago. They attacked from the sea. It was so quick, so brutal." She paused for a moment, recalling the shouts, the cries, the clash of metal and the pounding of booted feet as the Norsemen stormed their farm. "They slew my father, and they raped my mother. I hid in the forest until they left or they would have…"

His arm tightened around her shoulders. "Go on. I am listening."

"I hid for two days. When I returned, the farm was in ruins. My father was dead, and my mother barely alive though I nursed her and she survived. My two older brothers were gone. I later learnt from my mother that the Vikings took them as slaves…"

Encouraged by Mathios' gentle probing, Merewyn was able to recount the struggle she and Ronat had put up in order to survive that first winter, the hardship they endured. She described Ronat's pregnancy, Connell's birth, and her mother's death. By the time she concluded her tale she was weeping. “I have tried, for my mother’s sake I have done my best. But it is difficult. I cannot leave Connell at home while I tend the fields so I must carry him with me. I love him, of course, but…”

“But what, Merewyn?”

“It is lonely. I long for others to talk to, someone to share the work perhaps, but there are no neighbours close and I fear they might attempt to take the farm if they think I cannot manage. You yourself said that a woman alone is vulnerable…”

“Yes, and this is a hard enough life as it is. You have done well.”

She shook her head. “No, I have not. We did some repairs and rebuilding, my mother and I, but I have achieved nothing since she died. It is too hard…”

“You have survived. No one could have done more.” He fell silent, then, “I understand now why you feared and hated us. You must have been terrified when we arrived and took over your home.”

“Yes,” she agreed. “I was. I was sure that all Vikings were the same, and that at any moment you would… would…”

“And now? Now that you know us? Do you still believe we are a threat to you? To your brother?”

“No, not any longer. I think I knew from the beginning that Connell was in no danger from you. All your men are kind to him and he enjoys being with you. It has only been a couple of weeks, but he is thriving in a way he did not before. He laughs, he plays, he…”

“He is a fine boy.”

“Yes. He is.”

“Had I known of this I would have better understood your actions. You must hate us, resent us, blame us for the hardships you have faced, the destruction of your family. You have every right to do so.”

“I did, at first. I still do blame the vile men who were here two years ago, but I realise you are different.”

"Not so different. We, too, have raided villages up and down this coast, burned homes and taken slaves. I do not condone rape, though, nor would we murder without cause. But we have killed."

"You have been kind to me."

"Yes. We made an exception for you."

CHAPTER NINE

Merewyn shivered as he reached around her to open the cottage door. Mathios did not believe that she was cold as he had wrapped his own thick cloak about her for the short walk back from the barn. It was apprehension that caused her to tremble, that and the prospect of having to make her apology to seven Vikings who she still thought might seek to exact retribution for her misdeeds.

Mathios knew that they would not. Apart from anything else he would not permit it. However, he was reasonably certain that once they knew her story the other Norsemen would accept that the Celtic female had good cause to fear them and this had driven her actions. He ushered her before him into the warmth of the dwelling.

All the others were there, seated around the table whilst Vikarr stirred the pot over the fire. Arne balanced Connell upon his knee. They all glanced in his direction as he entered, the diminutive wench before him.

"Go and be seated," he instructed her. "If you can."

He smiled at the faint flush that crept up from her neck. Ivar and Ywan moved along the bench to make a space for her and Merewyn gingerly lowered herself onto the seat. She continued to hug the cloak about her body as though that could offer protection from more than merely the cold.

"Merewyn has something she wishes to say." Mathios moved to stand behind her, and placed his hands on her shoulders. She turned her head to look up at him, her expression one of gratitude. "Go on," he prompted. "I shall translate."

"I… I am sorry… very, very sorry for what I did."

She hesitated, and Mathios used the opportunity to translate her words into the Norse tongue. His men regarded her, then looked to each other. Her apology needed to be more convincing. "Go on," he urged.

"I should never have tried to deceive you. I gave you a potion without your knowledge, and I deeply regret it."

Mathios translated that also.

Ormarr grinned. "Aye, she regrets it right enough, but only because her arse is smarting. How many switches did you get through, Jarl? Olav told us he left a dozen there."

"Just four were sufficient. I believe Merewyn has more to say." He squeezed her shoulders. "Go on, little Celt."

"I… I swear that I will never do anything like that again. I know it was wrong and… and… I hope you can forgive me."

Mathios repeated her sentiment in the Norse tongue, then bent to speak softly into her ear. "They need to know the rest, about your family, about what happened here. Only then can all properly understand."

Merewyn nodded. "I… I will try."

"Shall I explain to them? It will be easier."

"Thank you," she murmured.

Mathios remained behind her, his hands on her shoulders as he related the tale. The expressions on the faces of his warriors suggested that whilst they might not entirely condemn the brutal and senseless acts of their countrymen—they were Vikings after all—neither did they condone all that had taken place. It was not Mathios' belief that any man in the room would have treated a defenceless woman as Merewyn's mother had been treated, though many a Viking would. Neither, probably, would they have slain her father unless they had to. Her brothers would have been taken though. It was the Viking way.

He concluded his explanation, reminding them that Merewyn had acted out of fear, and that she had been understandably confused. She found their promises that she would not be harmed difficult to accept, given what had gone before. He was satisfied that she was truly contrite, and the matter was now closed. They would not speak of it again. He looked about the room, inviting any man who chose to dispute their Jarl's conclusion to make his objections known. None did.

"So, she is not mother to the lad, then?" This from Vikarr.

"No," confirmed Mathios. "He is her brother."

"It is a pity about the potion," bemoaned Hakon. "I enjoyed the meals she cooked."

"Aye, well, I daresay Vikarr's flavourless slop will have to do," observed Ivar. "Is it ready yet? I am famished."

Bowls were passed around the table, and lumps of bread that had been purchased from Alfred's stores. Mathios wondered if they might contrive to make more loaves from the grain he had bought on their trading expedition. The conversation soon turned to the other pressing matters facing them—the repairs to their ship, the need to ensure that the barn was watertight before the weather worsened much further, who was to attempt to milk the cow in the morning. He slid into the seat next to Merewyn and caught her gaze. Her eyes glistened, but she managed a smile.

This would probably be all right.

• • • • • • •

Days became weeks, and weeks grew to become months. The weather closed in, the snows started and there were days when it seemed to Mathios the blizzards would never stop. He was no stranger to bad weather, his homeland saw its share, but that did not mean he had to like it. He always found the winter months dragged and he longed for the return of spring.

Now, he had more reason than ever to watch the skies, eager for the first glimmer of warmth. More cause than usual to examine the frigid earth for the first shoots of new growth. Yet he did not. He found he enjoyed the enforced idleness as he and his men clustered around the fire pit, Merewyn and Connell too, sharing mugs of mead or buttermilk, and tales of heroic deeds.

Merewyn had managed to learn enough of their tongue to be able to join in the conversation, though she still struggled a little with it. Connell had become quite sturdy on his feet, and he had uttered his first words. They were in Norse. On the occasional fine days that they saw, Olav would go out hunting or fishing. They ate well, their diet now supplemented with the additional eggs and the dairy produce that Merewyn was able to provide. She was a decent cheese maker, and the butter churn had been repaired and was in regular use. She had even taken over most of the cooking again, after a decent interval, of course.

The repairs to the barn had been completed before the winter really set in, and apart from providing accommodation for their livestock it afforded more places for his warriors to sleep. They no longer piled on top of each other in the tiny cottage, a fact particularly to Mathios' liking since it afforded him the privacy he required to properly enjoy Merewyn's company.

He shared her bed, had done so since that first night after they returned from the barn, but she was reluctant to spread her thighs for him whilst the other men were present. He respected her wishes and contrived to find reasons to send his warriors from the cottage whenever he could. But since they had their nights to themselves, matters had eased. He no longer found it necessary to insist that firewood be chopped or the cow fed at such regular intervals.

Merewyn was an enthusiastic and responsive lover, and

eager to learn. On the first night they found themselves alone—apart from Connell who slept soundly in his cot on the other side of the room—she had slid the bar across on the door then stripped off her clothing. He watched from his seat at the table, his lip quirking in silent appreciation at her nude body. He would never tire of looking at her. She came to kneel between his legs, then, wordless, she opened the fastenings of his trousers and released his cock. Gently, reverently, she cradled it in her hands, stroked her fingers up and down the length of it as he leaned back and moaned. She swiped her thumb over the head, smearing his juices across the shiny dome, at the same time as she cupped his balls in her other hand. He had considered himself in paradise until she bobbed her head forward to take him in her mouth.

Where the fuck did she learn that?

He let out a groan and closed his eyes. His little Celt was perfect, absolutely fucking perfect. He tangled his fingers in her hair as she rocked back and forth, each time taking him deeper. She hollowed out her cheeks and the suction sent waves of pure lust from his cock to his balls. She wrapped her tongue around the head, then stroked the tip along the groove that surrounded the shiny crown. He thrust hard, unable to remain still. She opened her mouth wider, took even more of him inside. His balls ached, he was about to shoot his seed into her throat.

"Merewyn, stop."

She looked up at him, her brow furrowing in confusion. Her expression was one of consternation as she released him and sat back on her heels.

"Did I do something wrong?"

Fuck, no!

Mathios groaned and cupped her chin, then used his thumb to wipe away the drops of saliva that escaped from her lips.

"Not wrong, little one. It was perfect. So perfect, in fact, that you were about to receive a mouthful of my seed."

"Oh…" Her lovely eyes widened. "Is that not how…?"

"Do you want that, Merewyn? Do you want to swallow my seed?"

"I… I think that I would not mind, unless it is something which you would dislike. I want to please you…"

"By Odin's teeth, girl, you do please me."

Her features cleared. Merewyn smiled up at him, a playful, teasing grin as her confidence returned. "Do I please you when I do this, my Viking?" She bobbed her head forward to take him deep within the warm recess of her mouth again, and she sucked…

It was too much. His balls contracted and semen surged from his cock to fill her mouth, her throat. She never took her eyes from his as she swallowed, gasped for air, then swallowed again to clear her airway. Then she licked him clean. She was thorough, her tongue reaching every fold and crease, every inch of him. Only when she had completed her task did she sit back on her heels and smile up at him.

"I waited to do that. Since that first day, in the barn, when you said I would learn to clean you with my tongue. I wanted to do it, but there was never an opportunity."

He leaned forward to cradle her face between his hands, brushed his lips across hers and tasted the saltiness of his own tang. Could anything be more erotic? He inhaled, savouring the aroma of his own release just moments earlier.

"I would have rebuilt your barn with my own bare hands had I known what my reward would be."

"I would have helped you."

He laughed out loud and scooped her up from the floor. She clung to him as he carried her to the pallet and laid her on it. Mathios rid himself of his own clothing and resolved to speak to Ormarr about making a proper bed for them. He stretched out alongside her and cupped her breast in his palm, kneaded the soft flesh between his fingers.

"Your body is perfect, so pretty…"

"Mathios, please…"

"And so eager."

"Yes."

"You must learn patience, or I shall have to spank you. Again."

"That would wake up Connell."

"Maybe he should sleep in the barn also…"

"No, he is too little."

"In that case, you will present yourself to me, after the *dagmal* tomorrow when all are about their duties. You bottom will be bared and ready to accept your punishment."

"Yes, Jarl."

He slid his hand between her thighs to explore her slick folds. She was dripping, her moisture coated his fingers as he thrust them between her nether lips. First two, then three digits penetrated her.

"So wet, and just from the promise of a spanking."

She was panting, her head tilted back against the mattress, her brown eyes dark with passion. She would soon find her climax.

He stilled his hand. "Do not take your release without my permission."

She opened her eyes to regard him in puzzlement. "What do you mean? I cannot—"

"You can, if you try. And you must try, because if you do not control yourself, your spanking will become a switching, and we both know that is not nearly so much fun."

"Mathios…?"

He started to move his fingers again, angling his hand to ensure he reached the spot just within her tight channel that never failed to arouse her.

"Please, do not…"

"You wish me to stop?"

"No, but… I cannot help myself."

"Not even to spare yourself a sore bottom?"

"No, not even for that."

"You are a harlot, Merewyn."

"It seems so. Perhaps you should—"

"Spread your legs, Merewyn. As wide as you are able."

She did as he commanded and he positioned himself between her thighs. It had only been a few minutes since he deposited his seed in her throat but his cock was hard again, ready to sink into her. He could not get enough of this little Celt. He sank balls-deep into her hot, tight channel.

"You may take your release now, Merewyn."

"Thank you," she whispered as her body convulsed around him, ripples of pleasure rolling the length of his cock. He took his weight on his arms and thrust hard, each stroke long and deep, riding out her climax and building toward his own. He was able to maintain the rhythm longer as she had already taken the edge off his urgency, and soon she clenched hard again, a signal she was finding her second release. He slowed, slipped his hand between their bodies to seek out the responsive little pleasure bud and stroked there until she writhed and squirmed beneath him. Only then did he withdraw, almost pulling right out of her, then drove his cock deep again.

Merewyn cried out, her back arched as she shuddered and gave herself over to the pleasure. He was there with her this time, his cock twitching violently as his seed surged forth to fill her again.

•••••••

Merewyn was content. She could not recall ever feeling quite like this, even when she was surrounded by her family. She had almost forgotten what it was to be hungry. Or cold. A plentiful supply of firewood was stacked outside the door of her cottage, salted meat hung from the beams above her head and a regular supply of fresh fish arrived on her table almost daily. Mathios had said she could keep the cow and the goat when the Vikings left, so she would continue to enjoy butter and cheese. And Connell could have milk.

A new bed stood in the corner, large enough for her and Mathios, and several sturdy chairs were arranged around her table. Even her mother's loom had been repaired and now stood beside the door where it could benefit from the best daylight.

The Vikings had their own reasons for fixing the loom, but still Merewyn appreciated it. She had agreed to weave the necessary woollen cloth that would serve as the replacement sail for their vessel. Already the spun wool had been purchased and was stored ready for use. She lacked her mother's dexterity at the craft, but she could manage well enough and the task was a simple one. All that was required was a large square of stout fabric, which would be attached to the mast that Ivar and Ywan had fashioned from a trunk of pine. She could probably weave it in the space of a month or so, especially as the Vikings invariably took Connell with them when they went out about their tasks.

Today, though, the baby was in the cottage with her. It had been snowing for the last three days but there had been a welcome break in the weather. Whilst it was not possible to stray far from the cottage, the Vikings took advantage of the opportunity to replenish their stock of firewood from the woodland close by. No one considered it safe for Connell to be playing in the vicinity of a swinging axe so he remained safely indoors. Olav was in the cottage also, as were Vikarr and Hakon. The rest were in the forest with Mathios, chopping logs.

Merewyn dropped several pieces of rabbit meat into the pot. The stew would simmer for the next few hours. She would spend the time baking bread, and if she had a few minutes to spare she might make a start on setting up the loom in readiness to commence weaving tomorrow. She gave the pot a quick stir and turned her attention to the flour she had ground the day before.

Connell tugged at her skirt. She bent to untangle his tiny fingers from her clothing. "Are you hungry?"

He shook his head.

"What then?"

He clutched the small boat that Olav had made for him

and held it up to her.

"You want to sail your boat?"

He nodded.

"We shall. Soon. If it does not start to snow again. We can go out and sail it in the trough. But first I must put this bread in the pan by the fire so we can have something to eat later. You like bread, do you not?"

He nodded again. Connell loved his toy boat, but he loved food even more. He sat down on the floor with a thump and Merewyn returned to her task.

Moments later a shrill shriek rent the air. She spun around at the same time as the three Vikings leapt to their feet. Merewyn cried out in dismay at the sight of the wildly swinging cauldron and the pool of boiling stew that had splashed onto the floor. Connell sat in the mess, screaming at the top of his small lungs, steaming broth dripping from his arm. His boat floated on the surface of the liquid that remained within the pot.

Oh, dear lord. He has tried to sail his boat in the boiling cauldron! The realisation struck Merewyn instantly, but it was too late to prevent the tragedy.

Olav shouted something in their Norse tongue. Merewyn had no idea what he said but Vikarr sprinted for the door and flung it open as Olav grabbed the pail of cold water that stood beside the fire pit in readiness to be added to the pot. He flung the contents of the bucket over the child, then scooped Connell up and ran outside with him. Merewyn followed, wringing her hands, moaning.

He was scalded. Burnt. Her little brother, the only blood relative she had left. How badly was he hurt? What had she done? Why had she not taken proper care of him?

Olav ignored the baby's pathetic wails as he tugged the garments from his tiny body and heaped handfuls of snow onto the reddening skin and torso. His arm, his side, both glowed with a deep, angry-looking pink. Vikarr helped to pile the snow on, and they replenished any that melted with more, crisp and fresh and cold.

"What are you doing? You are hurting him even more!" Merewyn rushed to grab the baby from them but Hakon held her back.

"They are helping him. The cold snow will stop the burning, reduce the damage."

"But…"

"It is a remedy used often in our land, and it does work."

Already the baby's cries were quieting. He sniffled, whimpered occasionally, but seemed calmer. Merewyn knelt beside him in the snow and took hold of his uninjured hand. She was weeping herself now. "You will be all right. We will take care of you."

"What happened?" Other Vikings, alerted by the screams, came charging from the forest, Mathios at their head.

Merewyn leapt to her feet and rushed to meet him. "It was my fault. I should have been watching, I never thought…"

"The lad met with a little accident, that is all. He'll be fine." Olav stood, picked up the now shivering child and handed him to Merewyn. "Best get him back inside where it's warm. We'll bring some snow in with us, better still ice if we can find some. The worst of it is over now though."

Merewyn was not convinced. "But, he will be scarred. Burns are so painful, I know, and he is so little…"

Olav pulled off his own shirt and draped it over the child. "It is fortunate we were there. He may have some marks left after his adventure, but not much. Snow and ice can ease a burn considerably if applied quickly enough. It cools the burn down, you will see. He is going to be fine by tomorrow."

"Are you sure?"

Olav nodded.

Mathios put his arm around Merewyn. She was still shaking. "You can trust him. Olav has six children of his own and there's not a day goes by that one or other of them isn't in some sort of mess. To my knowledge he has not lost one yet."

Merewyn looked from Mathios to Olav to Connell. The baby already looked to be more or less back to his cheerful self and enjoying all the attention. Perhaps the Vikings were right.

"Thank you. Thank you so much. I… am glad you were here."

Only after the words were out did she realise how strange, how incongruous they sounded from her lips. But it was true. She did, in that moment, bless the day these Nordic raiders had arrived in her home.

CHAPTER TEN

The dwelling was quiet when Mathios entered. His warriors were in the barn and settled for the night, and Connell slept peacefully in his cot close to the fire pit. Olav's ministrations appeared to have been successful and the angry redness was already fading from the child's flesh. Mathios thought it unlikely that any lasting damage had been done.

He shed his clothing quickly and slipped into the bed in the corner, Merewyn was already snuggled within the furs and blankets, her back turned to him.

"Little Celt?" He reached for her and she rolled over to face him. In the dim lamplight he could see she had been crying. She had barely ceased weeping since the baby's accident. "He will be fine," Mathios assured her. "You will see."

"I know," sniffled Merewyn. "His arm seems to barely pain him at all, not more than a few hours after the scalding."

"So, why the tears then?"

"If Olav had not been there…"

"Then Hakon would have done what was required. Or even Vikarr."

"What if no one but me was present? I would not have known what to do. What if there had not been snow outside?"

"And now you do know. Cold spring water would have worked almost as well and you have an abundance of that in all seasons. You will remember, for next time."

"I will remember, I shall never forget…"

"Maybe I can find a way to help put this day's unpleasantness from your mind."

"I am not sure…"

He stemmed her protest by slanting his mouth across hers. Merewyn parted her lips and accepted his questing tongue. Mathios tasted her, savoured the sensual play of his tongue against hers, the sweet taste that was unique to his Celtic lover. She permitted his exploration, compliant as always, but he sensed he did not have her wholehearted participation.

"Merewyn?" He broke the kiss. "You do not want this?"

"I… I do not intend to… I mean, of course, if you wish…"

"What do *you* wish?" He propped himself up on one elbow and scrutinised her features with care. Even in the dim light her indecision, her uncertainty, were writ plain across her face. "Tell me what you want. Or do not want."

"I… I want to be forgiven."

"Forgiven?" This he had not expected. "Forgiven for what?"

"I swore to my mother as she lay dying in my arms that I would take care of Connell. I failed her."

Mathios frowned and shook his head. "You have not failed anyone. You mother would have been proud of what you have achieved, of the care you have given your brother."

"It is my fault that he was hurt. I should have protected him."

"It was *not* your fault," Mathios argued. "There was nothing you could have done."

Merewyn grasped his arm. "I was distracted, too busy to play with him. I should have been watching Connell, I should have seen him get too close to the pot."

"As should Olav, and Hakon. Even Vikarr. All bear equal responsibility, but however careful we are, the young are vulnerable. We will all be more vigilant in future. We do our best, and can offer no more. Even you, little Celt."

"You do not understand…"

Mathios sighed. She was correct, he did not understand all this self-blame.

"I deserve to be punished for failing to keep my promise."

"Merewyn, I do not think—"

"Please." She grasped his arm even tighter. "Please, you can help me."

"In what way?" He regarded her earnest features, the distress and guilt evident in her brown eyes.

"You could spank me. It is what I deserve."

"I do not believe that it is. No one here thinks that."

"I think it. I cannot forgive myself."

"Ah, now that is different," he agreed, "but even so I consider your judgement to be over-harsh."

"Please. It… it worked before… in the barn. I felt guilty, deeply ashamed of my foolishness, the danger I created for all. You punished me, then forgave me. So, I thought…"

He raised one eyebrow. "You want me to take you out to the barn for a switching? Do I understand you correctly?"

"Yes," she whispered. "I do."

"That would have to wait until tomorrow, since my men are asleep and I expect your caterwauling would disturb them. We would have an audience, for sure."

"I… I know that."

"Can you wait?"

"I suppose so, if we must."

"There is an alternative, if you prefer."

"What?"

"My belt, and you bent over yonder table, your bottom

bared. I would need to gag you, I daresay, because you would likely wake everyone with your din."

She gazed up at him, her lips parted. "Your belt? Would that hurt? As much as the switch did?"

"Yes, it could. If I chose to make it so."

"It has to hurt. You do understand…?"

"Oh, yes, I understand. I do not agree that today's incident merits this, but I do understand. If you are bent on this course I will do my part to aid you. And after, when your head is again clear and your guilt assuaged, I intend to fuck you until you forget your own name. Do I make myself plain?

"You do, sir. Shall I… shall I remove my nightshirt now?"

Mathios sighed again. "Yes. If we must do this then let us be getting on with it."

He rolled from the bed and reached for his clothes, which he had discarded scant minutes before. Mathios dragged his own trousers back on and picked up the stout leather belt that usually held his dagger and often enough his sword. He set his weapons aside though, and doubled the strap in his hands. It made a formidable implement of discipline and his little Celt would remember this night for a long time.

She slipped from the bed also, and tugged the long woollen shirt that she usually wore to sleep in over her head. Merewyn was naked beneath, a sight he never tired of, but on this occasion, he would not make her wait while he enjoyed the view. He tilted his head in the direction of the table.

Displaying obedience that bordered on eagerness, she stepped past him and draped herself over the rough oak board. Mathios was reasonably certain that her enthusiasm for this endeavour would evaporate by the third stroke of his belt, but he admired her fortitude. First, though, he needed to see to her safety and to ensure that the rest of their household were not unduly disturbed.

He pulled a chair in front of Connell's cot and draped a blanket over it to obstruct the boy's view of the rest of the cottage. The child would not see what was happening, even if he did awaken. Mathios thought that unlikely, the child slept like the dead, but the precaution seemed necessary.

Next, he returned to their bed and used his dagger to slice a narrow strip of fabric from one of the blankets, which he then cut in half again. He returned to where Merewyn awaited him.

"I will tie your hands behind you to keep them out of the way."

She nodded and allowed him to draw her hands into the small of her back, and to bind her wrists.

"And now, the gag. Open your mouth, if you would, Merewyn."

She obeyed, and he balled the other fabric strip up and stuffed it between her lips.

"Ten strokes," he announced.

She turned her head to look at him, and he wondered if she might argue had she been free to do so. He rather suspected she might have tried to make the case for more, certainly he had delivered many more than ten strokes with the switch before he considered her suitably chastened, but then he had believed her to be culpable. Whatever she might wish to say, it would have availed her nothing. His mind was made up, and although she had requested this punishment, the doing of it was up to him. He would determine what was needed. Ten strokes would be concluded quickly, Connell would likely sleep through it, and Merewyn would achieve the suitably throbbing backside she deemed necessary. And, he hoped, a wet and needy cunny.

"Ready?"

She nodded, and clenched her delectable bottom. He laid his palm on her left cheek and squeezed hard.

"Keep this soft and relaxed for me or I might be minded to insert a piece of ginger into your arse to remind you not to clench."

Her eyes widened, her shock at the lewd suggestion apparent. She shook her head vigorously and made inarticulate sounds behind the gag.

Mathios chuckled. "Not on this occasion, but perhaps the next time I have cause to take issue with your behaviour. It will be an educative experience for you."

She continued to regard him over her shoulder as he positioned himself behind her. Mathios met her gaze once more, offered her a brief nod to signal that he was about to start, and he picked his spot on her arse.

The first stroke landed on her right cheek. Merewyn jerked hard and grunted into the gag. It had been a relatively benign introduction to his belt, and Mathios followed it up with three more strokes in rapid succession. Merewyn danced on the balls of her feet, her muffled squeals echoing around the dwelling. Mathios cast a glance across to Connell's cot, relieved to see that the little lad still slept peacefully. Even with his view blocked, Mathios would not continue if the child was disturbed.

"Spread your legs for me, Merewyn," he commanded.

She turned to look at him, panic in her tear-filled eyes.

"Fear not, I do not intend to hit you there. I merely wish you to show me how wet you are."

Seemingly mollified, slowly she inched her thighs apart.

"Wider," he instructed. "And lift your bottom up so that I can see."

She obeyed, treating him to a beautiful view of her swollen cunny, her sweet little clitty already peeping out from beneath its hood. Her juices glistened, dampening her inner thighs and threatening to leave a pool on the earthen floor before much longer.

"Ah, I see you are enjoying yourself, my Celt." He swiped his palm along the length of her slit, pausing to dip two fingers into her entrance. The sounds of her wetness now filled the dwelling, decadent and dirty and wondrously erotic. Mathios' cock leapt within the confines of his trousers. "So eager. I look forward to burying my rod deep in here. Do you think you might like that too, little wench?"

Merewyn nodded, her hips writhing as he thrust his fingers in and out of her tight, slick channel. Her punished bottom glowed in the meagre light cast by the oil lamp and Mathios admired his work so far. Four bright crimson welts bloomed on her creamy skin.

"Ah, but we have work to finish, do we not? The matter of your suitable chastisement remains. Six more strokes, I believe. Do you agree?"

He continued to drive his fingers in and out of her cunny, adding a third digit when she failed to respond to his question. Then, as suddenly as he had started, he stopped and withdrew.

"Settle down, girl and lift your bottom for my belt." He hardened his voice, injecting a note of stern authority. "I do not believe you are suitably punished yet."

She panted through the gag as she waited for the next stroke but this time Mathios took his time. It would do her no harm to reflect on the reason they were here. She wanted to be absolved of her guilt over Connell's misadventure and he intended to achieve exactly that.

The fifth and sixth strokes were harder than the ones that had preceded them. Livid welts blossomed at once, and Mathios paused to draw his fingers along the length of each new stripe. Merewyn sobbed quietly. He believed they were making progress.

The next two were harder still. She let out a muffled yelp as each fell, her body lurching forward against the unrelenting oak of the table. Tears flowed across her cheeks and her slender form shuddered as she struggled to absorb the pain. She did well, he acknowledged. The wench had courage and resilience.

He laid the final two stripes across the backs of her thighs. Merewyn screamed soundlessly behind the gag but she lay still, her surrender absolute.

They were done.

Mathios released her hands, then pulled the rag from her

mouth. Her jaw worked and she hollowed her cheeks as she peered up at him through her tears. Mathios bent to kiss her forehead, then returned to his position behind her. Merewyn's legs were still spread wide, her readiness and arousal if anything more apparent and framed by her beautifully punished bottom.

He parted her buttocks with his fingers and admired her swollen nether lips before using the fingers of one hand to spread her entrance open. Her clitty was plump and pink but he ignored the quivering nub for now. Instead he plunged three fingers deep into her cunny and relished the way her inner muscles convulsed around his digits. She moaned, rolled her hips, and squeezed him hard.

He unfastened his trousers to release his engorged cock, the solid length jutting forward to nudge her bottom. Clear liquid seeped from the end, the head swollen and smooth and aching to be driven deep inside her. His balls throbbed, his rod twitched. This would not take long.

He continued to fuck her with his fingers, building her arousal. She thrust back against his hand, her incoherent moans and pleas signalling her need.

Mathios withdrew his fingers and placed the crown of his cock against her entrance. He drove it forward, at the same time taking her clit between his finger and thumb and tugging hard. He squeezed the sensitive bud as he impaled her on his wide cock, then held still, his rod buried balls-deep inside her, as she convulsed around him.

Merewyn's release was swift and powerful. He treated her to several rapid, shallow thrusts to help prolong the climax, then succumbed to his own. Mathios let out a guttural growl and buried himself to the hilt as his balls contracted and his semen filled her hot, tight channel.

He took a few moments to collect his wits, then withdrew his now softening cock. Merewyn lay boneless across the table. He kissed the sensitive spot between her shoulder blades.

"Tell me, my Celt, are you quite satisfied now? In every

way?"

She nodded, a small smile curling her lips.

"Might we get some sleep now, do you imagine?"

"Yes, sir, I think we could."

Mathios lifted her and carried her back to the bed. When she would have reached for her nightshirt, he shook his head.

"You will not require that. I believe I may not be quite finished with you yet."

CHAPTER ELEVEN

It was a long winter. Snow continued to blanket the frozen earth well into February that year, and even when the blizzards finally ceased, the biting winds and driving rain contrived to hamper the repair work to the Viking ship. The men ventured out on those days when the elements permitted it, but progress was slow. Mathios found he was in no particular hurry, but he knew his warriors yearned to return to their homes and families. Their womenfolk would presume them perished, lost to the seas, if they did not return in the early spring.

Mathios had no wife waiting by his hearth. He had been married briefly, but Gudrun had been a delicate woman and it had not surprised him greatly when she had succumbed at her second childbirth. His two sons, on the other hand, had both entered the world in rude good health and had thrived during the three years since in the care of his stepmother. The efficient Rowena now ran his household, and she would ignore all rumours of her stepson's possible demise until faced with undeniable proof.

Now, in the final week of March, the weather was milder though a stiff breeze stirred the waves of the North Sea as Mathios stood on the beach and gazed out across the grey-blue waters. His home lay perhaps four or five days sailing away, and if the weather continued to be clement he and his men would be able to attempt the trip in the coming days. He shifted his gaze to the newly repaired dragon ship, which sat proud and menacing upon the golden sand, its shallow hull designed to be beached and put to sea at speed. The new mast stood tall and majestic, and the most careful scrutiny would be required to discern where the damage to the timbers of the hull had been. New oars had been carved and now poked through the openings in the side of his ship. Only the sail remained to be added, and he knew Merewyn was well advanced with that. They would need to load supplies, but those were stacked in Merewyn's barn awaiting the day they would be hoisted onto broad shoulders and transferred to the vessel. They would be ready to leave these shores any day now.

Ivar and Ywan scrambled across the gleaming timbers, checking this, tightening that. A shout from the trees that edged the beach attracted their attention. The men on the ship waved as Arne strode across the sand, young Connell sitting astride his shoulders. The child laughed, his high-pitched cries of excitement reached Mathios even across the distance of a couple of hundred yards or so. Arne passed the small boy up to Ivar then leaped onto the ship himself.

The three Vikings would guard the vessel this night. Since their ship had been rendered seaworthy once more, Mathios had ordered that she be guarded at all times. They could not risk an attack, whether from inland or from the sea. It would appear that Connell was to join their vigil. It did not surprise Mathios to see the child here, he was seldom far away from Arne's side.

Mathios sighed. He could not put off the inevitable any longer. He had to speak with Merewyn.

• • • • • • •

The light was failing. Merewyn leaned forward to peer at

the fabric taking form under her fingers and adjusted the lamp to throw a little more illumination on her efforts. It did not help much so she sighed and stepped away from the loom. She had hoped to finish the sail this day, but had been disturbed by various chores that required her attention. The work would be finished tomorrow, for sure.

And the Vikings would leave. They would have no further need to remain here. She should rejoice.

Merewyn gulped, fought back the sadness that threatened to overwhelm her at the thought of her now crowded and bustling cottage falling silent again but for her voice and that of Connell. She dashed the tears from her eyes and moved toward the fire pit to stir the broth she had prepared for this evening's meal. At the sound of the door opening behind her, she glanced around to see which of the Vikings had returned early from their day's chores.

"The meal is not yet ready, Jarl." She offered Mathios a quick smile as she picked up her large wooden spoon. "I had not expected you so soon. I trust all is well?"

"Aye, it is." The Viking chief removed his heavy cloak and slung it aside, then took a seat at the table. "Come, join me. I need to speak with you." He gestured to the bench next to him.

"I have work to do. The food—"

"The food will be fine. We will eat well, as we always do. Come, sit."

Merewyn's heart sank. His expression was serious. This was the day she had longed for with a fervency that now seemed incomprehensible. For weeks she had prayed that the Norsemen would depart and leave her and her home in peace. Now that the moment was upon her, she was filled with dread. And sorrow. They had not yet departed and already she missed the Norsemen with all her heart. One, in particular, she would remember for the rest of her days. She set aside her cooking implement and went to join him.

"I have almost finished the fabric for the sail. I had hoped to be done by today, but there was cheese to make, and Hakon's tunic was ripped, so…" She trailed off into silence. Babbling would not help to delay the Vikings' inevitable departure.

"I am not here to discuss the sail, though I appreciate your work and I have no doubt it will be ready when it is needed. There is another matter I must raise with you. It… it concerns Connell."

"Connell?" Merewyn furrowed her brow. "Is he all right? He went with Arne to view the latest work to your vessel."

"Yes, I saw him there. He seemed to be enjoying the excursion. Arne too."

Merewyn nodded. She was under no illusions about how deeply the little boy would feel the loss of his gruff playmates. He had thrived whilst the Vikings had been here, and not only because of their ability to provide plentiful food. The rough Norsemen were kind to the small boy, they made time for him, played with him, taught him. They had enriched his little world in ways she could never have achieved alone as she toiled to scrabble out a meagre existence for them. Connell had formed a particular attachment to Arne and was never happier than when he was hoisted onto the large Norseman's shoulders and included in some expedition or other.

Mathios cleared his throat. He seemed ill at ease, which was unusual. The Viking Jarl was usually so confident, so commanding.

"Is there a problem? Something concerning Connell?"

Mathios met her gaze. "Arne is very fond of the child. You will have seen this."

"Of course. He has been most kind. All of your warriors have, but Arne in particular…"

"Arne has no children of his own. He and his wife have been married for twelve years and no one expects it now. It is a shame, but not all unions are blessed by the gods."

"I suppose not. Arne would have made a good father."

"Aye, I know it. He… has spoken to me. Of Connell."

"Of Connell?" Merewyn was genuinely perplexed. "What of Connell?"

"Arne wishes to adopt him and raise him as his son."

The words were gently spoken, but Merewyn's world started to collapse about her ears.

"A-adopt…? But… how?" She backed away along the bench, shaking her head. This was impossible, it could not happen. It just could not.

Mathios took her chin in his hand and tilted her face up so she had to meet his gaze. "Arne wants to take Connell with us when we leave here. The child would return to our home with us and be raised as a Viking. Arne has sought my permission for this."

"You cannot. You promised. You gave me your word that you would not take us, that when you left we could remain here, unharmed. Free."

"I am not threatening your freedom, nor that of Connell. To be raised as the son of a Viking is not at all the same as being taken as a thrall."

"You swore," she accused, unable to get past the broken promise, unheeding of the rest of his words. "You cannot take him. I… I will fight you. I shall—"

Mathios laid a hand across her mouth to still her protests. "I know. I know what I promised and I will keep my word. If you do not agree to this, then I shall not give my permission." She made as if to speak again but he shook his head. "No, listen to me first. Before you make your decision, think of what this opportunity might mean for your brother. What is best for Connell?"

"He belongs here. This is his home. Someday, when he is grown, the farm will be his." Merewyn could conceive of no circumstances in which this unthinkable notion might make sense. She could never allow Connell to be carried off by the Vikings to a foreign land, never to be seen again. "That is what is best for him."

"Arne is my cousin, my kinsman. He is of the Jarl, a man of wealth and standing in our homeland. His wife, too, has wealth of her own. Sigrunn is a good woman, she would be kind to the boy. Indeed, she would dote upon him. They have no other children, nor are they likely to. Connell will be their heir. Their sole heir. In time, he will be wealthy too, and powerful. He will learn the skills needed to be a Viking, a leader of men. I swear to you that he will be happy, and he will be loved."

"He is loved already. He means everything to me."

Mathios took her in his arms. "I know. We all know that and this is why it is so difficult. I know you don't want your brother to leave, but think of all that Arne is able to offer him. Can you really turn that down on Connell's behalf?"

"I... I promised my mother I would look after Connell. I cannot let him go." She was sobbing now, struggling to be free but Mathios held her firm.

"You would not be letting him go. You would be sending him to a better future. Please, at least consider it."

She shook her head, unable to articulate coherent words any more. Her heart was breaking.

The worst of it was, Mathios was right. Connell need not be condemned to the miserable existence she could eke out for him, a life of struggle and poverty, hunger and back-breaking toil. Of course he would be better off with the Vikings. Of course Arne would make a perfect father for him, and the unknown Sigrunn would replace the mother he had lost so young. She knew all of this, had known it as soon as Mathios started to speak.

But how could she live without him? Her brother was all she had left.

"There is more that you might consider." Mathios murmured the words into her hair. "You need not stay here, alone. You could come with us. With me. Arne's longhouse is not far from mine; if you come with us, you could see your brother every day."

She lifted her tearstained face to look up at him. His handsome features were blurred, shimmering before her. "Come with you? You want to take me too?"

"Only if you agree to come. Not by force."

"Then… if not a slave, what would I be? What would be my station in your land?"

Mathios shrugged. "You would be found a place, work to do which you would enjoy. You can weave, or you might cook. We have need of a healer and your skill with herbs would be welcomed."

"I would share your bed?"

"Yes. Of course. Just as we are here."

"But not as your wife?"

"My wife? I had not—"

"You have no wife at home. Vikarr told me. Why not wed me, if I am to share your bed?"

"Merewyn, it is not so simple. I have responsibilities, my people expect—"

She wriggled from his embrace. "I, too, have a right to expect." She dashed the tears from her eyes and stiffened her spine as she faced him. "I am not a fool, nor am I selfish. I recognise the opportunity offered to Connell and however much I might long for him to stay here, I will not stand between him and the future you and your people can give him. But… but you insult me, Jarl, if you think I will come with you and live with you as your… your whore."

"Whore? Merewyn, you would not be that." His features betrayed his shock at her condemnation. "Never that. I respect you, I care deeply for you. I merely wish to be certain that you are all right, that you are safe, and—"

"If you cared for me, truly cared for me, you would not make such a demeaning offer."

He frowned, shock receding and irritation starting to show. "I fail to see how it would differ greatly from the life we have here. You have found pleasure in my bed and I have certainly enjoyed your company. I see no reason for it not to continue."

"This…" Merewyn swung her arm out to indicate the cottage, their surroundings, "this was temporary. One winter, a few short months when fate threw unlikely companions together. We found a way to be, you and I, all of us, but it was never meant to last forever. It was just a winter, not a life. Now you are offering me a life, but not one of honour and respect. You may not consider me a whore, but your people will. At best I will be a figure of fun, or perhaps someone to be pitied. At worst they will revile me. I will be an outsider, a foreigner who speaks almost nothing of their tongue and has no status in their land. So, thank you, Jarl, but no. I shall remain here, my self-respect intact."

She turned her back on him and started to stir the pot once more.

"Merewyn, we need to talk. You should—"

"Are you still here, Viking?"

She had no notion how she managed it, but Merewyn succeeded in stemming the flood of tears until after the door slammed behind him. Only then did she sink to her knees and weep for the life she used to have, and for the one she had just turned down.

• • • • • • •

She hated him. Merewyn harboured no doubt of that, reminded herself of the vile and brutal nature of his kind, the damage all Vikings wrought with their violence, their greed. Worse still, and as she now knew to her cost, the utter devastation they could create with their soft and gentle ways, their easy charm and generosity, their humour, their companionship.

Mathios was a bastard, she reiterated lest she might forget. He was mean and faithless and quite without scruples. He had seduced her, teased her with his clever fingers, his skilled tongue, not to mention his wondrous cock that filled her nightly and often enough during the day too, whenever they were alone. He had promised her nothing but her freedom, her safety as long as the Vikings were here. He had sworn she would not be hurt, yet she lay in her bed unable to drag herself from it to face the daylight. Her heart was shattered, her hopes and dreams in a pile at her feet, trampled by the careless words of a Viking who had meant to treat her kindly yet had no concept of what she wanted, needed from him.

How could he? She had not known herself until the moment he dismissed her dreams and barely formed hopes as mere nonsense, the romantic ramblings of a lovesick wench. He genuinely thought the prospect of returning to his homeland at his side and sharing his bed was a good one. He had expected her to accept.

Now, a lifetime alone stretched endlessly before her. She faced the gnawing, aching loneliness of trying to carry on without even her small brother's needs to lend purpose to her existence. Merewyn wondered why she did not accept Mathios' offer. Surely nothing could be worse that the misery that awaited her in just a few short days.

They would be gone. He would be gone.

Yes, she hated Mathios for bringing her to this, but it was not so simple. She knew, too, that this was what love felt like and she did not care for it. Not at all.

• • • • • • •

The rest of the Vikings picked up on the mood. They eyed Merewyn with sympathy and concern, but only Mathios possessed a good enough command of her language to properly speak to her and she refused to exchange so much as a word with him. Their meals were now taken in near silence. Connell fretted, also sensing the frigid atmosphere, and Arne tended to him. Merewyn permitted that; after all, it was how matters would be in the future and she could not fault Arne's care of the child.

She finished the sail and removed the fabric from her loom. Ivar and Ywan carried it to the longship and attached it to the mast. From their grateful, happy smiles she had to assume it suited their needs well enough. The day after the sail was fitted, the Vikings started to haul their supplies down to the beach. They had collected barrels of fresh water, sacks of grain, pitchers of milk, some cheese, a leg of salted ham. Merewyn watched from the door of her dwelling, knowing that their preparations meant their departure was imminent.

She should not complain. The Vikings left her with her home and outbuildings in a fine state of repair. She had crops in her fields, a cow and a goat in her barn, and more chickens than she knew what to do with. She could even contemplate selling her spare eggs or trading them for other goods. Olav had shown her how to catch fish and set traps for rabbits. If her crops failed she would not starve. She might die of loneliness, but she would do so with ample food in her belly.

Since their fateful conversation Mathios had not shared her bed. He slept in the barn with the other warriors. Even Connell had deserted her to share Arne's rough pallet of hay. After their evening meal on the day she knew would be the last the Vikings would spend on her shores, Merewyn bade each goodnight as they filed out. She reserved a curt nod for Mathios and would not answer when he asked her if she had all she needed.

Of course she did not, but she would not ask him again, not for anything.

When she was alone she wandered about her cottage in the dim lamplight, setting things to rights, clearing away the day's debris. Anything to stave off the awful stretch of misery that was the night. She would not sleep, had not done so since she quarrelled with Mathios. If she did manage to doze off she would waken again shortly after, fitful, chilled, unable to settle. She had spent most of the last two nights perching on a stool beside the dying embers of her fire and expected to do so again.

The next morning dawned, and even before thin shafts of sunlight crested the horizon the men could be heard moving about in the barn. They would seek an early departure, hope to make good progress while the light held. Merewyn prepared their *dagmal* and waited for them to crowd into the cottage, to cram their big, hard bodies around her table one last time, demanding food, nudging and elbowing each other for the best seats, the biggest helpings. They did not disappoint her, and this morning, despite her own abject misery, their anticipation, their longing to be at last on their way home permeated the mood of despondency. Merewyn ladled the thick porridge into the rough bowls and even pretended to take a few mouthfuls herself rather than allow Mathios to witness her despair.

Too soon, the Jarl got to his feet. She did not fully comprehend his Norse tongue, though a few words had sunk in over the weeks and months. She now knew enough to understand that Mathios commanded them to assemble at the longship in readiness to set sail. The Vikings did not need telling twice. They were on their feet, milling about, grabbing cloaks, weapons, anything they needed to take with them, then each in turn embraced Merewyn. Arne hung back, Connell nestling in his arms, tucked within the warmth of the Viking's cloak. The large Viking warrior also hugged Merewyn, then bent to kiss her cold cheek. His smile was sad, yet grateful. He knew the child was only his because she had consented to it.

Merewyn's lips quivered as she kissed her baby brother for the last time. She could not speak, her silent wishes and heartfelt prayers for his safe deliverance across the water and subsequent happiness among foreigners quite beyond her remaining powers of speech. Arne left, and only Mathios remained.

"Will you not come?" He rested his hands on her shoulders as she set her back to him and gently turned her around. She was weeping now and he wiped away her tears with his thumbs. "I would take care of you, I swear it. You will want for nothing, and if you do not wish to live with me you need not. I will find somewhere…"

"No." She shook her head. That would be even worse,

to live close to him and eventually to watch as he took another for his wife. No, she must find a way to manage. Here. Alone.

Mathios kissed her forehead. "I will not forget you, little Celt. Neither will Connell. I will make sure of it, Arne too. And some day, if we pass this way again, then maybe…"

"No," she repeated. "No, you must not come back, I could not bear it. Please, just… I want…" She raised her gaze to meet his. "Do not make this harder that it is. Please."

He kissed her again, a light brush of his lips across hers. Then he reached for his cloak, and he was gone.

Merewyn stood for a long while, staring at the door, wishing, willing him to come back through it. He did not. Eventually she had to accept the truth of the matter. She was quite, quite alone.

CHAPTER TWELVE

The deck swayed under his feet, the rhythmic rise and swell of the waves failing to soothe him as they usually did. The wind was fresh, the furled sail fluttering against the ties that held it in place, the confined fabric seeking to be free. Once unleashed the swift longship would fly across the glimmering sea, carrying Mathios and his warriors back to the homes and loved ones they had not seen for months. He should be more enthusiastic. He should share the delight of his men that they had come safe through the winter, all who reached the shore had survived and their homeland was but a few short days away.

Mathios had first gone to sea aged no more than six or seven years old and had loved it his entire life. He had always lived within sight and sound of the roiling waves and he adored the music of it, whether the gentle splash of water against the hull or even the wilder, ominous crash of heavy swell that would toss a small craft about like tinder. All the sea's mercurial moods excited and exhilarated him. The scents, too, the salty tang that filled his nostrils and the taste that lingered on his lips. He adored the endless motion of the planks beneath him, the sense that he was at one with his ship. But this day the usual joy, the anticipation, the tingle of excitement eluded him.

He was overwhelmed by sadness and the near-crushing weight of loss. He felt guilt, regret at the misery Merewyn had failed to conceal and for which he felt responsible. He had never intended to hurt her. At first, he had not thought their dalliance would amount to much, just a brief liaison to while away a cold winter and the enforced proximity of their situation. He had never expected her to be a virgin, and perhaps that had been his fatal error. He should have apologised, then left her alone. He should never have prised her story from her, nor made it his business to make amends for the wrongs committed by his countrymen. Without doubt he should not have held her in the night, buried his cock in her slick, hot channel at every opportunity, revelled in her artless but fervent response. Quite simply, she had delighted him, his little Celt. He had parted from her not two hours ago and already he missed her.

"So, you could not convince her to come along with us?" Olav materialised at his side and the pair of them surveyed the foaming waves ahead of the swift ship.

"I could not. Her mind was made up."

Olav grimaced. "That farm of hers is fine enough, I daresay, but a patch of land is only that. I would have expected her to come with us for her brother, if not for you."

"She did not choose to."

"Was it because you punished her, over the matter of the mandrake? I had thought that was done with."

"It was."

"Did you lay hands on her again after that? Does she have reason to fear you?"

"No. Well, yes, but that was not the same. She does not fear me."

"Then why? You and she… well, I thought… We all did."

"She expected me to wed her."

"Aye. Well?" Olav sounded unsurprised.

Mathios turned to glare at his companion. "'Well'? What do you mean, 'well'? The idea is ridiculous. You must see that."

Olav shrugged. "I do not see a line of other women clamouring for your hand. If there is another you might wish to wed you have failed to mention this fact to me. What is wrong with Merewyn? Was she not to your liking after all?"

Mathios snorted. "Of course she was to my liking, I would not have fucked her every night for four months were she not pleasing to me. But even so, a wife…"

"A wife is a woman you *can* fuck every night should that be your wish. It sounds as though the wench was perfect."

Mathios could not believe what he was hearing. "You believe I should have agreed to wed her? A Celt? We make thralls of her people, not wives."

"It does not have to be so. You among all of us should know this."

"You refer to my stepmother."

"Of course. Your father developed a fondness for his female thrall and was determined to make her his wife. Despite your hostility to your father's choice at first, has Rowena not proven to be an asset to your family? And now, though she is a widow and could have returned to her people since your father freed her, she chooses to remain in your longhouse. She cares for your boys well enough, and keeps your house for you."

"Rowena is different, not typical. I was wrong about her, I have said as much."

"I know that. You made your peace long ago. Your father loved Rowena and she was accepted as his wife."

"Yes, but—"

Olav was not yet finished. "And the boy, Connell, will not be a slave."

"He is half Viking."

"So we understand, but that is not the reason Arne wants the lad. It is not usual for a Viking to take a bride from another people, especially among the Jarl, but neither is it unheard of."

"Rowena is Welsh. They are more… biddable. You think a marriage between a Viking and Celt could work? Especially given what happened in the past, to Merewyn's family?"

"She obviously thought so or she would not have suggested it to you."

"You are saying I should have agreed to this… this madness?"

"If that would have been sufficient to convince her to come with us, if that was what it took, then yes. But if you do not want her, then I suppose—"

"Of course I fucking want her. It's too late now though."

"Aye, I suppose it must be, if you say so." Olav turned, swaying, his movements graceful and agile for a man of his size. "Best get that sail properly unfurled. There's a decent breeze getting up and if we look sharp we can catch it. Hey, Ormarr, to me…"

"Wait." Mathios' tone was harsh, tortured, even to his own ears.

Olav paused. "Yes, Jarl?"

"You really think I should have wed her?" Mathios growled the words over his shoulder, catching the attention not only of his second in command but the rest of his crew too. Several heads turned, ears pricked with interest.

"I see no compelling reason why not, Jarl. If you had wanted her."

"I did. Do."

"Do you love her?"

Mathios paused, then, "Aye, I suppose I do."

A murmur of conversation rippled around the longship. It was Arne who spoke for the crew. "We could go back for her. We would lose a day, no more…"

Mathios shook his head. "She would not agree to come."

"Then we will bring her anyway," suggested Olav. "You could settle the details later."

"No." He had promised her, given his word on that at least and Mathios would not break it.

"Very well." Olav shrugged. He had tried.

"Do you see that structure over there, on the shore?" Mathios pointed to the English coastline, still clearly visible as they skimmed the waves on their journey north. "It is a church, is it not?"

Olav squinted into the morning sun. "It looks to be, for sure."

"What does a church usually have?"

"Treasure? Are you not more eager to see your home again, my friend, that you would suggest a spot of Viking to pass the time?"

"No, my friend, I am not interested in their gold plate, not this time. But a church usually has a priest and I believe I could make use of one of those."

"You mean to abduct one of their holy men?" Olav feigned surprise. "You are considering a ransom, perhaps?"

Mathios shook his head. "No, I am considering a wedding." He turned to Ivar and Ywan, each one at an oar. Behind them Ormarr and Hakon also rowed. "Bring us ashore on that outcrop. And be quick about it. They will see us approaching and doubtless they will make a run for it. I do not want to be chasing the fucking priest halfway across Northumbria."

• • • • • • •

It was dusk when the Viking longship once again slithered to a halt on the stretch of shingle close to Merewyn's small homestead. Father Allred, as they now knew the priest to be called, had been most reluctant to aid Mathios in his endeavour and had indeed made off across the meadow at first sight of the Viking ship approaching his shore. The Norsemen landed and gave chase. Eventually they caught the fleeing cleric cowering in a disused cattle shelter and clutching his crucifix. They had marched him back to their longship where it had taken the better part of an hour and several draughts of their finest mead before the man had eventually agreed to aid Mathios' cause. Even so, he was adamant that he would not preside over a forced marriage, unless of course there was the possibility that the wench was with child. That would change everything.

Mathios believed such a circumstance could be arranged if it came to that. He assisted the priest aboard the longship and gave the order to return to Merewyn's farm. He had a bride to claim.

As usual, Ivar and Ywan were left to guard the ship whilst the rest accompanied their leader up the steep cliff path that led to Merewyn's cottage. The dwelling was in darkness when they arrived, and no smoke spiralled from the hole in the thatch roof.

"What the…?" Mathios shouldered the door open. The cottage was empty. He turned to the priest. "You, stay here. Vikarr too, and the baby. Get the fire going again. It's fucking freezing in here. The rest of you, come with me. I want her found."

They separated into two groups and started the search. Olav led Ormarr and Hakon back in the direction of the beach, while Mathios and Arne headed into the thickly wooded forest that surrounded the rear of the dwelling. He had an instinct, a feeling he could not quite define, but he was drawn to the clearing where he had first encountered his little Celt all those months before. Why she would come here, at night, alone, he had no idea, but it was in that spot he would seek her out.

And it was there he found her. He almost trod on the small figure hunched against a tree, her cloak huddled about her. She shivered as he crouched before her, peered at him, disbelief writ across her features.

Mathios reached for her, laid his palm on her cold cheek. "I have returned."

"Why?" she whispered. "There is nothing you need here."

"I need you," he replied simply. "Come with me."

She shook her head. "You do not need me and you do not want me, apart from in your bed."

"I never said that. I said things which I should not have, but never that. Come home with me, to the cottage. I have a priest waiting for us there. We shall be wed, if that is what you want. I do not mind, I just want you."

"You… you would wed me?"

"Aye, I would. I will, this very night. Then we will set sail again in the morning. I daresay we will have to return Father Allred to his church or he will make my ears bleed with his complaining, but after that we shall go to my land. Together."

"But—"

He laid his fingers over her lips. "No. No arguments now. You have set out your conditions and I will meet them. It is done."

• • • • • • •

The wedding was conducted with little fuss and even less ceremony. Father Allred insisted upon having a few words in private with Merewyn, following which he declared himself satisfied and willing to perform the nuptials. The exchange of vows took place in the clearing in front of Merewyn's cottage and was witnessed by seven Vikings and a small boy, none of whom understood the strange and solemn Latin incantations recited by the priest. Despite this, they cheered and clapped their swords against their shields when the event was concluded and passed Merewyn among them to receive their hearty congratulations. Then they clattered back indoors to fill their bellies with some broth of indeterminate origins that had been hastily prepared by Vikarr, and ale that the Norsemen had left in the barn for Merewyn. She would not be requiring the supplies now and it was intended to load all they could carry and take it with them. Even the cow would accompany them to the

Norseland. The goat and chickens would be set free.

Merewyn herself owned little in the way of personal possessions that she wished to take, with the exception of her mother's chest, which was now empty since the disposal of her herbs and spices. "May I bring it with us anyway?" she asked Mathios. "It is not especially large, and…"

"Of course. It is yours. I am sure you will find a use for it."

The meal concluded, Mathios issued a low command. Olav got to his feet and led the men from the cottage to take up residence for one final time in the barn. Father Allred would have remained, but Olav was insistent that the cleric accompany the rest. Connell, too, slept with the men. Alone with his new bride, Mathios reached across the table to take Merewyn's hand.

"Why were you in the forest? It was not safe…"

She lowered her gaze to study their joined hands. "I… I found I did not care for safety, not after you had gone. I did not much care about anything at all."

"I appreciate what it must have cost you to part from Connell."

"Yes," agreed Merewyn. "That was hard."

"You were courageous and unselfish. I am proud of you."

Merewyn shook her head. "I am neither. It broke my heart to let Connell go, but it was not only him I missed. I lost heart, lacked the courage to go on. As soon as you had left, I lost the will to do anything. I… I had thought I would manage, that I could cope alone. I cannot. I found I no longer wished to even try so I returned to the place where it began. I believed it would end there. As it did. You returned."

"Few of us can manage alone, little Celt." He paused, then, "I should never have expected you to, nor permitted you to try. I should have insisted that you accompany us."

"You invited me."

"It was not enough."

"If you had taken me from here by force I would have fought you. I would not have forgiven you."

"I believe you might have, eventually. But I should have met your conditions without argument."

"You had no wish to wed me. I do realise that, and—"

"I love you, little Celt."

"What?"

"I love you, Merewyn. And now, because you insisted upon it, you find yourself wife to a Viking. I know you fear and mistrust my people, so how will your hasty marriage suit you, do you think?"

"I believe I shall cope, Jarl."

"You will have to, because I intend to keep you beside me. Always."

She raised her gaze to smile at him. "That is as it should be."

Mathios inclined his head. "I am glad we have that settled. There only remains the matter of your foolish wanderings in the forest. I believe you know what will happen now."

"You will spank me." It was a statement, not a question.

"Aye. For your own good. You must learn to keep yourself safe, especially now that you belong to me."

"I did not belong to you when—"

"You split hairs which are quite narrow enough, Merewyn."

"You will require me to remove my clothes and lie across the table?"

"The clothes, yes. But you shall lie over my lap this time."

"I would prefer that."

He smiled and leaned across the table to kiss her mouth. "Good." He rose and crossed to the bed where he sat down. "Come now, my bride. Let us waste no time this night. We have an early start in the morning."

Mathios watched as his wife of but a couple of hours undressed. The flickering lamplight cast enticing shadows over the contours and valleys of her body, a body now filled out from a winter of decent food and sufficient warmth. He had never thought her lovelier. Her breasts were firm, the peaks just slightly upturned and stiffening as she bared them to the air and to him. Her mound bore the soft brown curls he loved to twist between his fingers and as she moved toward him he caught a brief glimpse of the nether lips concealed between her thighs. She stood beside him, her hands behind her back in silent submission.

Mathios patted his lap. He had no need of words as she arranged herself across his thighs, her long, dark hair unbound and flowing to the earthen floor. Once in position, she returned her hands to the small of her back.

Mathios wrapped his larger hand around her slender wrists to hold her still and to offer her the contact, the reassurance, she seemed to desire and he longed to give. He raised his right leg just a little, enough to elevate her heart-shaped bottom and better present it to him.

"Part your thighs, Merewyn," he murmured.

She did so, quick to obey.

Her cunny was moist, her juices already flowing in anticipation of what was to come. His little Merewyn took a spanking well, and she would improve every time she experienced a trip over his knee. Mathios intended her opportunities for betterment to be frequent, since she responded so prettily.

He started slow, dropping a series of light slaps over her buttocks, causing them to blush a pale, delicate shade of pink. Merewyn lay still, her breathing barely elevated. Mathios increased the intensity, adding weight to the spanks. He peppered her curved cheeks and the backs of her thighs. The flush deepened. Merewyn let out the occasional squeal, and started to wriggle.

"Be still, wench," he commanded.

She settled, her breath now coming in quick pants as she fought to control her movements. Mathios continued to spank her.

The heat warmed his palm. He paused, briefly, to caress her now crimson buttocks and was gratified at the low moan she emitted. She was hurting—and loving it. Mathios slipped his hand between her legs to explore her drenched slit, and found her to be hot and slick and needy. He thrust two fingers inside her tight channel and finger fucked her hard for several seconds. Merewyn writhed and gasped, her inner muscles contracting to squeeze his digits. He added a third finger and twisted his hand to ensure he made contact with that most sensitive place he knew to be concealed within her depths.

He was aware when she came close to her release. He recognised the tell-tale moans, the increasingly desperate manner in which her hips rocked from side to side, the near frantic clenching of her inner walls. He pushed her to the very edge, then when he was certain she could take no more, he slid his fingers out.

"Mathios..." she wailed. "Jarl, please..."

"Please what, my Celt? You want me to spank you again, perhaps?"

"Yes, if you wish. If you think..."

"Very well." He raised his hand again, and this time he slapped her hard enough to cause her skin to ripple. She let out an anguished wail, enough to bring his men running had they truly feared for her. "Hush, my sweet Celt. You would not wish to alert my warriors and the good father to your plight, would you? It would be a pity if we were interrupted."

She shook her head. "I... I am sorry. I will be quiet."

Mathios grinned. He was sure she would try.

He continued to rain hard, sharp spanks across her buttocks and thighs. Merewyn's vow of silence lasted just three slaps, then she was shrieking again. Mathios ignored the din and continued to drop slap after sharp slap onto her naked buttocks.

"Why is this happening, Merewyn?" he demanded, pausing to allow her to answer.

"B-because I went into the forest," she managed, between gulping sobs.

"So far, so good," he agreed, then started to spank her again, the slaps heavier now, faster and harder. Merewyn screeched and squirmed, but he only tightened his grip and held her in place as he rained swat after swat onto her bright crimson behind.

"Why should you not go in the forest, Merewyn?"

"I should not go there alone. It is dangerous. Oh, please… I am sorry. I will not do it again. Please stop."

"I shall decide when you have been sufficiently punished, not you. I intend to make quite certain you do not do something so foolhardy in the future. Why do you suppose that is, my little bride?"

"I do not understand. Please, you are hurting me, oh! Aaagh!" She let out a particularly loud scream when he delivered a hard slap to the back of her thigh. Now they were getting somewhere.

"What did I tell you, not more than a few minutes ago?"

"I cannot remember. Please, Mathios, I cannot bear it…"

He shook his head in mock disappointment though of course from her position across his lap she could not see it. "I tell you that I love you, and within mere minutes my declaration has escaped you entirely. Perhaps I should take a switch to you for your lamentably poor memory also."

"No! Please, I did hear you say that. Of course, I remember it…"

"Then perhaps with that in mind you can now explain to me why you are not permitted to endanger yourself in such a manner. Indeed, in any manner."

"B-because you love me, and I am yours to keep safe."

"Exactly so, my little Celt. Now that we have that clear understanding between us, I believe a few more slaps will suffice to press the message home."

Merewyn whimpered, sniffling against his thigh. But her struggles had ceased. She still grunted painfully with each additional slap he delivered to her quivering buttocks, but she no longer protested, no longer begged him to stop.

His own hand was smarting by the time she quieted fully at last and lay soft and yielding across his thighs, accepting her punishment with perfect submission.

He slowed the swats as she lay motionless, eventually laying his palm on her heated skin and pressing hard. His fingers left paler spots on her buttocks when he lifted his hand. She sobbed quietly, her breath now coming in gulps. She had earned her release.

Mathios parted her thighs, used his hands to push her legs apart. Merewyn did not resist. The lamp was dying, but still cast enough light for him to admire her glistening nether lips, and the plump bud that waited for his attention. She was close, hovering on the very edge of the precipice. The moment he touched her, anywhere, in any way, she would fly.

Gentle would have sufficed, but he opted for intense. This was, after all, their wedding night and he intended to create a memory his Celtic bride would cherish. He parted her lips with his fingers, causing the swollen pleasure nub to stand more erect, greedier. He took it between his finger and thumb and he pulled.

Merewyn let out a startled "Ooh!"

Mathios flicked his fingertip across the very top, his touch feather-light at first, then heavier. She started to shudder as her body responded to this final sensual assault.

He pressed, then rolled the sensitive nub between his fingers at the same time as he plunged the digits of his other hand deep inside her. Merewyn's entire body convulsed, she shook, went stiff then relaxed as the tremors seized her. She thrust her hips helplessly against his thighs as he stroked and drove his fingers in and out of her cunny. He didn't cease, didn't even slow until the final, yearning sob escaped her lips and she lay still, sprawled across his lap, sated and spent. Only then did he lift her and roll her onto the bed.

Merewyn whimpered as her punished bottom pressed

against the mattress. She rolled onto her stomach and turned her head to peer at him over her shoulder.

Mathios grinned. If she preferred it that way… He shed his own clothes in moments, then came to lay beside her.

He kissed her, taking the time to explore her mouth with his tongue, to savour this first taste of his wife. She was willing, wet, eager. She reached for him and draped her arm around his shoulders. He deepened the kiss as he caressed her heated buttocks, loving the soft murmurs she made as she spread her legs for him.

He broke the kiss and moved to kneel between her legs, then he took hold of her by the waist and lifted her hips up. His cock was hard, leaking from the tip as he positioned it at her entrance. She twisted her neck to continue to meet his gaze as he drove his rod inside her. Merewyn's body parted to accept him, to welcome him. She gasped, her brow furrowing and her beautiful dark eyes widening. Then she smiled, that slow, sensual, knowing smile she reserved just for him.

Mathios leaned over her, his weight braced on his hands, which he planted on either side of her shoulders. He treated her to short, jabbing strokes at first, which he knew she loved. She rotated her hips and pushed back against him, oblivious now to any residual discomfort. He lengthened the strokes, finding a demanding rhythm as he pounded into her. Merewyn grasped at the blanket beneath her, her fingers closing around the coarse fabric as she crumpled it in her small fists. Mathios drove harder, deeper, burying his cock right to the hilt. Each stroke sent Merewyn plunging forward but he wrapped an arm around her waist to hold her still. She was tight, so tight and so wet. He grasped a hank of her flowing hair with his free hand and twisted it around his fingers. As he tightened his grip her head was dragged back, her neck stretching, her throat exposed to his kiss.

She muttered something. He thought he heard her but was unsure.

"What was that, Merewyn?" He gripped her hair harder, pulled on the dark locks until her eyes watered.

"I… I love you, Viking." She ground the words through gritted teeth as her second release surged forth and her cunny quivered around him.

That was what he thought she had said, Now, he was certain. He kissed her mouth as he seated his cock as deep as he could. The crown of his erection nudged her womb, he was convinced of it. Merewyn let out a ragged moan as she convulsed and shuddered in his arms. Mathios' balls twisted, contracted painfully. His semen surged forth to fill her tight channel until at last he was still.

Mathios rolled to his side, his cock still buried within his bride's lush body. He was exhausted, and in moments Merewyn's breathing slowed, deepened. He knew she slept. He did not withdraw his softening cock, he found he liked it just where it was. Contented and more than a little pleased with this day's work, Mathios pulled his Celtic bride closer and held her tight, then drew the blankets up to cover them both.

CHAPTER THIRTEEN

Merewyn had lived beside the sea her entire life but had no experience of sailing upon it. Her father had been a farmer, not a fisherman. She had no notion what to expect but it was not this. The never-ending motion, the tossing, the churning of the waves caused her stomach to heave and her throat to retch. Her legs would not hold her upright, her limbs were not her own. She either lay on the bottom of the longship, a groaning, heaving knot of abject misery wrapped in blankets that Mathios tucked about her, or hung over the side of the ship casting up whatever sustenance she had managed to swallow. Rarely did she retain anything in her stomach for more than a few minutes before the awful gurgling started again and she rushed for the rail as fast as her ridiculously weak legs would take her.

Olav patted her on the back as she clung to the mast. "It will pass, girl. In a day or so. Maybe a week…"

"How… how long before we reach your land?" She hoped her voice did not sound as desperate as she felt.

Olav shrugged. "A week, perhaps."

Merewyn groaned and rested her forehead on the smooth wood, then clasped her hand over her mouth and dashed past the grinning Viking.

• • • • • • •

Olav was right, as it turned out, on both counts. The horrible sickness did ease after a few days, and as dawn broke on her fourth morning at sea Merewyn was able to gaze across the waves without being overwhelmed by nausea. She even began to enjoy the sense of motion, of speed as the longship flew across the waves. Whatever else might be said of these Vikings, they knew how to build swift ships. And how to sail them. Mathios strode from bow to stern, his long-legged gait sure and steady, his voice strong and confident, his authority absolute as he issued instructions, advice, warnings. His men obeyed without hesitation; no one questioned the Jarl, they just scurried to do his bidding.

Yet this stern master was unfailingly kind and considerate to her. Merewyn had feared he would lose patience as she continued to be wretchedly sick, but he did not. She wondered if he had been quite so solicitous when first the Vikings arrived in her home and she was too ill to be aware of what was happening. She knew he had cared for her then, but had not dwelt upon the details. She did now, as she recalled the countless times he had crouched beside her to offer a cup of cool water, a damp cloth to clean her face, a steadying arm about her shoulders as she moaned over the heaving waves and wished she were dead. Now, as the sun rose to cast a warm, pink glow over the horizon, she returned his concerned enquiry with a tremulous smile.

"I… I believe I feel a little better, Jarl."

"I am glad of it. Could you manage a few mouthfuls of bread, some cheese, perhaps?"

Her stomach growled, but in hunger now. She had barely eaten since her wedding night. Merewyn nodded and Mathios beckoned Vikarr over.

"My wife is hungry. Could you find her something to eat? Something light, and perhaps a little milk if there is some."

The youth gave his chief a rueful grin. "I shall try to milk the heifer now, Jarl, if I can get near the beast. She appears to dislike being tethered to the mast and has kicked me the last three times I attempted it."

Mathios was sympathetic, to a point. "I know. I saw. Try again, lad."

"Maybe I could help," offered Merewyn. "Ermenilda is more accustomed to me." She and the temperamental animal had managed to strike some sort of accord whilst at the farm and the cow generally acquiesced more readily to being milked by Merewyn than by anyone else.

"Ermenilda?" Mathios lifted one eyebrow. "You have named the beast Ermenilda?"

Merewyn tilted her chin at him. "It is a fine name and befits her perfectly. Saint Ermenilda was an abbess, a woman of holiness, piety, and peace. I believe the saint's fine qualities might bring about a calming influence upon our heifer."

"It has not worked so far, lady," observed Vikarr. "She remains bad-tempered and vicious."

"Perhaps we should name her for a Norse goddess," mused Merewyn, "since she will be among Vikings. Do you have a suggestion, Mathios?"

"Freya might be a good choice since she is the goddess of love and beauty as well as war. I expect the contrary animal could find something she might identify with in that."

"I shall discuss it with her." Merewyn made to get up.

Mathios offered her his hand and pulled her to her feet. "Good luck with that, my love." He kissed her on the cheek and ambled off to inspect the sails.

• • • • • • •

Ermenilda appeared unimpressed with suggestions that she might change her name. She stamped and snorted as

Merewyn attempted to milk her, and managed to upend the pail twice during the process. Merewyn persevered, and at last was able to produce a quarter of a bucket of rich, fresh milk to share among the men. The cow seemed less than enthusiastic about any aspect of this journey. Merewyn sympathised. Her own acute bouts of sickness might have ended but she longed for dry land and was convinced Ermenilda's spirits would be lifted also once she had her hooves firmly planted upon some lush meadow in the Norseland.

"It will not be long now," she murmured to the discontented bovine. "When we arrive, you shall have fine hay to eat and a warm stable, I promise." Merewyn patted the cow's shoulder and moved over to the rail to watch for any sign of land.

She saw nothing that first day, but on the second that she kept watch, their fifth at sea, she spotted a dark smudge on the horizon to her right. Olav was the man closest to her and she called out to him. "Is that land? Over there?"

The Viking warrior shielded his eyes with his hand as he peered across the glimmering waves. "Aye, you have sharp eyes, lady. It is. You have had your first glimpse of our homeland."

Others crowded about them to look. Shouts and cheers went up as they sighted land. Arne lifted Connell up high so that he, too, could view his new home.

"Where will we land? How much longer before we reach your village?" She directed her questions now to Mathios, who leaned on the rail to her left.

"Another day's sailing up the coast, though we will come in closer to the shore. My settlement is called Agnartved, which in your tongue means the place cleared by Agnar. Agnar was my grandfather. He chose the place and had his warriors fell trees to make space beside the cove, then he built the first longhouses in our settlement. My father, Agnarsson, added more dwellings as our numbers grew and he built the harbour."

Merewyn was puzzled. "You were not named for them? For your father and grandfather?"

Mathios shook his head. "My brother bore their names but he died, lost at sea when he was aged just fourteen. I did not grow up expecting to be Jarl but fate has a way of forming her own plans for us. My surname is Agnarsson and my sons bear that name also."

"Your sons? You have not spoken of them before."

"Have I not? I am father to two boys; the eldest, Galinn is five summers of age. Petrus is but three. They run their grandmother ragged, and me too when I am at home. I believe you will like them, though they are more of a handful than Connell."

"What happened to their mother?"

"Gudrun did not survive the birth of my second son."

"You… you must miss her."

Mathios frowned, his expression thoughtful. "I did, at first, especially with two young boys to rear, one an infant. Luckily the other women of Agnartved were willing to assist and both my sons thrived."

"But, what about in other ways? You lost a companion as well as the mother of your young children."

Mathios shrugged. "I confess, I was at home so seldom during my marriage that I did not consider Gudrun my companion. We were married for barely more than three years and I spent all but four months of that time away trading."

"Trading?"

"Aye, mostly, though there was a little Viking too. It is in the blood, Merewyn. My stepmother missed Gudrun though. They were friends."

"She runs your household now? Your stepmother?"

"She does, and she cares for my boys. Rowena will be pleased that I have taken another wife."

"Rowena? That is not a Viking name."

"My stepmother is from Wales originally, an Anglo-Saxon thrall who caught my father's eye."

"Oh. I see…" Merewyn had wondered about the new family she had married into, but had not expected such a revelation. "Your stepmother was once a slave?"

"She was, though that was many years ago. She has been a free woman for as long as I can recall. Rowena was my father's bed slave, then I suppose you would say she was his lover since he freed her and she was no longer a slave. He took her as his wife when my mother died. I confess I was not the most welcoming stepson. I resented Rowena, mainly out of misplaced loyalty to my mother."

"Misplaced?"

"My mother accepted Rowena in her lifetime. Who was I to object after her death? They were friends, up to a point. Certainly, there was not enmity between them. They shared the household and my father, and he treated both well enough. Eventually I came to my senses and made my peace with both my father and Rowena. I am glad I did for he died not many months later and I would not have wished our last words to be uttered in anger. Rowena, too, is very dear to me. I have no idea how I would have managed without her since Gudrun's death."

"It sounds a rather strange arrangement."

"Perhaps, but it is practical and ours is a happy family, I believe. I hope you will find it so."

"I… I will try. I am looking forward to meeting Rowena."

"You shall, soon enough. She will no doubt complain that she was not present at our wedding. Perhaps we could repeat the ceremony, in the Norse tradition this time."

"Of course, if you think it needful, though I have no idea what I would have to do."

He laughed. "Me neither. It is a complex and lengthy process but I believe we can rely upon Rowena to arrange matters. Despite her own heritage she has become well versed in our traditions. It is a matter of great pride to her that she straddles two cultures and does so effortlessly. I seem to recall being sent to the bathhouse just before the ceremony when I was wed the first time, and there was much discussion of the bride-price and the dowry."

"I bring no dowry but I will try to adapt to the Nordic culture."

"I know that. It is fortunate I have sufficient wealth and can manage well enough without your dowry though I think payment of a bride-price will be needful. A woman should not be without personal means."

"I do not understand."

"I will settle a sum of money on you. It will be your property and will remain yours throughout your life. Normally the bride-price is paid to a bride's family, but in this case you shall have it. There are other rituals but we shall impress upon Rowena that the process must be simple and the whole affair concluded in no more than a few days."

"A few days?" Merewyn gasped.

"Yes. That will allow ample time to introduce you as my bride and establish your place in Agnartved."

•••••••

Merewyn stood beside her tall Viking husband as the longship turned east and headed for the steeply cliff-lined coast of the Norseland. Mathios had navigated their course whilst at sea, but once they came in sight of land he passed the responsibility on to Hakon, who steered them in using landmarks. Now they were headed straight for a sizable coastal village consisting of several dozen dwellings and some larger buildings too. A jetty snaked out from the timber harbour and a plethora of small boats were fastened to that, bobbing cheerily in the waves.

"Our fishermen have not set out today," observed Mathios. "It is Friday, the traditional day of rest and worship."

"Your settlement is large," commented Merewyn. "How many live here?"

"Three hundred. Four, perhaps including the thralls."

"You keep slaves? Celts?"

"I do not think I possess any Celtic thralls. Our slaves here at Agnartved are mainly taken from Normandy, and a handful which were purchased from traders will have come from further afield. The lands to the east, mostly."

"Are… are they well-treated?"

"Yes, as long as they do as they are told and cause no trouble."

"But they are not free."

"How many of us are truly free, Merewyn?" He took her hand. "Look, there is Rowena, at the end of the jetty. My boys are with her."

Merewyn picked out the female wrapped in a heavy blue cloak and the two small figures dancing beside her. "They look to be excited at seeing their father's safe return."

"Yes. My stepmother will not have accepted that I was dead, but there are always rumours, always someone ready to ferment unease."

The longship slid onto the soft sand and continued on up the beach. Villagers swarmed about them, shouting, pointing, their faces full of glee. As soon as the dragon ship was moored, Mathios' men vaulted over the side to splash ashore and greet their joyful families. Merewyn saw Vikarr grabbed by a middle-aged woman and seized in a hug. Olav was subjected to similar treatment. The fierce Viking laughed as he bent to pick up a small boy and girl and waded ashore with them clinging to his neck. Arne bore Connell on his shoulders and made his way to where a woman of perhaps thirty summers awaited him, her expression bemused. He reached her and spoke to her for a few moments. Her features split in a beaming smile and she reached up to take Connell in her arms.

Tears pricked Merewyn's eyes. She had made the right choice, for Connell at least.

Mathios slung an arm across her shoulders. "Come, I shall carry you ashore."

"Really, there is no need—"

"Do as I say, wench." He leapt over the side and turned, his arms outstretched. "Jump over the rail, sweetheart. I shall catch you."

Merewyn could see nothing else for it. She clambered up and perched on the edge of the longship, then launched herself forward into her husband's arms.

Mathios strode out of the water and up onto the harbour where Rowena awaited him. The tall, brown-haired woman held herself with a regal air though her smile was pleasant enough. She was flanked by two small, blond-haired boys who Merewyn thought looked like smaller versions of their father.

Mathios set Merewyn on her feet and bent to kiss Rowena. The older woman, Merewyn would have judged her to be perhaps forty summers of age, smiled at him and released her hold on the boys to return his hug. The small boys seized the opportunity to attach themselves to each of Mathios' legs, both clamouring for his attention. Merewyn could not understand their rapid Norse, but the high-pitched demands as each sought to shout above the other were so funny she laughed out loud at their antics. Rowena turned to regard her quizzically and spoke softly to Mathios, also in Norse.

"Merewyn does not yet speak our tongue, though she is learning," Mathios replied in the slightly accented English Merewyn had grown to love. She wondered if Rowena had taught him it. "I trust you will help her in that. Rowena, this is Merewyn of Northumbria. My wife."

Rowena's eyes widened. She took a half pace back then regarded Merewyn closely for a few moments as Mathios sought to disengage the small boys from his lower limbs. She extended her hand in a polite greeting.

"I am pleased to meet you, Merewyn of Northumbria."

"Thank you. I have heard much about you."

"I hope our Jarl has spoken well of me." Rowena inclined her head in a graceful gesture. "You must be hungry, and tired. I am anxious to hear more of your story but first, shall we return to our longhouse? I have food prepared…"

"That will be excellent," agreed Mathios, now crouching in front of his two sons. "First though, let us complete the introductions. Galinn, Petrus, please greet your new stepmother."

Both boys peered up at her. They made no attempt to conceal their curiosity. Merewyn bent forward to offer her hand. "I hope we shall become friends, as your father and Rowena have."

Neither child gave any indication that they understood her words but one of the boys took her hand and shook solemnly. "I am delighted to meet you…" Merewyn continued, looking to Mathios to identify which child she was addressing.

"This is Galinn." Mathios laid his hand on the head of the boy who shook Merewyn's hand, "and this is Petrus." He spoke to the boys in Norse and Galinn stepped back to allow his brother to also greet Merewyn.

The social niceties concluded, Mathios took each of his sons by the hand. He grinned at Merewyn over their excited chatter. "Come, we will show you your new home." He set off along the harbour.

Merewyn started to follow. She had taken but two steps before Rowena slipped her arm through Merewyn's to link them at the elbow. No longer caught by surprise, her smile now seemed genuine and warm. "I really am delighted to meet you, Merewyn. It is time Mathios took another bride and I hope we can become friends."

"I hope so too." And Merewyn truly believed that it might be so.

Perhaps her fears of the Norsemen and their way of life had been unfounded. Maybe she could find happiness here.

CHAPTER FOURTEEN

It came as something of a surprise to Merewyn to realise that the Vikings lived in many ways just as the Celts did. The people of Agnartved were farmers for the most part, and traders. Their clothing was not dissimilar to the garments Merewyn had been accustomed to at home, their diet reasonably familiar. Their Nordic language was proving less difficult to master than she had feared, especially with Mathios and Rowena to aid her. Within just a few weeks Merewyn was able to understand much of what she heard about the settlement and could make herself understood, more or less.

Many of Mathios' people remained wary of the stranger in their midst. Foreigners were common enough in the settlement, but as thralls, not equals. Certainly not as the bride of their Jarl. The women viewed her with suspicion, the men with curiosity. Merewyn suspected that the men who had wintered in her cottage would have spoken of her to their comrades and families and she hoped their accounts were favourable. Perhaps the matter of the mandrake would not be mentioned.

Rowena was distant at first, though polite enough. She continued to manage the household and the boys, though after the first few days Merewyn was permitted to assist her around the longhouse.

Mathios' home was huge in comparison to the one-roomed cottage where Merewyn grew up. The longhouse was of similar construction to her farm, though the footings were of stone rather than wood. The dwelling was wood-framed and the outer walls were made of planks, a few stout logs, and in places wattle and daub. The roof was thatched, with no hole for smoke to escape. The fumes from the fire that burned night and day in the central fire pit rose up into the rafters and eventually dispersed through the thatch. The scent of wood smoke permeated everywhere. There were no windows. The only illumination came from the door, which stood open for most of the day whatever the weather in order to let in enough light to complete daily tasks. They used lamps too, fuelled by oil, but they were inefficient for close work.

She suspected the building had been extended over the years, and now the dimensions measured some eight paces in width and over sixty paces in length. A series of thick wooden poles ran down the centre, spaced perhaps twenty feet apart. From the apex the roof sloped down, and at the outer edges the walls were no more than five feet in height. This space was mainly used for storage, and for sleeping, with most of the activity of the household conducted in the centre or close to the door. Some areas were partitioned off with curtains to afford a degree of privacy. The sleeping area she was to share with Mathios was an example of such a concession, and Merewyn was glad of it.

Rowena, too, had her own quarters. The boys slept on pallets close to the fire, as did the three house thralls who served their Jarl's needs. All were female, aged from perhaps twelve years to middle age. They spoke the Norse tongue when conversing with Rowena or Mathios, but used a language of their own when they spoke among themselves.

"They are from France," explained Rowena. "Three generations of the same family, taken together on a raid and brought to market here in the Norseland. Mathios purchased all three and has allowed them to remain together."

"But even if they are together, to be enslaved seems so cruel," protested Merewyn. "Can we not—"

Rowena patted her hand. "Our slaves are safe here, well fed, and treated kindly. Their tasks are not especially onerous, as you can see for yourself. Would the life of a peasant in their homeland be any better?"

Merewyn had to admit that her own existence in the months following the raid by the Vikings had been infinitely worse, and even before the attack, her family's lives were harsh and unpredictable. One poor harvest could spell disaster. They had to work hard, toiling for long, back-breaking hours in the fields to scrape out a living. Mathios' thralls enjoyed a life of relative ease in comparison.

On her second morning at Agnartved, Merewyn, Mathios, Rowena and the two boys took their *dagmal* together. The meal consisted of honey, porridge, and dried fruit. The boys had buttermilk to drink and the adults a mug of mead.

"Are you busy today?" Merewyn set down her cup and gazed across the table at Mathios.

"I was intending to accompany Olav on the hunt. Our stores are depleted following the winter and now that we have returned, it is a priority to ensure we have enough food for all."

"Of course. I see that."

"Was there something you wished to do, Merewyn?" He gnawed on a hunk of bread as he regarded her. "If it is important, then I am sure—"

"No, no, you must hunt as you have said. I would not wish to interfere."

"Merewyn…" His tone had lowered and he managed to inject a note of warning into it. "If you want something, you must say so."

She stiffened her spine. He was right, of course, and

could only say 'no.' "I was hoping to see Connell today, but I do not know Arne's wife, Sigrunn, and I am unsure of my welcome in her home. I thought that perhaps you could accompany me on this first visit."

"Ah, I see. There is no need. Their longhouse is but a couple of minutes' walk away and Sigrunn will welcome you. Arne will be with us on the hunt so she may appreciate the company."

"Of course." Merewyn lowered her eyes. She had always been of a shy disposition and could not contemplate visiting a woman who was a stranger, especially knowing that she would find conversation difficult if not impossible since Sigrunn was unlikely to speak English. But if Mathios could not spare the time today she would postpone the visit.

"I will go with you." Rowena made the offer as she smeared honey onto bread for Galinn. "We will all go. I wish to consult Sigrunn regarding the wedding ritual, so it will be good to talk whilst the men are otherwise occupied, do you not agree?"

"What? You will come with me?" It had not occurred to Merewyn to ask Rowena. The other woman always seemed so busy.

"I would love to. Galinn and Petrus would enjoy the outing too and they should get to know their new cousin."

"Their cousin?" Merewyn was bemused.

"Well, strictly speaking I believe Connell is now their uncle by marriage, but cousin seems more apt. We shall complete our tasks here, then walk over to Arne and Sigrunn's longhouse by midmorning. Does that suit you?"

"It… it suits me very well. Thank you."

"Then that is settled." Mathios got to his feet. "I must be off. Enjoy your visit and do not allow Rowena and Sigrunn to get carried away with their plans for our wedding. Remember, it is to be a simple affair, and I will agree to three days of feasting, no more."

Three days? Merewyn could not imagine sufficient food assembled in one place to sustain three days of feasting but these Vikings clearly had other ideas. "Of course," she agreed, "no more than three days."

• • • • • • •

Despite being accompanied by her new family, Merewyn was apprehensive as they crossed the settlement in the direction of the longhouse occupied by Arne and his now expanded family. A lad of perhaps thirteen summers perched upon a stool in the doorway of the dwelling, three fat trout on the ground at his feet. He was busily engaged in gutting and cleaning the fish and glanced up as they arrived before him. Rowena spoke to him and he scurried indoors. A moment later Sigrunn appeared, Connell balanced upon her hip. She flung the door open wide and gestured them inside.

Cautious, Merewyn followed Rowena in, and sat beside her new friend on a bench close to the fire pit. Sigrunn chatted nonstop but the words were lost on Merewyn. Occasionally Rowena leaned toward her with a rapid translation.

"She is happy to see us, was intending to come and visit you before much longer."

"Sigrunn has broth and fresh-baked flatbread and invites us to eat with her."

"She thanks you for the gift of her child."

"Oh, no," Merewyn protested. "Connell was not intended as a gift. I know he will be better off here and I wanted what was best for him."

"She is grateful even so and loves him dearly."

Merewyn could see that. Connell appeared contented and happy. She was reassured that her choice had been the right one, however painful.

"Please, could you ask if I may hold him? Just for a few moments?"

Rowena conveyed the request and at once Sigrunn bustled across from the fire pit where she was busily hurling logs to feed the already cheery blaze. She deposited the squirming child on Merewyn's lap and delivered a torrent of rapid Norse.

"She says that you have no need to ask for anything within this longhouse. You are family."

"But I didn't want to interfere, now that Connell has a new family."

Rowena exchanged a few more words with Sigrunn then turned to face Merewyn. "It is important that you understand how Sigrunn views this matter. She loves Connell and will be a good mother to him. Arne will be a good and loving father also and Connell will want for nothing. But he will always need his sister. Sigrunn wishes to think of you as a daughter to her, and you will always be welcome in her home."

Merewyn could only stare at the two women, strangers to her but scant days previously but who had welcomed her and shown her the warmth and love she had almost forgotten existed between women. Ronat, her own mother, would have liked these two, she was certain of it.

"Thank you," Merewyn managed. "I… I… you have been very kind."

Rowena patted her hand, then reached to stroke Connell's rosy cheek. "He is a fine boy. You must be very proud of him."

"I am, yes."

Rowena nodded. "He will grow to be a strong and courageous warrior. Now, shall we turn to the pressing matter of your wedding?"

Much of the rest of the conversation was conducted in Norse and Merewyn caught but snatches of it. Occasionally Rowena explained what they were saying, but for the most part Merewyn was content to let them arrange matters as they saw fit. After all, what did she know of Viking wedding rituals? Merewyn played with Connell, and with her new stepsons, and was delighted when Rowena suggested that she go with the three little ones for a stroll around the settlement. "It will be a chance get to know the village, to chat to the women when the men are not about, and our settlement is not so large that you could get lost. We shall see you later."

"But what if someone wants to talk to me? I cannot—"

"You can smile, they will soon realise. Go on, there is nothing to fear. You are Mathios' bride so everyone will want to see you."

It seemed they did. Merewyn could not progress more than a few paces before she was waylaid by one villager after another. On each occasion she gave an apologetic little grin, which usually earned her a beaming smile or perhaps a piece of fruit or horn of ale. All were generous, keen to display their welcoming hospitality. The two small boys were also pleasant if demanding company with their never-ending stream of lively chatter and boisterous play. Connell was, of course, keen to join in and insisted on making the circuit of the settlement on his own far from steady feet. Their progress was slow but Merewyn enjoyed the excursion and managed to exchange pleasantries with many of the women of the village.

Once more, Vikings had managed to surprise her. She was starting to feel she belonged here.

• • • • • • •

"So," Rowena announced when Merewyn arrived back at Sigrunn's longhouse, "we have decided it would be best not to delay the wedding. You and Mathios already share a bed, so it is imperative we get the formalities concluded."

"We are already wed, it was done before we left…"

"Of course, we know that, but it does no harm to repeat the process, for good measure. Arne has explained that you and Mathios have been… are… well, you have known each other for some time, several months in fact. It would not do to wait until the first child is well on the way, would it?"

"A child? But no, I am not—"

Rowena waved away her protests. "These things happen. We shall make haste. It is what Mathios wishes also."

"I know that. Very well, but not too much feasting. That is also Mathios' wish."

Sigrunn set platters of food before them, sliced goat's meat and salted pork, bread cooked over the hearth, and a bowl of dried fruit and honey for the children. She poured each of them a mug of mead whilst Rowena continued to explain the emerging plan.

"Nordic weddings usually take place on a Friday as that is the sacred day for Frigga, the goddess of marriage. Next Friday is too soon. Just five days away… even Mathios could not conclude the matters of property which will be required to have been settled before the ceremony can commence. There is not much to accomplish, just the bride-price, but the coins will need to be presented and accepted."

"I am sure that whatever he decides will be more than adequate." Indeed, Merewyn had not expected anything at all.

"No doubt," agreed Rowena. "We shall arrange the ceremony for the following Friday, which will give us twelve days in which to summon guests and prepare sufficient food to sustain the feasting."

"No more than three days of feasting," Merewyn reminded the other women, "Mathios was most clear on that."

Rowena merely nodded and pressed on. "We will require meat, fish, fruit, breads, and cheeses, and of course a great deal of ale. Weddings always require copious amounts of ale. The men will have to hunt and fish, the children can gather the fruit. It is fortunate that Mathios brought ale back with him or we might not have had enough."

Sigrunn offered a comment that brought a smile to Rowena's face. "There is a tradition in this land that a bride should visit the bathhouse, attended by her female relatives, and wash away her virginity in readiness for her marriage. We assume such measures will not be necessary."

"No," muttered Merewyn, "they will not."

"In the Christian tradition a bride usually wears fine clothes. Do you have a preferred garment you would like to wear for the ceremony, Merewyn?"

"No, I do not, I... I have very few clothes. Perhaps I could—"

"We will make sure you have something new to wear. Sigrunn has some fine, soft wool in a delightful shade of blue which would fashion a decent gown. Your hair must be dressed, of course. I shall do that. And it is traditional for a bride to wear a gold circlet. I have mine still, from when I wed Agnarsson. You may borrow it if you wish."

"Yes, please. That would be most kind. As for the dress, perhaps I could find a way to pay Sigrunn for it, once I have the money Mathios has said he will give me."

Rowena waved away that suggestion. "It is our duty and our pleasure to ensure you are suitably attired for your wedding. As for the day itself, we shall select the finest goat to sacrifice, since it is important to attract the attention of the gods and goddesses but you need not concern yourself with any of that. Agnartved will be crowded with guests and all you need do is smile and make your husband proud."

"I shall do my best. Are you sure this can all be accomplished in just a few days?"

"Of course. We shall send out messengers at once to summon the guests and you must return here tomorrow in order that Sigrunn may start to fit your gown. I shall examine our food stores personally and inform Mathios of what is still required. Our fishermen will be kept busy, but the seas are calm just now so there should be ample opportunity to land the catch we need." She got to her feet and brushed a few creases from the front of her tunic. "We should be getting started."

Rowena gathered the boys up while Merewyn took her leave of Connell and Sigrunn.

"I shall see you tomorrow." She kissed her brother's cheek, then gave Sigrunn a quick hug. They had much to do.

• • • • • • •

The following days passed in a blur. Merewyn presented herself at Sigrunn's dwelling every day for a week, until Sigrunn declared the new gown ready. It was a fine garment of soft blue wool, decorated with a brooch of silver at the shoulder, a gift from Mathios, and a belt fashioned from strands of fine silk. The silk had come from the east, Sigrunn informed her, brought back from a trading expedition the previous year.

Rowena harassed Mathios into setting out almost every other day to hunt and fish, and their larders were overflowing. It was not considered needful to salt and preserve the meat as they had the boar back at her cottage because the flesh would be eaten within a matter of days. However, it required to be prepared and flavoured, and cooked to perfection if the feasting was to meet the required standards befitting a respected Viking chief. All the women of the settlement were tasked with producing their finest dishes. Thralls scurried about fetching and carrying, chopping wood for fires, washing stained clothing and bed linens, ensuring all would be in pristine readiness for the great day.

Merewyn watched the frenzy of activity in something of a daze. Her offers to help were usually declined, politely but firmly. Rowena explained that the people of Agnartved wanted to do this for her, for their Jarl. Mathios was liked and respected, and there were those among the villagers who had believed him lost at sea when he did not return home the previous autumn. This wedding was their way of celebrating their Jarl's safe return, they were determined to enjoy themselves and glad to do all that was required.

From the fifth day prior to the wedding, guests started to converge on the settlement. The Jarls of other villages, some close by, some as far as three or four days' ride from Agnartved, arrived with their followers. Some brought their families too. All needed to be housed and the longhouses were filling up fast as pallets were laid out on every spare inch of floor. Mathios' own dwelling was reserved for the most important visitors. His uncle, Magnus, second son of Agnar and brother to Agnarsson, arrived two days before the ceremony accompanied by a dozen warriors. All were found a place to sleep within Mathios' own dwelling.

On the day prior to the wedding Mathios' childhood friend, Torsteinn Haraldson, now Jarl of his own settlement and gaining fame as a prosperous trader, rode into Agnartved at the head of a column of wagons. He had brought his family, several thralls, and gifts of silks and spices to mark this auspicious occasion.

Mathios strode to the stables to greet his old friend, Merewyn at his side.

"It has been too long, my friend," he called as Torsteinn slithered from his mount. The two embraced, slapped each other on the back, and exchanged playful punches.

"It has indeed," agreed the newcomer. "Let me greet your new bride." He seized Merewyn and planted a kiss on each of her cheeks before sealing his mouth across hers. Mathios tolerated that for a few seconds then applied his fist none too gently to the other man's ear.

"You should find your own bride if you have a mind to eat a wench alive. I'll thank you to leave mine alone."

Torsteinn grinned at him. "You are right, of course. It is just that these Celtic females are so hard to resist." He turned to the wagon that had trundled into the settlement behind his massive horse. "Deva, come and meet our host."

Merewyn waited, curious, as a diminutive figure was helped by one of Torsteinn's men to disembark from the rear of the vehicle. She wore a thick cloak in a dark fabric, the hood shielding her from the stiff spring breeze as she came to stand beside her tall Viking companion. Torsteinn wrapped an arm about her shoulders and smiled at Merewyn. "You two will get along, I am sure. Deva is a Celt too."

The hood slipped from the other woman's face and Merewyn's knees gave way. She stumbled, would have fallen to the ground but for Mathios' quick reaction. He caught her and steadied her.

"Sweetheart, are you ill? You look pale as death."

So she might, for had she not just looked death in the face. She had seen a ghost, a woman she had presumed perished.

Trembling, Merewyn peered around Mathios to look again, to leave no room for doubt. "Deva," she croaked, reverting to her native Celtic tongue. "Is it you? Is it really you?"

"It is," came the whispered reply.

Merewyn was certain now. She recognised the voice, the low, gentle tone of the woman who in another life almost forgotten was to have been her sister. Deva was to have married her brother, Nyle, but instead she had been carried off with him and many others on that fateful day. She had been lost, enslaved or killed, with the others of their community, in the Viking raid on their home.

"You are alive. You survived." Merewyn could not believe that her childhood friend really stood before her, seemingly unharmed.

Deva nodded slowly. "I did."

"But... how? I thought... I never imagined..."

"I have been fortunate." Deva moved closer to Torsteinn's side but did not use the Nordic tongue that would have ensured he understood what was being said.

Merewyn ignored their guest's bemused expression as she reached for Deva's hands. "What about...? Do you know if... if...?"

"Bowdyn lives still. He is a thrall in my master's settlement and is well. I am afraid I have no news of Nyle."

CHAPTER FIFTEEN

Mathios had always considered himself to be moderately quick-witted, a quality that had served him well over the years. It was clear that Merewyn and Deva were acquainted, and that the reunion was one that neither had expected. Both women appeared shocked, stunned even. Mathios had followed the whispered exchange, which was more than his long-time friend had been able to manage, so he had some notion of what was happening.

Merewyn trembled as she leaned against him, unconsciously seeking his support. Torsteinn, too, appeared bemused, and who could blame him?

"Come, we will discuss matters further in private. My longhouse is but a few minutes away and we have yet to offer you refreshment after your journey..." Mathios spoke in the Norse language in order to include Torsteinn. He had to assume that Deva, like Merewyn, had learned enough to get by. He ushered Merewyn away from the stables and in the direction of their dwelling. Glancing back, he was relieved to see that Torsteinn was at his heels, the pale Deva clinging to his arm. No one spoke again until Mathios closed the door of his longhouse behind them.

"Please, be seated," he invited as Rowena hurried from

her sleeping quarters, a pile of blankets in her arms. "Ah, Rowena, we have guests."

"Yes, I saw them arrive and was about to make up pallets…" She looked from one ashen-faced woman to the other. "Is everything all right?"

Mathios shrugged. Really, he did not know. "Perhaps some ale? Or mead…"

"Yes, of course." Rowena dropped her blankets in a corner and rushed to find drinking horns and a pitcher of their good ale. Meanwhile the women sat down, while he and Torsteinn exchanged puzzled glances.

"You mentioned a thrall," began Mathios.

"Yes," whispered Merewyn. "Bowdyn. He is my brother." She turned to regard Deva closely. "You say he is well?"

"He is. He works with the Jarl's horses."

"Your brother?" The disjointed pieces began to fall into place for Mathios. "One of those taken as slaves?"

"Yes," breathed Merewyn. "I had not dared to hope that Bowdyn and Nyle might survive. But Nyle…?"

Deva shook her head. "I do not know his fate. He was taken away soon after we landed. He struck one of the guards and they… they…"

"He was hurt? Killed?"

"I did not see that, but I would not have thought they would kill him. He was—is—a strong worker, and valuable…"

Mathios directed his next question at Torsteinn, and spoke in Norse. "What do you know of this?"

His friend met his level gaze. "I purchased a number of thralls in Holvik." Torsteinn took a long draught of the ale provided by Rowena before continuing. "I had returned from a lucrative trading expedition laden with silks and spices from the eastern lands and found myself in need of workers to construct new dwellings, and to serve my growing band of followers. Deva was among the new slaves, as was this Bowdyn." Torsteinn paused and shook his head.

"In truth, he has been nothing but trouble and I would have sold him on within days had Deva not pleaded his case so prettily. They were from the same village in Northumbria, I gather. Anyway, I kept him locked in my slave barn for long enough, but we managed to arrive at some sort of understanding eventually. Now, he tends my horses and is remarkably good at it when he feels so minded. Most of the time he glares at me and seeks to stir up trouble among my thralls."

"Not much of an understanding, by the sound of it," observed Mathios. He noted that his friend did not disagree. "So, you will not have any objection then, should I seek to take this bothersome thrall off your hands?"

"None whatsoever," confirmed Torsteinn.

"Your price?"

"You may have the man as a wedding gift. I will send for him."

"Thank you. I appreciate your generosity and my wife will be most grateful. Her brothers are dear to her."

Torsteinn nodded. "What of the other? I understand they are twins and that my Deva was at one time betrothed to the brother of Bowdyn."

My Deva? "I see." Mathios considered this an awkward circumstance to say the least.

Torsteinn did not, apparently, share his concerns. "Her affections are now otherwise engaged and I have no quarrel with the Celt she was to wed. All I can tell you of him is that I purchased my thralls from a trader by the name of Nikulas Njallson. He is well known in Holvik and would be easy enough to locate there I imagine. Njallson may have knowledge of what became of the man who attacked the guard. It is likely he would recall the incident."

Mathios tended to agree. He got to his feet and smiled at his wife. "Merewyn, you will remain here with Deva. I am sure you both have much to discuss. Torsteinn and I have matters of some urgency to attend to."

Merewyn grabbed his sleeve. "But…what of my

brothers? Please, Mathios, could you not—?"

He crouched beside her seat in order to look up into her still pale features and raised a hand to sweep her hair back from her face. "Torsteinn has kindly agreed to relinquish Bowdyn to me. Your brother will be brought to Agnartved within the coming days."

"Oh, that is wonderful. But what of Nyle? We must find him, too."

"I shall make enquiries, but if he has not been seen for over a year the trail will not be a warm one."

"I know, but—"

Mathios rose to his feet. "I shall let you know if I discover anything. Now, I must go."

"Of course. Thank you." She offered a smile to Torsteinn also. "And thank you too."

Once outside the longhouse, Mathios summoned Olav and briefly explained to him what had taken place. "Torsteinn has already dispatched men to his settlement to bring Bowdyn here. I would like you to take five or six warriors and go to Holvik. Seek out the slave trader and question him. You may bribe Njallson if necessary, threaten him as you see fit but extract any information you are able as to the whereabouts of this missing thrall. If you are able to discern the new owner you will seek him out and purchase the slave from him. I will provide the necessary funds and you will pay whatever it costs to secure the man and bring him back to me here. Needless to say, he is not to be harmed regardless of how reluctant he may be to cooperate. Merewyn would not forgive either of us should her brother meet with any sort of mishap at our hands."

"I understand, Jarl. We shall leave at once."

"Thank you. I am sorry that you will miss the feasting."

Olav shrugged, unconcerned. "As long as some ale remains for when we return, I shall not complain."

• • • • • • •

Mathios had not greatly enjoyed his first wedding and no particularly high expectations of his second one. The purpose of the event was to secure Merewyn's place here and establish her as his wife. A Celt would not be readily accepted, though his bride's early progress was more than he could have hoped for. He intended to do all he could to ensure that his people were in no doubt as to her status at Agnartved. Mathios was surprised, therefore, to find pleasure in the traditional rituals and practises. Perhaps it was the smile on his bride's face that made the difference. Since he had told her that she was soon to be reunited with one of her brothers she had not stopped smiling. He found her joy infectious.

The wedding was to take place in a cleared area in the heart of his settlement. The people of Agnartved and the many guests who had descended upon the village gathered in the morning and formed a huge circle. Those at the back shoved and jostled, craning their necks to get a better view of the main participants. The bride-price was the first matter to be addressed.

She gaped at the bag of silver coins he deposited at her feet on the morning of their wedding, witnessed by the hundreds of Vikings gathered to share the event. She reached out to lift a handful of the glittering silver pennies and allowed them to trickle through her fingers.

"You cannot mean me to have this? All of it?"

"All of it," he confirmed. "It is yours."

"I have never before seen even one silver coin, let alone so many," she murmured. "It is too much."

"The bride-price has been recorded. We shall proceed with the ceremony now." Mathios nodded to Magnus, his uncle, who as his oldest and most elevated male relative had the honour of making the sacrifice to the gods and goddesses required to ensure a happy and fertile union. A quick flash of a blade was all it took, and the hapless goat collapsed on the stone altar. Magnus collected a small pool of blood in a bowl and approached Mathios and Merewyn.

He chanted the ancient words of blessing, at the same time using fir twigs to flick droplets of the still warm blood over them. Merewyn flinched, no doubt mindful of her lovely new dress, but Mathios' hand on her shoulder kept her in place to receive the ritual. Mercifully that part was quickly concluded, and he was quite convinced the gown could be washed. Magnus led the chants and incantations required to gain the blessings of the gods and goddesses and thus protect their union.

The formalities at an end, Mathios led Merewyn through the settlement to receive the jubilant good wishes of their friends and guests, and at last the feasting could start. Long tables had been erected outdoors, close to his longhouse, but there was nowhere near enough space at the tables for all who were there. Most sat on the ground or on upturned barrels, stools, fences, and low walls as female thralls rushed to and fro refilling mugs and drinking horns. The prepared food was set out upon the tables, again by thralls, and guests could help themselves. The boards groaned under the weight of roasted meat, fish, and vegetables. Platters piled high with flatbreads sat at regular intervals, beside steaming pots containing broths of beef, pork, and lamb. The aroma of spices and herbs filled the air, along with the piquant scent of nuts and fried fruits soaked in honey. It was clear that the women had been busy.

"Eat slowly," he advised Merewyn. "We shall be here for hours at least, then all day tomorrow."

"There is so much food," she breathed. "Surely we do not need all of this."

"A wedding has little enough to do with need and everything to do with tradition and flamboyant display." He assisted her into one of the two large chairs set at the head of one of the tables. "So we sit here, we smile, we sip our ale and nibble on succulent pork, and look forward to the time when we will be permitted to retire to our longhouse and savour the more personal delights of the married state."

He loved the way she reddened, even now. He would

enjoy even more fucking her later and intended to take all night over it despite the throng of bodies likely to be sprawled all over the floors of his home. Judging by the quantities of ale and mead being swigged, few would be in any state to take notice of the sounds emanating from behind the curtain that shielded his sleeping quarters. Even so, he had plans that would ensure the privacy he required.

The hours passed slowly but Mathios could summon up reserves of patience when the occasion called for it. He introduced Merewyn to the guests whose acquaintance she had not yet met, and, in truth, even he struggled on more than a few occasions to recall everybody's name. Rowena hovered near at hand and assisted him whenever she could. Magnus also, and once or twice Torsteinn, stepped in. He noted that Deva was not present at the feast and found an opportunity to ask his friend about her absence.

"She is with the other thralls, preparing and serving food. It is what she prefers."

"Really? I had assumed that you and she were close."

"She shares my bed if that is what you mean."

"And that is all?" Mathios had thought their relationship appeared to be more.

"For now," explained Torsteinn. "I confess being rid of the slave Bowdyn will likely ease matters. My little Celtic bed slave harbours a certain loyalty to him although it was the other twin she was destined to wed."

"When might we expect Bowdyn to arrive here?"

"Tomorrow perhaps, or the day after provided the weather remains good for travelling."

"Ah, then he shall be in time to join our wedding feast." He signalled for a passing servant to refill his mug and that of his bride. "Let us drink to clement weather and dry roads."

• • • • • • •

Darkness had long since fallen by the time Mathios

deemed it reasonable to withdraw from the feast. Merewyn was exhausted. So was he, but their guests had travelled long distances over inhospitable terrain and at very short notice so the least they could do as hosts was observe the social niceties. Still, he considered their duty done, at least for now. He leaned over to murmur in his wife's ear, "It is time for us to retire, I believe."

"Jarl?" She turned to smile up at him. "Yes, please."

He stood and offered her his hand. They made their way cautiously between the tables, taking care not to step on anyone as they passed. One or two of his men lifted a weary hand or mug in salute, but most of those still present were already asleep, their drunken snoring loud enough to drown the sound of footsteps as Mathios and Merewyn crept away.

"We shall have to present ourselves again tomorrow, but the celebrations will be less raucous by then," he advised.

"Christian weddings are more sedate than this," Merewyn observed, "though there is feasting and usually music too. And dancing."

"There will be music tomorrow, and dancing probably. Hakon plays the pan pipes and Vikarr the lyre. I shall instruct them to treat us to some lively tunes."

"I would enjoy that." She glanced about her. "Why are we going this way? Our house is over there, to the left."

"We are not going to our longhouse since it is already full to overflowing. I know of another place which will be... quieter."

"Oh." She made no further comment as he lifted a torch from its mounting in a wall and used it to light their way as he steered her in the direction of the harbour and the beach.

Mathios stopped at the entrance to the boathouse that protected his precious longship when not at sea. Following their arrival, the vessel had been dragged across the sand and into the tall, timber structure in order that Ivar and Ywan could treat the external hull with tallow to make it more watertight. They had made do as best they could to enable their voyage home, but now the craft would be meticulously maintained and made seaworthy. The scent of the tallow filled his nostrils as Mathios opened the large doors and slipped inside, towing Merewyn behind him.

"Why are we here?" she whispered in the darkness.

"You shall see." Mathios had been here the previous day to make his preparations and had taken the precaution of leaving a lamp close to the door. He reached for and lit the wick from the torch, which he then secured to the outside of the boathouse. They ventured inside, their way lit by the flickering lamplight and Mathios assisted Merewyn in scrambling up the rough wooden framework that cradled the ship. He scaled the hull with ease and vaulted onto the deck, then leaned over to draw his wife up behind him. "Follow me."

He led her between the narrow ribs of the ship that served as seating for the oarsmen, right to the raised platform at the prow. This was the spot where he would stand and direct his warriors in a raid, or view the stars to plot his course in the darkness, but this night the vantage point was equipped for entirely different purposes. A pile of furs and blankets lay on the planks, and a pitcher of fresh water stood close by.

"Our bed for the night," he announced. "I trust it is to your liking."

"Oh, it is perfect. Thank you."

"My motives were not entirely selfless. A degree of privacy will aid my plans for our wedding night."

"Our second wedding night," she corrected. "Our first started with a spanking."

"That is not my intention this time. In truth, I prefer to sleep, at least initially."

"Oh." She smiled and settled herself on the pile of furs. "Do you think we shall be warm enough? There is no fire…"

He eased his larger body alongside hers. "I am sure we will be. Come, move closer to me, little Celt."

She wriggled up against him and he wrapped his arms

about her. "This is a beautiful gown, Merewyn. I have been meaning to say so."

"It is," she agreed happily. "Sigrunn made it for me. She refused any payment. I hope the bloodstains will wash out." She wrinkled her nose and Mathios sympathised. The goat's blood was his least favourite part of the ritual also.

"I am sure they will. Rowena will help. Sigrunn did well. You and she have become friends, then?"

"Yes, I believe we have. And I know Connell will be happy with Sigrunn and Arne. She had made me welcome in her longhouse so I shall see my brother growing up."

"I always imagined it would be so. I am glad. You are content here, then?"

Merewyn turned to face him. "Yes, I am. Thank you for returning for me."

"I should never have left without you. Olav believes I should have tossed you into my ship and set sail, your protests be damned. Perhaps he is right."

"I would not have forgiven you."

He eyed her doubtfully. "No? I believe I might have persuaded you, eventually, even if I had to spank you every day for the first year of our marriage."

"You would not have done that."

He grinned. "I consider it an opportunity squandered. Still, it is done now." He shifted so her back was again turned to him and he drew her up close to his chest. She sighed contentedly as he slid his hand down the front of the gown he so admired and cupped her naked breast. "Your body is beautiful, so fragile yet strong. Your flesh yields beneath my hand, then springs back as though untouched." He caressed the soft curve in his palm, squeezing gently then stroking his fingers over the pebbled tip.

Merewyn shifted and stretched, her eyes closed as she relaxed under his touch. "Would it be permissible for me to fall asleep now, my Jarl?"

He chuckled. "I would not strenuously object."

Merewyn stifled a yawn, then, "I offered to purchase

Deva."

This he had not expected. Mathios glanced down at the top of her silken head. "I doubt you could persuade Torsteinn to part with her. I am quite sure she is not for sale."

"I did not approach him. I spoke to Deva, asked her if she wished to be free."

"I see. I assume you would have used your bride-price to fund the purchase?"

"Yes. I hope there would have been enough. I do not know the value of a thrall."

"You could buy a thousand Devas with the money you now own. What was Deva's response?"

"She wishes to remain with Torsteinn and hopes that he will free her one day."

"He may."

"Even if he does not, she loves him."

"I believe he cares for her."

"Did you know that she accompanies him on his trading journeys?"

"I did not, though that does not surprise me. He would require thralls to attend him and as evidence of his prosperity when dealing with other merchants."

"Had she wed my brother, it is likely that Deva would have lived her entire life within five miles of the cottage in which she was born. But at Torsteinn's side she has already travelled to France in the south, and to the shores of the Black Sea to the east. I had not even known there was such a place."

"Ah, yes, the Byzantine Empire. They trade mainly in silks and spices. Would you like to go there?"

"I am not sure. Maybe. I confess, travel both intrigues and terrifies me. And I detest sailing, as you know."

"You would become accustomed to it. I am an explorer by nature, I believe, and I find I rather enjoy the notion of both intriguing and terrifying you. It is in the Viking blood to travel, to seek out new places, new adventures and we are good seafarers. And it is in Deva's too, by the sound of it. She and Torsteinn are well matched."

Merewyn was silent for a few minutes, then, "I will never be reconciled to what happened to my family. My father died a senseless death, and the destruction of our home was cruel and unnecessary. But all is not as simple as I once thought. Had she not become pregnant, I believe my mother would have survived the attack, but I would not have had my brother and Connell is very dear to me. As are my other brothers. Would you permit me to purchase Bowdyn from you? I have the money, as you know."

"You do, but you are too late. The thrall Bowdyn is not for sale."

"But—"

"When he arrives I intend to make him a free man."

"You would do that?"

"Of course. My wife's brother cannot serve as a thrall. Bowdyn will be at liberty to remain at Agnartved if he chooses, or to return to his home."

"He will wish to go home, I am sure of it."

"Perhaps. In that case we shall have reason to return to Northumbria ourselves from time to time to visit."

She twisted her neck to smile up at him. "I would like that, despite my seasickness. I fear though that our arrival would cause panic in the neighbouring countryside,"

"They will get used to us, I daresay." He yawned. "We should sleep now. Tomorrow will be another long day."

CHAPTER SIXTEEN

When Merewyn awoke it was to see slivers of silvery daylight spearing between the planks that made up the walls of the boathouse. She knew a brief moment of panic at the unfamiliar surroundings, then relaxed when she recalled where she was. And who she was with.

Mathios still slept, his breathing low and even behind her. His hand still rested on her breast, his fingers curled around the soft lower curve. At some stage he must have drawn the furs up and around the pair of them because she was warm and the fur tickled her nose.

She stretched, her limbs stiff from sleeping in a strange position. Her bodice tightened, pressing her husband's hand against her breast in a manner she found quite delightful. Soon they would have to return to the festivities, seat themselves upon those great chairs in front of their longhouse and be feted by her husband's people. His family, friends, the Jarls of neighbouring settlements would clamour to wish them well and share in the celebrations. But not yet. Not quite yet…

"Mathios, are you sleeping…?"

No answer.

"Mathios? Are you awake?" She wriggled her shoulders

against his solid chest. "Jarl…?"

"By Odin's balls, can you not keep still, woman?"

"It is morning. We must go back soon."

"I think not." He moved his fingers, as though only now recalling where his hand was situated. "Does this bodice open?"

"I believe it does, my husband. Shall I…?" She could think of no better way in which to prolong this precious time together.

Mathios waited patiently while she fumbled with the unfamiliar fastenings. She managed to loosen the silver brooch but he had to release the lacings at the back. Eventually the front of her beautiful blue gown gaped open and Mathios tugged it down to her waist to reveal her breasts. Her nipples were already stiff from the chill in the air but warmed when he fastened his lips around first one then the other.

"That feels wonderful," she sighed. "I want… I want…"

"Tell me," he pressed, his face buried between the soft mounds. "What do you want, little Celt?"

"I want you inside me. Deep, and hard."

"I can do that."

"Now. I want you now."

"Where do you want me, Merewyn?"

"Do not tease me. You know. I just said…"

"You want me to fuck you, and I shall do so. Gladly."

"Well, then…"

"I shall fuck your arse."

"My… oh!. Oh…" She was perplexed. Utterly dumbfounded.

"Quite. So now that is clear, and having woken me from a perfectly relaxing and well-deserved slumber, perhaps you would be so good as to present your delightful bottom."

"Will it hurt?" Despite her astonishment at the suggestion, and utter humiliation at the prospect of what he wished to do to her, Merewyn found herself actually considering the idea. She must be quite mad, she concluded.

Or perhaps it was the oddly disturbing way her cunny clenched and dampened when she thought of the forbidden, intimate act.

"Perhaps, a little at first. I intend to be very gentle with you however."

"How…? I mean, I cannot imagine…" Not entirely the truth. There was nothing much amiss with Merewyn's imagination.

"You will lean forward and rest your elbows on this bench. If you feel able to assist by reaching back and spreading the cheeks of your arse for me, so much the better. I shall manage the rest." He leaned to the side and reached under the bench he had pointed out to her. "I have rapeseed oil to hand which I took the precaution of leaving here yesterday. This will ease my entry, and I shall use my fingers to first open your entrance."

She considered the matter for a few moments, her mind whirling at the explicit nature of his description. "You have done this before."

"I have."

"That is a relief, Jarl, for I have not."

He gave her that lopsided, sensual grin that could turn her insides to water. "I know that. And you know, do you not, that I will never harm you?"

She did know that. Merewyn merely nodded. "Should… should I remove my clothes?"

"You may if you wish, though it will suffice for you to merely lift the back of your gown up out of the way."

"Very well. I… shall I do it now?"

His grin widened. "I would appreciate it, my sweet Celt. Do you need my assistance?"

She shook her head. "I do not think so." She shuffled around until she knelt before the bench, then leaned forward to rest her elbows upon it. She looked back at him over her shoulder. "Like this?"

He inclined his head, then raised an eyebrow, "The dress?"

"Yes, I know." Merewyn reached behind her to grab a handful of the woollen fabric and pulled it forward. That did not work, merely drew the gown tightly across her bottom. She tried again, this time drawing it up the backs of her thighs. The whisper of cool air over her exposed buttocks signalled her success. "Is this better?"

"Much. Now, if we just…" Mathios arranged the fabric in a bunch and laid it over her back in such a manner that she did not have to hold it in place. "There. Perfect."

Merewyn watched, her anxiety mounting as he poured a little of the oil onto his fingers. He regarded her under his lowered brows. "Are you intending to assist me?"

"I am not sure. I…"

"Face forward, Merewyn." His tone was soft, and achingly gentle. "Reach back as I told you and part the cheeks of your bottom for me. Then just close your eyes and hold still. You can do that."

He was right, she could. Surely she could. Merewyn balanced her shoulders on the edge of the bench and stretched her arms back. She sank her fingers into the soft flesh of her bottom and pulled the two globes apart. She believed she might actually die of embarrassment when Mathios moved to kneel directly behind her. The light had strengthened now and cast bright beams to illuminate the interior of the boathouse. He had a perfect view of her exposed arsehole, that private, secret place that even she had never seen.

"Thank you."

Merewyn was expecting him to touch her, but even so she flinched when his slick fingers circled her tight ring of muscle.

Oh, God. Oh, sweet Jesus. She remained in place by sheer force of will.

Mathios continued to swirl his fingertip around her anus, then started to press on the centre. He was gentle, as he had promised he would be, but insistent also. Her instinctive response was to tighten, to clench and prevent his entry.

Mathios tapped her lightly on her upturned buttock.

"Do not fight me, little Celt."

"I do not mean to. This is difficult..."

"Not so difficult. You have but to obey me. Am I hurting you?"

"No."

"You are embarrassed?"

"Of course!"

"You will get past that, and find the pleasure beyond."

He uttered the words with such confidence, such certainty that Merewyn began to believe that it might be so, eventually. But not yet.

Mathios increased the pressure. Merewyn made an effort to relax, though she did not succeed. Perhaps she should beg him to stop, suggest that they return to their guests and abandon this strange, invasive business. She opened her mouth, the words were there, hovering on the tip of her tongue, when her body capitulated and he sank his finger into her arse. Not the entire digit, perhaps as far as the first knuckle, but enough to elicit a startled "Oh!" from her.

"There, it will become easier now." He withdrew the finger and sank it into her rear hole again, then again. He repeated the action several times as she gasped at the indignity of it all. He withdrew altogether, but only to apply more oil, then he plunged his finger back again. He pressed harder, deeper, sinking more of that questing digit inside her until he had inserted the entire length.

It felt... indescribable. Not pleasurable, not exactly. But not painful either. It was dirty and wicked and forbidden—and glorious because of all of that. A wave of pure lust washed through her and Merewyn wished he would stroke her clitty, just once; that would feel utterly wonderful.

"Please..." She did not know what she wanted to plead for, just... something.

"Merewyn? Are you all right?"

"Yes. No."

He chuckled and reached beneath her to rub her

quivering bud. "And now?"

"Yes!" Pleasure assailed her, pleasure so intense she could only squirm and rotate her hips as her sudden, powerful release swept her senses aside. It was swift, lasted but a few moments, but when she regained her wits, it was to realise that her rear entrance was stretched impossibly tight. Her entrance burned as he drove his fingers in and out. He had slipped a second finger in next to the first whilst she was otherwise preoccupied and now treated her to long, even strokes.

Merewyn started to pant. It was not painful, but the sensation was intense and threatened to overwhelm her. Perhaps it was the intimacy of the moment, or maybe the dazzling degradation of the act but she could not contain her response. Her emotions were shredded, desire merged with humiliation and she sobbed even as she begged him not to stop. Mathios continued to finger-fuck her arse at the same time as he caressed her throbbing clitty to bring her to a second shuddering release. As she soared he withdrew his fingers again, but only to drizzle oil on his hard, thick cock and place the head of that at her entrance.

Even as she dreaded this final humiliation, Merewyn pressed back against him. The head breached her with an ease she had not expected. It hurt now, really hurt. She would have been terrified but for the knowledge that this was Mathios and she was safe. He would take care of her, as he always had from the moment they met.

She clutched at the bench, only now realising that at some stage she had relinquished her grip on her buttocks. When had that happened? No matter, she groaned then let out a small squeal as he sank the entire length of his cock into her narrow channel.

"Fuck, fuck, fuck," he murmured. "So tight, so fucking wonderful…"

She was stretching, impossibly tight, indescribably full. Even so, she managed to constrict her inner muscles around him, causing Mathios to groan then land a sharp slap on her buttock. "Be still, wench."

She might have apologised but could not form a coherent thought let alone words. He drew his cock back, almost out of her, then drove it deep again, right to the root. Merewyn was sure she would lose her wits once more if he continued, but she was past caring.

He shoved his hands under her shoulders and slowly eased her upright so that she settled upon his thighs, impaled on his cock with her legs splayed and trapped on the outside of his.

"Am I hurting you?" he asked her again.

Merewyn could do no more than shake her head.

He eased her back so she leaned her weight on him, then he reached down to lift the fabric of her gown, which covered her legs and his. He lifted it to her waist and rolled it into a rough ball. "Hold this," he commanded softly.

Merewyn did as she was told, holding the gown up and out of the way as her husband reached around her to part the lips of her cunny. Merewyn peered down over the bundle of blue fabric and watched as he stroked her swollen clitty slowly, deliberately. She writhed on his lap, intensely aware of the thickness of his cock seated deep inside her. He continued to stroke and tug on her pleasure bud at the same time as he drove three fingers into her cunny. Merewyn could take no more. Her body shuddered as wave after crashing wave of pleasure coursed through her body. She was vaguely aware of Mathios' low growl in her ear as he thrust his cock in and out of her arse. She squeezed, she convulsed, she let out a ragged cry as her arousal peaked, crested, then sent her spinning into oblivion.

Long minutes later her husband slid his cock from her still quivering channel. The wet heat of his semen dribbled down her thighs but she did not care. Mathios rearranged his own clothing quickly, then produced a piece of cloth with which he cleansed her as she lay inert on the pile of furs and bedding. When he was done he took her in his arms again and they lay motionless, silent, absorbing the sensual intimacy of this moment.

Mathios was the first to break the silence. "We must return or they will start to seek us out."

"I know."

"If you prefer to remain in the longhouse, I can make your excuses. There is sufficient ale to occupy our guests, no one will mind."

"I wish to be there, at your side."

He kissed her tousled locks. "In that case, my sweet Celt, we should set your gown to rights, then seek out Rowena in the hope that she might contrive some way of making your hair respectable."

"Oh…" Merewyn patted her tangled mane. "Do I look dreadful?"

"You look beautiful, and very well fucked."

Merewyn sat up. She ached, and when she considered the matter further she found her bottom felt decidedly odd, though not uncomfortable.

Mathios' smile was warm and on a sudden rush of emotion she flung her arms about his neck. "I love you," she murmured. "I love you so much it hurts."

He chuckled and kissed her hair. "I love you too, my Celt."

• • • • • • •

When she was to cast her mind back later, Merewyn found she could recall little of the detail from the early part of the second day of feasting She and Mathios presided over more platters of succulent meats and fish than she had ever seen in her life, interminable drunken squabbles that would break out between the rowdy Vikings, frequent squeals of alarm and sometimes giggles of excitement from females caught up in the lust- and ale-fuelled festivities. Hours passed, they ate a little and drank sparingly, conversed with those who remained sufficiently sober to do so and received the effusive good wishes of all who passed their elevated seats situated close to the tables that still groaned under the unending dishes of food. By midday Merewyn was exhausted but she refused to leave Mathios' side.

"As your wife I must become accustomed to your Viking traditions and take part in the celebrations. How can I claim to do so if I cannot even manage to find the fortitude to attend my own wedding?"

"It is customary for a bride to spend time with her female relatives. It is their role to instruct you in the art of pleasuring your new husband. Perhaps you could use the time to rest since you please me greatly and I prefer to see to the matter of your education myself."

"I see. Then perhaps…"

"Ah, here is Rowena." Mathios summoned his stepmother to their side. "Rowena, could you accompany Merewyn back to the longhouse. She is badly in need of quiet in which to rest. I trust our private sleeping quarters are not occupied by our guests."

"No, though we may have to pick our way across the main hall with care for there are many slumbering there and little in the way of empty space to put our feet." She helped Merewyn from her lofty seat and the pair made their way between the raucous groups of still-celebrating Norsemen. Once back in their own home Merewyn saw that Rowena had not exaggerated. There was barely an inch of the earthen floor still visible, almost the entire area was occupied by slumbering chieftains and their followers. Only warriors of the Jarl, the most exalted status in the Viking world, and their wives, thralls, and children were permitted to use Mathios' own dwelling. The rest, those of the karl class and their kin, found shelter from the stiff easterly wind in the homes of lesser Norse families.

As Rowena had promised, the sleeping quarters Merewyn shared with Mathios were unoccupied. She slipped behind the curtain that divided the narrow chamber from the rest of the longhouse. There was barely enough room for a large pallet and space for some personal items of clothing. Rowena followed and helped her out of her lovely blue gown.

"I shall attend to the stains, beat the dust from this, and freshen it for you. By the time you awaken it will be as new again."

"Thank you." Merewyn sank onto the pile of furs. "Perhaps you could wake me in an hour or so."

Rowena merely smiled and left her to her rest.

Dusk was falling when Merewyn opened her eyes. The first thing she noticed was silence from the outer chamber. She rose from the bedding and peeped around the curtain. The room was deserted but for the trio of female thralls who helped Rowena with the domestic tasks. They tended the fire and stirred the huge cauldron. One looked up when the movement of the curtain caught her eye.

"Where is Rowena?" asked Merewyn.

The women regarded each other, then her, with consternation, reminding Merewyn once more that she must learn their tongue for she could not rely on Mathios or Rowena to translate for her.

"Rowena?" she repeated. They would at least know their mistress's name.

One responded in rapid and incomprehensible Norse. The other shot out of the longhouse, presumably in search of Rowena. Sure enough, Mathios' stepmother arrived after a few minutes, bearing the blue gown.

"Ah, you are awake. I was on my way to rouse you as the Jarl has requested that you join him to greet our latest guests."

"There are more people arriving? But I thought—"

"Mathios suggests that you make haste. You will be eager to greet this particular guest."

"Who…? Oh!" She pressed her hand to her chest as realisation dawned. "Is it Bowdyn? He is here? Already?"

"The party sent by Torsteinn to bring him to Agnartved has been sighted. They are perhaps an hour's ride away."

"Does he know? Have they told him that I am here?"

"I cannot say, Merewyn. But I do know that your husband wishes to greet the man with you at his side, so perhaps we could…"

"Yes, yes. I will get ready and come at once."

Rowena assisted her into the now freshened dress, which was a blessing as Merewyn could not have achieved the feat unaided. Her fingers were leaden, her mind unable to focus on anything but the coming reunion. She dashed from the longhouse before Rowena had time to drape her cloak about her shoulders, causing the older woman to hurry in her wake with the forgotten garment. By the time Rowena caught up with her and fastened the cloak about her shivering form, Merewyn was once more beside Mathios. Her husband drew the cloak about her and assisted her back into her seat.

"I trust you are refreshed? You certainly appear so."

"Yes, I slept for hours. Rowena said… Is he here yet?"

"They are expected to enter the settlement in the next few minutes. My men made good time and the weather has been clement." Torsteinn stood behind Mathios' chair, Deva at his side. Even as he spoke, a clattering of hooves heralded the arrival of several men on horseback. Torsteinn issued a short command to one of his warriors. "They will dismount and leave their horses at the stables, then present themselves before us."

"Bowdyn too? He will not remain to tend the horses?"

"Not on this occasion," confirmed the Viking chief.

The four of them—Merewyn and Mathios, Torsteinn and Deva—waited in silence though Merewyn was convinced the entire settlement could hear the pounding of her heart. At last she heard the voices of men approaching, perhaps a half dozen or so, and speaking in the Norse language.

She would have known him anywhere. As tall as the warriors who flanked him, Bowdyn now sported a beard and his features were darker than when she saw him last. He had clearly spent much time outdoors and lacked the facilities to shave. His clothing was plain, serviceable, but decent enough she supposed. In the few weeks she had spent in this land she had witnessed thralls who appeared far less content than her brother now did.

"The thrall, Bowdyn, Jarl. As you commanded." One of the men gestured to Bowdyn as he bowed to his lord.

Torsteinn gave a curt nod. "You did well. There is food and ale, make yourselves comfortable."

The warriors strode off to join what was left of the celebrations, heading straight for the closest cask of mead. Bowdyn remained where he was and eyed his Viking master with caution.

"You wanted me?" he demanded, not a trace of servility in his tone.

Torsteinn shook his head. "Not me so much as your new master and his lady. You now belong to Mathios of Agnartved."

Bowdyn's eyes narrowed a fraction, the only sign he was at all moved by this shift in his circumstances. He did not so much as cast a glance in the direction of Mathios or Merewyn.

"You are welcome here, Bowdyn of Northumbria." Mathios rose and went to stand immediately before the thrall. "However, Torsteinn's words are not accurate. I have decided to make you a free man. No one here is your master."

Now this did elicit a response. "What the fuck is going on?" Bowdyn regarded the Viking with undisguised hostility and suspicion. "Why have you brought me here?"

"You are here at my wife's request." Mathios turned to extend his hand to Merewyn. "My Celt, your brother has arrived."

Unable to contain herself a moment longer, Merewyn leaped from the chair and rushed past Mathios to greet her brother. An expression of incredulity flickered across his features and she knew he recognised her instantly. Bowdyn had no opportunity to speak before she flung her arms about his waist and clung on. He settled for hugging her, then lifted her from her feet and swung her around.

CHAPTER SEVENTEEN

"Perhaps when you have finished hurling my wife about the settlement I might make proper introductions."

The exuberant pair ignored him so Mathios cleared his throat and tried again.

"This is a most touching reunion but I would also like to properly make the acquaintance of my new brother. Merewyn, if you might—"

She broke free and rushed at Mathios to grab him in a hug too. "Thank you, thank you, thank you. I know you said, you promised, but I never thought…"

He kissed her hair and did his best to extend his hand to Bowdyn. "My name is Mathios, Jarl of Agnartved. Merewyn, your sister, is now my wife."

The man took his hand, though the suspicion was back in his hooded brown eyes. The man shared Merewyn's dark hair, though his was cropped short. The family resemblance was unmistakeable, as was the undisguised hostility. Mathios was reminded of those early weeks with Merewyn.

"Come, we shall retire to my longhouse where we can speak more privately. Torsteinn, you will accompany us in order that we may complete the formalities." Mathios released Merewyn, who immediately linked her arm through that of her brother to steer him in the direction of their dwelling. Mathios hung back and walked beside Torsteinn. He would leave her to it. The Celtic thrall would have questions and she could answer them as well as he might. He was thankful when Rowena fell into step on his other side.

"Where are my sons?" he enquired. He would explain later but for now, whilst circumstances still appeared somewhat volatile, he would prefer them to be absent.

"With Sigrunn," murmured Rowena.

Satisfied, Mathios turned his attention to other matters. "You will have ale, I daresay, and of course we have food. You will need to find a sleeping space for him also, since he should share our longhouse while he is here."

"I believe I can manage that, Jarl." As they neared the Jarl's dwelling, Rowena summoned her house thralls and sent them scurrying in search of suitable refreshment. Meanwhile Mathios ushered his companions into his home and bade everyone be seated. Merewyn sat beside her brother, and Deva on the Celt's other side. He and Torsteinn sat on the opposite side of the table that ran down the middle of the hall. Rowena directed the servants and within moments they all had full drinking horns and a platter of breads and cheese was set before them. Mathios thanked his stepmother, who herded her thralls from the longhouse and closed the door behind them.

"I trust your journey here was not too arduous." Mathios pushed the plate of cheese toward Bowdyn. "Please, help yourself."

"I am not hungry."

Mathios accepted that, though he surmised the man must be thirsty as the horn was quickly emptied. Rowena had left the pitcher on the table and he reached to refill Bowdyn's drinking vessel.

"Have they harmed you? Our parents? Our home…?" Bowdyn turned to face his sister. "You say you are wed to this Viking, but how?"

"Mathios is not one of those who attacked us. He came to Northumbria a year after the raid in which you and Deva were taken."

"Another attempt to loot and pillage and destroy." His tone was flat.

"No, though at first I feared it was so. Mathios and his men were shipwrecked on our coast and sought shelter. They were stranded over the winter."

"What became of our parents?"

"They… they perished. Our father died during the raid, our mother some months later."

"So, you were left alone?"

"Yes. No… I… we have a brother. A baby brother. He is called Connell."

Bowdyn frowned. "Our father's name?"

"Yes, though the baby was sired by one of the Viking raiders. Our mother was… I mean they…"

Bowdyn took her hand. "I know how these Vikings treat captive females. I can well imagine how this came about. So, the child survived?"

"Yes. Connell is here, at Agnartved, and has been adopted into a Viking family. He is well cared for."

Bowdyn ignored Mathios as he held his sister's gaze. "And you, Merewyn? Are you well cared for?"

Mathios remained silent, waiting for his wife's response. He did not have to wait long.

"I am. Mathios is a good man. He loves me, and I love him. You have arrived amid our marriage celebrations but you should know we were wed before we left our home."

"Yes, you said as much. Am I to understand that you have truly wed this Viking by your own choice? After what they did to us? You know of their foul deeds, their violence, their vicious cruelty. Our family was slain, our mother raped. My brother and I were taken as slaves, yet still you marry this man…" Bowdyn sprang to his feet as though he would reach across the table and throttle Mathios with his bare hands.

Mathios held his ground, and gestured to Torsteinn to do likewise. "I understand your anger, your sense of loss, of injustice, but none of this is Merewyn's fault so you should not blame her. She is my wife, I love her and I will protect her. This is my house and I have welcomed you here so you will oblige me by taking your seat once more. We are a family, however unlikely that may seem, and however painful the circumstances which made it so."

Bowdyn glowered at Mathios under his lowered eyebrows for several long moments, then slowly sank back onto the bench. "My sister may accept you as her husband, but I never will."

Mathios hoped that would not always be so, but did not say as much. Instead he returned to the legal matters before them.

"I told you of my intention to free you. For this we will require Torsteinn to formally affirm that he relinquishes his right to you as his thrall and that he freely delivers you into my ownership. I will, in turn, declare you a free man. This will take place tomorrow, before the assembled karls and members of the Jarl who are present for our wedding. Thus our laws will be satisfied and no one will later challenge your status here. You will be free to remain at Agnartved, or to leave as you choose."

"Remain here? Why would I wish to remain here?"

"I understand, and as I have said you will be free to leave whenever you choose to. However, I know your sister, my wife, would appreciate your company, at least for a while."

"Merewyn will understand that I cannot stay. I have to find my brother. *Our* brother. Nyle is still a slave and I cannot—"

"I am aware of your brother's fate and I have instigated a search. I hope to be able to locate him."

"You… you have done that?" Beside him Merewyn gasped. "But I thought… I never imagined… How will you find Nyle?"

"Torsteinn was able to tell me where he was last seen, in

the slave market in Holvik, so I sent Olav to question the slave trader who sold your brother. If we are able to trace him I shall purchase Nyle and free him also."

"You would do that? Why?" Now it was Bowdyn who contemplated him, his features mirroring his confusion.

"For your sister, my wife. I cannot undo what was done at your farm, and I make no apology for the actions of others of my people. We are what we are, though I hope you will believe that neither I nor my warriors would have wreaked such destruction without cause. But I love Merewyn and I will do what I can to make this right. For her." He paused, contemplated those gathered about him for several moments, then directed his words at Bowdyn. "Your parents are gone, and for what it may be worth I do regret that. But you live still and I hope the same will be true of your brother. If so, you will see him again and you can both choose what to do next. You will have your lives back."

• • • • • • •

The rest of the evening passed in relative peace. Mathios returned to the feasting, received yet more hearty felicitations from those who had been too inebriated to offer their good wishes previously. Merewyn joined him for part of it, her surly brother in attendance. Bowdyn locked gazes with Mathios from time to time and seemed perhaps marginally less hostile though Mathios could not be certain. He supposed the man was entitled. He had no doubt whatsoever of his wife's jubilation though. She chattered without ceasing, delighted at the prospect of being reunited with her other brother also. Mathios hoped that would come to pass. Deva had been correct when she pointed out that a strong, able-bodied slave was a valuable commodity, but a belligerent thrall would not last long in most Viking settlements. He could only hope that the man had come to his senses and not provoked his masters unduly.

It was late by the time Mathios led his wife back to their longhouse. Bowdyn followed, though he appeared uncomfortable. Mathios was aware that the Celt had lived among the Norsemen long enough to know that a thrall's place was in a barn, or maybe the darkest corners of the roughest longhouses, with the animals. A thrall was generally considered to be little better than cattle and most certainly a slave did not accompany the Jarl to his home and sleep within those salubrious walls.

Well, mused Mathios, as he eyed his reluctant new brother, he'd better fucking well get used to it.

• • • • • • •

The legal formalities were concluded the following morning, before the assembled Jarls and karls. Mathios' actions clearly surprised more than a few of them, but they muttered and shrugged and returned to their drinking horns soon enough. Mathios gestured to the closest thrall and bid her bring them food and ale. When the refreshments were delivered, he handed a mug of foaming ale to his new brother.

"You will drink to my marriage?"

Bowdyn's snort of derision was answer enough.

"I see. Then to your freedom, and to the future?"

Bowdyn took the mug and raised it. "Aye, to the future." He took a long draught, as did Mathios. It was progress of a sort and would have to do. And at least this bloody feasting was nearing its end.

• • • • • • •

Three days had passed since the conclusion of the wedding celebrations. Their guests had departed and the settlement was returning to normal. Rowena fretted about their depleted food stores and urged Mathios to assemble a hunting party to replenish their supplies. Already their fishermen were at sea and the weather was kind so they would have food for their own needs and plenty with which to trade. Mathios welcomed the return to the usual routine, though he was sorry to say goodbye to Torsteinn.

His friend was among the last to leave but had promised to make a detour to visit Agnartved again on his return from the Byzantine a few months hence. Merewyn was delighted. She and Deva were firm friends. Bowdyn's view on the matter was less easy to discern. Although Torsteinn had been his master, Mathios detected a grudging respect between the pair. Perhaps they had arrived at an understanding after all, though that was more than could be said for his own efforts to make peace with Merewyn's taciturn brother.

The man stalked around the settlement exchanging a few words here and there. He had picked up sufficient of the Norse tongue during his years in captivity to be able to converse, but was short of people to talk to. The other thralls avoided him, and the karls of Agnartved were equally uncertain. Bowdyn was not one of them since he slept in the Jarl's longhouse and was brother to the Jarl's wife, yet neither was he of the Viking ruling class. There was nothing Mathios could do to assist Bowdyn; the Celt would have to find his own place here, or he would leave. At least as a free man the choice was his.

"You will hunt with us?" He issued the invitation to Bowdyn as they shared the *dagmal*. "The day looks fine, we should be able to take down a stag or perhaps a wild boar."

Rowena, Merewyn, and the two boys were also present. Petrus chirped in at once.

"I will come, Papa. I can ride my pony better than Galinn and I can spear a boar."

"You cannot!" Galinn was outraged by the slur and demonstrated his disgust with a punch to his brother's ribs. "I am the better rider, and I can lift a heavier sword that you can. Papa will take me, not you."

Mathios grinned. He had this argument every time a

hunting expedition was mentioned. "Neither of you is coming hunting. You are too small still. It is too dangerous."

Petrus was not giving up. "But Papa, we could—"

"No. And you, Galinn, will stop laying into your brother if you please. When you are both tall enough to sit a full-size mount we will discuss the matter again."

"That will not be long," observed Merewyn. "I swear you have both grown a hand's width in the time I have been here." She handed a mug of buttermilk to Petrus. "Here, let this aid you in your quest to grow big enough to hunt. And you too, Galinn, since however much you two may fight, you will go together or not at all. It is so with brothers. Bowdyn will tell you."

The Celt furrowed his brow, clearly displeased at being dragged into the family banter. However he did answer. "Aye. My brother and I fought incessantly all our lives, but we did everything together even so."

"You will miss him," observed Rowena, her voice soft.

"Aye, I do." Now he met Mathios' gaze. "When might we expect news from Holvik?"

"Soon, I hope, though it depends on whether my warriors had to journey far to locate the man who purchased your brother. They will return as soon as they are able, and we will consider whatever news they bring." He paused. "So, you will join us for the hunt? I understand you are good with horses and I have a mount which might suit you."

Bowdyn shrugged. Mathios took that as assent.

•••••••

The day went well. Bowdyn turned out to be a skilled horseman and an asset to their party, which would aid him in becoming accepted. Vikings respected strength and skill, and neither did it hurt that he had the stamina of two men and was willing to do his share of the work when it came to hoisting the stag they brought down onto a pole and hauling it back to Agnartved. It was a raucously jubilant band of hunters who made their triumphant way back as dusk fell.

Olav was waiting for them at the stables. Mathios dismounted, flung the reins to a lad hovering close by, and clapped his comrade on the shoulder.

"It is good to see you, my friend. Do you have news for me?"

"I do, Jarl, though not the news you hoped for."

Mathios' heart sank. He did not relish the prospect of informing Merewyn and Bowdyn that their brother had perished before he could be rescued. "The man, Nyle, is he dead?"

Olav shrugged. "I cannot be sure. The news was not promising at first. We found the trader Nikulas Njallson…"

"Mathios! I saw Olav return. What news is there?" Merewyn came running across the hard-packed earth underfoot, her skirt flying in the wind. She had rushed out of the longhouse without her cloak but seem oblivious to the stiffening breeze.

Mathios removed his own cloak and wrapped it around her. "We were just coming to that. Shall we get inside where it is warm and we shall all hear the report? Rowena…" He beckoned over his stepmother who had followed Merewyn at a more sedate pace. "Perhaps you could supervise the storage of our fine stag, ready for butchering when it is light again."

"Of course." She hastened off to instruct her thralls.

Meanwhile Bowdyn had returned his mount to the stables and now approached them. He took in his sister's agitated demeanour at a glance. "There is news?"

"Yes." Mathios tilted his head in the direction of the newly returned Viking. "This is Olav, my warrior who I sent to Holvik. Let us all return to the longhouse where we shall hear his account."

"Nikulas Njallson did not at first recall a slave by the name of Nyle, but he did remember the incident when a Celt struck a guard. Apparently, your brother took exception to being prodded with the butt of a whip and grabbed the implement intending to use it on the guard. He was overpowered, naturally, and spent a few nights in the keeping pit where Njallson imagined he might learn better manners. Seemingly it did not work as the man was no less aggressive when he was brought up from the pit to be sold to Arkyn Arkynson."

"Keeping pit? What is this?" Merewyn grasped Mathios' arm. "How would it teach my brother manners?"

"The keeping pit is a large hole, perhaps six or seven paces wide and equally long, and maybe ten feet in depth, with a cover over the top to keep out the light and prevent escape. The cover is usually weighed down with rocks for good measure. Troublesome thralls and other criminals are imprisoned in the pit to await whatever fate is considered appropriate." Mathios turned to Olav. "A few days, you say?"

"Aye. He was hungry when he was pulled out, and thirsty too, though there was apparently an underground stream which kept the place damp and cold but also provided a few drops to drink. The Celt came out fighting but was subdued again, this time by his new owner."

"Yes. Arkynson. I know of this Jarl. His settlement is to the south."

Olav nodded. "We went to Arkynsund in search of the Jarl. We were fortunate to encounter him just as he was about to embark on a Viking expedition to the western coast of Scotland. However, the thrall Nyle was no longer with him."

"He was sold again?"

"No, Jarl. He escaped."

"Escaped! By Odin's balls, this we did not need." Mathios was well aware that an escaped thrall was a fugitive, reviled by all Norsemen. The man he sought would be in hiding, legitimate prey to any who came across him. Nyle would find little in the way of aid and his fate was unlikely to be a good one. He would either be killed by other Norsemen or perish in the inhospitable terrain with neither shelter nor food to sustain him. "How long has he been on the run?"

"Only two weeks, Jarl. We were given to understand that Arkynson purchased him to work as an oarsman, and the Celt survived three arduous voyages aboard his master's dragon ships. It appears he did not much fancy a fourth, and when an opportunity presented itself in the form of a drunken guard he slipped away. Arkynson sent men after him, but though they found tracks they soon lost the trail. He is gone."

"Two weeks. He could be anywhere. Did Arkynson post a reward?"

"He did, and it has not been claimed so we can assume that the slave has not been found, whether alive or dead."

"How much?"

"Twenty silver pennies, Jarl."

"I shall double that, for information or the return of this slave. Send word out to the other settlements, especially those between here and Arkynsund, and up to fifty miles south of Arkynsund also."

Olav rose to do the Jarl's bidding. "Is there anything else, Jarl?"

"No, I—"

"Yes!" Bowdyn had listened intently. Now he rose to his feet also. "We must find him. I am not prepared to sit here and wait for news. Where is this place, Arkynsund? I shall go there and—"

"No, it is not safe." Merewyn spoke quietly but still managed to make herself heard. "You run the risk of being mistaken for a runaway thrall yourself, despite the pronouncements made at our wedding. I could not bear to lose you too, not now."

"I must try to find Nyle. Surely you see that."

"I do, but…"

"Where would he go?" Mathios silenced the rest by raising his own voice above the babble. Bowdyn and Merewyn turned to regard him. Mathios fixed his gaze on

Bowdyn. "You are his twin. You know him better than anyone. If you were in his situation, what would you do once you had escaped? Where would you head for?"

"I am not sure. He does not know this land, and…" Bowdyn paused, then grinned widely. "He would make for a port. He would want to return home, so would need to find passage somehow on a ship. So, he would stay close to the coast and seek out a port where he might contrive to get aboard a vessel of some sort."

That made sense. Mathios nodded. "Olav, when you have sent out word of the reward you will assemble another party of men, fresh ones this time. We shall call at every port, harbour, and coastal village from here to Arkynsund to make sure they know that I will pay handsomely for any information, better still anyone who can return this thrall to me unharmed." He turned to face Bowdyn. "You will come with us. Your brother is your twin, yes? Identical to you?"

"He is, though he may not have a beard now."

"We cannot know that, but whether he does or not I am hoping the similarity is striking enough that someone having seen you may recognise him. Do you think it is so?"

"Yes, it would be so," agreed Bowdyn.

"Then you shall go with us. Olav, how soon could we leave? I do not wish to miss our quarry if he does manage to scramble aboard some fishing ship."

"First light, Jarl."

"Very well. I shall see you by the stables at dawn."

CHAPTER EIGHTEEN

"Six weeks. It has been six weeks since Nyle was last seen. How can he survive on his own for so long?" Merewyn lay beside Mathios, the bedclothes pulled up to her chin to keep out the chill. Mathios tossed another log on the small fire in the pit in their sleeping quarters. Merewyn knew that would be enough to warm the space within a few minutes, but her missing brother could call upon no such comfort.

"We must be patient, my Celt. And remember your brother is a resourceful man, and not one who gives in easily. He survived three outings as an oars slave so I have every confidence he can take care of himself."

"Are you quite certain that no one had seen him? In any of the places you visited?"

"Yes. No one has any reason to conceal him, and my reward is more than generous. Thanks to Bowdyn he is now likely to be recognised if he does show up anywhere. We must wait. And hope." Mathios joined her in the bed.

Merewyn shifted along to make room for him, then snuggled up against his hard, warm torso. She adored the sensation of her naked breasts pressed up close to his chest, the soft mounds flattened against his muscled body. Of late, however, her breasts had been tender to the touch and she shifted a little, less comfortable that usual. Mathios rolled her onto her back then propped himself above her.

"Is something wrong, Merewyn?"

"No, Jarl. I am concerned for my brother, that is all."

"There is more. You flinch from me. See?" He cupped her breast in his hand and though his touch was gentle, she tensed. "Tell me what ails you, sweetheart."

"Nothing, I swear. I am well, and—"

"When are your courses due?"

"My…? Jarl, what is that to you?" Her husband was always sympathetic during her monthly courses, but never saw fit to engage her in conversation about them.

"Think. When did you last bleed?"

"A month ago, of course."

"Are you certain? That would have been the week of our marriage and I do not recall the inconvenience occurring then."

"Well, after that, perhaps…"

He shook his head. "No, not since our wedding. In fact, I am reasonably certain that you have not bled since those final days before we left your home in Northumbria. I do remember that quite clearly as it convinced me that you were not pregnant at that stage. I would not have left you otherwise."

"That is impossible. That would mean…"

"Almost two months. I suspect the matter is settled."

She lay in silence as the awesome truth sank in. "No, I cannot be…"

"You can. Indeed, it would be a surprise if you were not, either now or in the near future. It is the natural outcome, is it not?"

"I thought, maybe the stress of the voyage, and my horrible sickness whilst we were at sea. The wedding, and Bowdyn and… and…"

"Time will tell, and I am confident I shall be proved right. We are to have a child, my Celt." He grinned at her as though the accomplishment was his alone. "A brother or sister for my boys. I hope for a sister if that can be arranged."

"I do not believe we would have any choice in the matter."

"No, that is my understanding too." His features became serious and he caressed her tender breast again. "Are you in any discomfort?"

She considered this for a few moments then shook her head. "Not exactly. I am tender, but if you are gentle…"

"When am I not?"

Often enough, she could retort, though usually she found his rough lovemaking entirely to her taste. Mathios was a demanding, exciting lover. It had been so from the start and she had always responded to the dominance in his touch but now she craved a more muted and tranquil approach. It was as though he read her mind when he leaned down to take her stiff, hard nipple in his mouth. He pressed it with his tongue, then flicked the end as he hollowed his cheeks to create just enough suction to…

"Aaagh!"

He released her at once when she groaned. "Did I hurt you?"

"No. It just feels so intense."

He applied his mouth to her other nipple and elicited the identical response.

"Do you prefer to stop? If you are tired…?"

"I am tired, but… no. Do not stop. Please."

Mathios made his way slowly but surely down her body, tracing a row of kisses between her breasts and across her stomach. He paused at her belly button to dip his tongue into the small hollow and Merewyn imagined a time in the months to come when her belly would swell and he would no longer find her attractive. Men often preferred to stay away from their wives in the later stages of pregnancy, or so she had heard. She had no experience of her own to draw upon. She would miss him, she decided. She would miss him very much indeed.

He resumed his journey, trailing more kisses over her mound, combing his fingers through the soft curls at the apex of her thighs then using his hands to gently part her legs.

"Do you think we should? I mean, what if it harms the baby?" Mere minutes earlier she had been blissfully unaware that the tiny being even existed, and now she fretted about its wellbeing.

"I will do our baby no harm, I swear. Indeed, there are those who insist that the pleasure to be found in our bed is good for the growing child. I promise to do all I may to ensure she—or he—benefits from my attentions."

"But… oh!" Her protests were stifled when he took her engorged clitty between his lips and sucked on that as he had her nipples. No bothersome tenderness assailed her now as she thrust her pelvis up to press her pleasure nub against his teeth. She gasped as her arousal curled within, right at her very core where the baby now nestled. Her womb clenched, her inner channel convulsed then tightened around his exploring fingers. First one, then two, he drove them inside her but with aching gentleness.

"Harder," she muttered. "Harder and deeper."

"My greedy Celtish slut," he murmured against her inner thigh. "So demanding. Has pregnancy made a harlot of you?"

Has it indeed? Merewyn wondered if it might be so as she squirmed and writhed and bucked her hips as she sought her release. The sensations deepened, seemed to find focus at her centre, at the spot where he continued to suck and flick, working his clever tongue down one side of her clitty then the other, then curling it around the very tip.

Merewyn rocked from side to side as she chased the pleasure that dangled and danced just out of reach. One moment she had it, the next it cavorted away again. She tangled her fingers in his hair and gripped him tight as she at last soared.

"Oh! Oh! *Oh!*" she yelled, remembering too late the rest of the household slumbering beyond the curtain. But it was too late now, and she was past caring when her senses at last shattered and she found herself spinning, weightless, whirling like a leaf in autumn.

He entered her slowly, as her release still pulsed through her, while her muscles were liquid and her body boneless. She sighed, her contentment absolute. Where on previous occasions he might have drawn her knees up to her ears and pounded her with his thick, wide cock, this time each stroke was long and slow, an inner caress as gentle as the fluttering of angels' wings. Merewyn arched her back and reached for his shoulders. She dug her fingers into his solid flesh and clung on as a second release rushed to consume her. She contracted her internal walls as though she wished to grip him and hold him inside her for ever, as though she might prevent him from ever leaving her.

The warm wetness of his semen filled her, a sudden flush of inner heat, then another, and another. Merewyn imagined she was melting inside. Perhaps she truly was, perhaps it felt different, now.

Yes, that must be it. Everything seemed different now.

• • • • • • •

Rowena was delighted at their news, Bowdyn less so.

He scowled across the table at her over *dagmal*. Just the two of them remained in the longhouse as Mathios had departed early on a trading visit to a nearby settlement and was not expected back until the afternoon. Rowena was watching the boys at their swordplay practice with Olav.

"You will not wish to return to our home then, with Nyle and me? Not once you have a child here."

Merewyn gaped at him. It had never occurred to her that she might return to Northumbria without Mathios, or, indeed, that anyone would think such a thing.

"Mathios is my husband, I would never leave him. My

home is here now, though Mathios has said we might return to visit if you choose to go back. I… I hope we would be welcome. Both of us."

Her brother's noncommittal snort was less than encouraging, but even that could not dim Merewyn's happiness. She was to have a child. Her own child. And she would not be called upon to do so alone. She would have Rowena beside her, and Sigrunn. And Mathios, naturally. Perhaps even her elder brother, if he remained with them long enough and could quell his distaste for all things Viking. She understood his bitterness, but felt it was misplaced when directed against Mathios or any of the Vikings at Agnartved.

Childbirth was a perilous undertaking for women, she had no illusions about that. But she was surrounded by experienced women who would aid her. If she remained in good health, and of course if she offered up sufficient prayers to the Holy Virgin, then perhaps fate would deal kindly with her. She would hold on to that hope as the months progressed.

It was mid-afternoon, as Merewyn worked on her loom beside the open door of the longhouse, that she heard the rumble of wheels bumping over the hard-packed earth outside. She peered out of the dwelling to see who was here.

She did not recognise the tall Viking woman who drove the cart, which had by now rolled to a halt in the cleared area in front of their longhouse. Certainly, the woman was not from Agnartved. Since neither Rowena nor Sigrunn were anywhere to be seen, Merewyn left her weaving to greet the visitor and enquire as to what might have brought her to their village.

Her Norse was improved but far from perfect. She practised the phrases in her head as she hurried toward the wagon, which she now noted was covered with a length of sack cloth.

"Good day. Welcome to Agnartved. What is your business here?"

The newcomer narrowed her eyes and looked past Merewyn to the now empty longhouse.

"I am here to see the Jarl. Mathios Agnarsson." She tipped up her chin and regarded Merewyn haughtily. "You will summon him."

I will…? Merewyn allowed herself a private smile. The Norsewoman had mistaken her for a thrall. Clearly her dark hair and eyes marked her as not of Viking descent.

"Mathios… my husband," she could not resist adding, "is not here today. May I be of assistance?"

"Husband?" The woman glared at her, then raised one elegant blonde eyebrow. "I see. That may explain his interest in this man." She strode around to the back of her cart. "I am here to claim my reward. Twenty silver pennies, I understand, for the safe return of this thrall." She flung back the hessian cover to reveal the prone body lying within. "I suggest you restrain him before he regains his senses. He can be quite… unmanageable."

"Nyle!" Merewyn gripped the edge of the wagon and peered over the side at the large man who lay motionless before her. He was face down so she could not see his features. She did not need to. Tears streamed across her cheeks as she dropped to her knees murmuring her gratitude to any deity within earshot.

"Are you quite well?" The haughty Norsewoman appeared concerned now. She bent to take Merewyn's arm and help her to her feet. "Perhaps we should summon your husband's men…"

"No, that will not be necessary," Merewyn managed. "I think…" She broke off when she spotted Rowena hurrying in their direction. "This is my stepmother, she will aid me. We must get him from the wagon and into the longhouse."

"I cannot recommend it. I am sure that your husband will have a place where he secures thralls and other prisoners. Perhaps—"

"He is not a prisoner. He is my brother." She waited, allowed that fact to penetrate, then, "Now if you will assist us, I would be most grateful. Then you shall have your money."

"Is this true?" Rowena ignored the Norsewoman. She scrutinised the prone figure. "Is it truly your brother? Should we not turn him over to make sure?"

"It is true. This is Nyle." Merewyn hailed a hovering slave. "Please, run and find Bowdyn and bid him return to the longhouse at once." She gnawed on her lip as she contemplated the task before them. "Perhaps if we each grasp a leg and pull…"

They had succeeded in dragging Nyle halfway off the wagon by the time Bowdyn arrived and took over. The Celt had tears in his eyes and was grinning from ear to ear as he hauled his brother over his shoulder and made for the longhouse. Once inside he deposited the man on the closest pallet, which happened to be his own. Now that Nyle was face up they could all clearly see the large bruise on his forehead.

"What happened to him?" demanded Merewyn, already rushing across the room in search of a cloth and clean water with which to bathe the wound.

The Norsewoman tipped up her chin. "I told you, he is not a biddable man, not in the slightest. I had no choice but to subdue him in order to bring him here."

Bowdyn glared at her. "So you hit him? Knocked him unconscious?"

The woman returned his furious scowl, quite uncowed by Bowdyn's hostility. "It seemed the only way. I am sure he will recover his senses soon enough, such as they are. See, he is already stirring…"

It was true. Nyle let out a loud groan and rolled onto his side. Rowena crouched beside him. "You are safe now. Your sister is here, and your brother…"

She scuttled back to make room as Merewyn took her place and applied a damp cloth to the lump on his head. Nyle groaned again and attempted to shove her hand away.

"See, I did tell you…"

Rowena rose and faced the visitor. "I do not believe we have met. I am Rowena, stepmother to Mathios Agnarsson. And you have met Merewyn, the Jarl's wife."

"And I am Bowdyn, brother to the man you have almost done to death in your zeal to subdue him."

The woman wisely withdrew a pace before the glowering figure of the angry Celt. "Yes, I saw you, at Ravnklif. You spoke with my husband, Baldvin Ryggiason. I am Kristin Lofnsdottir."

"I do not remember you. In truth, I do not recall your husband either."

"He owned the trading fleet which sails from Ravnklif. Seven ships in all."

"Owned?"

"He died, three days ago."

Bowdyn said nothing. It fell to Rowena to express their condolences. Meanwhile Nyle was recovering his senses fast and seeking to get up from the pallet. It took the combined efforts of Bowdyn and Merewyn to keep him lying down, and then only long enough for her to finish bathing his head. Nyle struggled to sit upright, then gingerly tested the bruise on his forehead.

"Fuck, that hurts. What did that woman hit me with? A mallet?"

"It was an earthenware cooking pot, in fact. It broke." Kristin may be outnumbered but her pride and dignity remained undaunted as she positioned herself at the foot of the pallet. "Now, if I might have my silver pennies I shall be on my way and bother you no further."

"Yes, of course. My husband promised it and you have brought my brother home, so—"

"What the fuck is going on here? Merewyn? Is it you?" Nyle shook his head from side to side as though trying to clear some fogginess from his memory. "And Bowdyn? How is this possible?"

"Please, you should rest…" Merewyn began.

"I shall rest when I am dead, though I am amazed to find

that has not already come to pass. Or perhaps it has. Perhaps you are all apparitions conjured up to escort me to the afterlife, whatever that might amount to in this godforsaken land."

Bowdyn crouched beside the pallet and peered into his brother's features, identical to his own. "We are all real, and you are not dead, my brother. Look around you. I am here, Bowdyn, and our sister too. We are in a Viking longhouse, the dwelling of our sister's husband. He is the Jarl of this settlement…"

"Husband? Viking? Now I am convinced we have all descended into madness. Fuck off and allow me to die in peace." He closed his eyes and slumped back against the pillow that Merewyn had shoved under his shoulders.

"Nyle! Wake up. Please…" Merewyn clutched at his arm and shook it but to no avail.

"Let him rest. That is what he needs, and food as soon as he awakens." Rowena put her arm about Merewyn's shoulders. "The main thing, the thing which matters most, is that he is here with us and safe. The rest may wait."

"I cannot wait." Kristin stepped forward again. "I wish to be about my business so I will trouble you for the money I am entitled to, then I will leave you to your tender reunion."

Kristin stiffened her spine and managed to ignore Bowdyn's angry glower, though Merewyn could not fathom where she gained her fortitude from. But the woman was quite correct. Even if she had found it necessary to knock Nyle senseless in order to fulfil the terms of Mathios' offer, she had met those terms. She had brought Nyle to them and she was entitled to her twenty silver pennies. In Mathios' absence, Merewyn would have to pay it from her bride-price. "If you will excuse me for a few moments, I shall get your money for you."

She hurried into the sleeping quarters she shared with Mathios, and where they both kept their most personal or valuable items. The chest that had once contained her mother's herbs now housed the coins that made up her bride-price. Merewyn kept it wedged behind their pallet and concealed beneath clothing. She uncovered it and opened the lid.

Merewyn was unfamiliar with Viking coins, or indeed any coins. Trade, when transacted at all at the farm, had always been in kind. A few eggs in exchange for a fish, grain in exchange for linen or herbs. She could count out twenty coins but did not know their value. Were these the pennies mentioned, or some other coin worth more? Or less? She was quite certain that Kristin Lofnsdottir would point out soon enough if the payment was insufficient. Merewyn counted first ten, then another ten coins and slipped them into a small linen bag before returning to the main hall.

"Here, your money." She handed the bag of coins to Kristin. "I thank you for your assistance in returning my brother to us. I know you have business to attend to, but if you have the time to remain and eat with us you will be welcome."

"I…"

Merewyn was convinced the woman intended to decline her invitation, and probably would have if Bowdyn had not chosen that moment to mutter something that sounded suspiciously like 'good riddance.'

Kristin's smile was wicked and Merewyn detected a distinct gleam in her azure eyes. "Why, thank you. I believe my business elsewhere may wait. I would be glad to share your meal."

"Excellent. Please be seated and take some refreshment now." Rowena took over the demands of hospitality, leaving Merewyn free to hover over her brother. "And perhaps Bowdyn could make himself useful by seeing to the safe stabling of your horse."

He shook his head. "I am not—"

Rowena stifled his protests with one of her most beatific smiles. "Yes, and then you could inform Sigrunn that we have guests for the *nattmal* and we would be delighted if she would join us. Oh, and she is to bring young Connell with her in order that he might meet his other brother." She ushered him toward the door. "Ah, yes, this is quite the homecoming. I wonder if we have any of that salted pork still…?"

CHAPTER NINETEEN

Mathios gazed about him, and wondered quite how he had managed to fill his longhouse with such a disparate bunch of people. Even more odd, they were all kin to him in some way or other.

Merewyn sat to his right, brimming with happiness. For that fact alone Mathios was prepared to endure the bizarre company in which he found himself. Beside her sat Nyle, the brother who Mathios had yet to come to know. He had almost fallen over the man when he returned from trading with his closest neighbour, Holmr, Jarl of Hraniborg. No introduction had been necessary; the man asleep on a pallet on the floor of his hall was identical to Bowdyn apart from the fact that he was clean shaven and his dark brown hair was cropped short. Mathios now knew that Nyle was possessed of a dry sense of humour also, another trait that set him apart from his brother. And his appetite was second to none. He had already consumed two bowls of Rowena's chicken broth and was asking for a third.

Opposite Nyle, Bowdyn ate with considerably less gusto, clearly brooding about something. When was he ever not? Mathios picked up the pitcher of ale that stood on the table. "Your horn is empty, my friend. Allow me…"

Bowdyn managed a curt nod of acknowledgement and abandoned his food in favour of cradling the drinking horn in his hands. It was clear he did not wish to be engaged in conversation so Mathios let him be.

Next to Bowdyn sat Sigrunn, with Connell balanced upon her knee. Despite his dark and brooding demeanour, Bowdyn could not help but smile at the attempts of the small boy to manage his own spoon. It was fortunate that Rowena had made plenty of broth for much of it did not find its way to Connell's ever-open mouth. Not for the first time Mathios had cause to be grateful to his stepmother for her artful handling of the most awkward situations. It was an inspired move to invite Sigrunn, Arne, and their adopted son to help alleviate the tension.

On the other side of Sigrunn, and opposite Arne, sat the source of the somewhat strained atmosphere. Kristin Lofnsdottir was a fine-looking woman, a fact not lost on either of the Celtic males at his table if Mathios did not miss his guess. But whilst Nyle treated the Viking female with his own brand of wry mockery, Bowdyn appeared to dislike her intensely and missed no opportunity to make that plain.

He had cause, of a sort. Kristin had brained Nyle with an earthenware jug if Mathios had understood the sequence of events correctly, but the Celt's skull was hard enough and no lasting damage seemed to have been done. And her scheme had worked. Nyle was here, delivered safe and more or less well. All in all, they could do without Bowdyn's antipathy.

Rowena was seated next to Kristin and made valiant efforts to engage the Viking woman in conversation.

"So, you are very recently widowed, we understand. Yet still you have found the time to bring Nyle to us. We are most grateful."

"It was nothing."

Rowena waved that away. "You must be grieving, and by aiding us you have allowed us to intrude upon your sorrow."

"Not in the slightest."

Bowdyn let out one of his characteristic snorts. "You mean to tell us you are not grieving in the slightest?"

Trust Bowdyn to arrive at the least sympathetic interpretation of the woman's words. Mathios sought to soothe matters. "Our guest means that we are not intruding in the slightest. Is that not so, Kristin?"

She flashed him a quick smile and gave an elegant little shrug. "Both interpretations are accurate, Jarl."

Ah. Right. Mathios cleared his throat and tried again. "How did your husband die, if the story is not too painful to share?"

"He died of a seizure, brought on, I suspect, by…" she glanced at the two small blond boys seated opposite her, on Rowena's right side, "… overexertion."

"I see." *So old Baldvin Ryggiason met his end whilst fucking?* Mathios vaguely remembered the man from his visit to Ravnklif when he and Bowdyn had laid the trail intended to find Nyle. Baldvin must have been sixty years old if he was a day and of a decidedly portly build. He could easily envisage the scene. What Mathios did not so readily understand was what a lovely young woman like Kristin Lofnsdottir was doing married to such an individual. He supposed it was a matter of business as much as anything, most marriages between Vikings of the Jarl were, though that rather undermined the theory that Baldvin had perished in the throes of passion. He was curious to learn more.

"I expect you had not been married long, given the difference in your ages."

"Less than two years, Jarl. I was Baldvin Ryggiason's fourth wife."

"It must have been a shock," observed Rowena. "Did he just… collapse?"

"I do not know the exact details. I was not present."

"I see. Then, how…?"

"My husband had many… friends. I believe he was in the company of a young man when he was taken ill."

Nyle had just taken a rather large mouthful of broth and was seized with a fit of violent coughing as he tried to dislodge the lump of chicken stuck in his windpipe. Merewyn thumped his back whilst the rest of those present gaped at Kristin in stunned silence. Even the children, who had not been privy to the underlying meaning of Kristin's words, observed a nervous quiet. Rowena was the first to remember her manners.

"A shocking end, no doubt, but mercifully swift. Has the funeral taken place already?"

"It has. My husband enjoyed a most glorious farewell, though I must regret the loss of one of our finest ships for the purpose. Still, that is now my stepson's problem rather than mine. I intend to use the twenty silver pennies that the Jarl was generous enough to provide to fund the purchase of another vessel, and I shall endeavour to continue to travel and trade for I find I have an aptitude for it."

Satisfied that Nyle was not, after all, on the point of choking to death, Merewyn resumed her seat and rejoined the conversation. "Do you not have sufficient ships already at your disposal, even with one used as a funeral pyre? Did you not say your husband owned seven ships in all?"

"I did say that. However the entire fleet is now the property of Eigil Baldvinson, my husband's eldest son. There are other half-siblings also, but none are to inherit anything. All my husband's wealth is now Eigil's and he has made it plain enough that I need not anticipate any aid from him. I confess I was somewhat at a loss regarding my future as I had no wealth of my own when I married, then when I encountered the missing Celtic thrall sniffing about our boats, I recalled the mention of a reward and decided I could make good use of the funds."

"So you clobbered me over the head and threw me onto a rickety old cart?" Nyle managed a glower to rival that of Bowdyn.

"Had I not done so, I doubt you would have agreed to accompany me. Further, you were behaving in a manner which could only be described as dishonourable. You deserved a clout to the head."

To Mathios' surprise, Nyle seemed not to wish to challenge this accusation. He shrugged and muttered something about not being blamed for trying.

Kristin's view of the matter was less sanguine. She pointed her small eating dagger at the unrepentant Celt and narrowed her eyes. "A thrall may not lay hands on a Viking female, not ever. The penalty is death and you knew that. However, tempting though it was to see you justly punished, I have no use for a corpse. You were worth twenty silver pennies to me alive and I would never turn my face away from a decent trading opportunity."

Mathios made a decent attempt at a straight face, and might have succeeded had he not caught sight of Merewyn's struggles to stifle her own mirth. He surrendered and in moments the entire table was laughing uproariously, even the bemused children. He thought afterwards that even Bowdyn managed to crack a smile, though he could not swear to it. When he was sufficiently in control once more, Mathios grinned at his unusual guest.

"Kristin Lofnsdottir, I believe we all find your company most entertaining. Am I to understand that your circumstances in your late husband's home have become difficult since his unfortunate passing?"

"I believe they would be described as strained, Jarl, yes."

"In that case, and if you would find it more convenient for your future plans, I would like to extend a welcome for you to use Agnartved as the base for your trading expeditions. I am sure you will find our harbour and jetty suitable, and we have boat builders here if you should wish to construct your own vessel. The twenty pennies may not suffice, but—"

"But if you require more funds I would be happy to loan you what is required." Merewyn turned to Mathios. "I do have enough, do I not? In my bride-price?"

Mathios smiled at her, genuinely pleased if somewhat

taken aback. "Certainly you do, my love, and it would be a shrewd investment. You and Kristin would make a fine partnership."

"I believe so too," Merewyn agreed, turning to face Kristin on the other side of the table, "provided you are willing to enter into an arrangement with a Celt."

The blonde Viking woman contemplated the dark-haired Celt for a few moments, then smiled. She extended her hand. "I am, and I believe we shall do very well together, lady."

EPILOGUE

One year later…

"Galinn, run and find your stepmother and bid her come to the harbour. Tell her that her brothers have returned." Mathios watched his son scamper off in search of Merewyn, then he turned to shield his eyes from the sun as he watched the approach of the knarr bearing his Celtic brothers and their enigmatic Viking partner.

With a hull wider, deeper, and shorter than his own dragon ships that were constructed for war, the knarr built by Ivar and Ywan to Kristin's exact specifications was more suited to exploration and the carrying of cargo. It required a crew of just seven or eight and yet could manage lengthy voyages. On this the new vessel's maiden voyage, they had travelled first to England and then it had been their intention to go on to continental Europe in search of new trade routes. Mathios wondered what they would bring back with them and he looked forward to the profit he—or rather Merewyn—might make.

His wife's footsteps could be heard approaching. He went to meet her, and to take the squirming bundle from her arms.

"Was Rowena not about that you had to carry our daughter all the way down here?" He drew back the fine wool blanket to reveal the tiny face he loved with a ferocity he had not believed possible. Perhaps it was because he was away when they were born and thus missed their earliest weeks, but Mathios did not recall being overwhelmed by such intensity of love for his boys, though he adored them now. A man should not have favourites among his children, he knew, but surely such decrees did not take account of this little scrap of pure sweetness who now gurgled up at him. He lifted her and kissed her smooth forehead.

"Come, little Ronat. You are to meet your uncles, provided of course that Kristin has not become truly exasperated and tossed the pair of them overboard."

"She would not do that," insisted Merewyn. "She likes them."

"Are you sure?" During the months that all three had spent in Agnartved whilst their boat was being built, Mathios had seen little evidence to support such an assertion. "Kristin and Nyle might manage a passing tolerance for each other, but Bowdyn…"

"She likes them," repeated his determined little wife. "I know she does, deep down."

Mathios decided to let it go. Perhaps the enforced proximity aboard the knarr would have necessitated a softening of attitudes. Time would tell. "I wonder what cargo they are bringing."

"Kristin told me she was seeking silver, or perhaps glass. She is also interested in wines and spices. I hope for some silk."

"We shall know soon enough. Come, we can wait for them on the jetty."

Mathios cradled baby Ronat in one arm, named for her Celtic grandmother, and the other arm rested across his wife's shoulders. His infant daughter had come squalling into the world four and a half months previously and he had been smitten from the first moment he laid eyes upon her.

He hoped for more children, though he would never say so. Ronat was healthy and thriving, and Merewyn had encountered no real difficulties either. They could not rely on it always being so. Childbirth was an uncertain undertaking for women, and he had already lost one wife to the capricious fates of procreation. He could not bear the thought of losing Merewyn in similar fashion but ultimately such matters were in the laps of the gods.

"I wonder if they managed to sell the farm. Or failing that, find a tenant."

He glanced down at her. "Will you miss it, if it is no longer yours?"

"It was never mine, not really."

"For a while I think it was."

"That was not a happy time. I would not wish to go back there now. If my brothers had decided to return, to grow crops there and make it our family home again, then perhaps…"

"I was as astonished as you when they opted to throw in their lot with Kristin. I was even more amazed that she agreed to it."

"It is as I said, she likes them. If they have been successful at making any wealth from the sale of our land, they will be able to build more ships, bigger ships perhaps, travel further. I know that is what they want, and Kristin too. They are well matched."

Not the description he might have applied, but Mathios did not comment. He heaved a relieved sigh as the knarr drew close enough for him to make out the features of those on board. Nyle, Bowdyn, and Kristin stood together at the prow of the vessel, the tall Viking woman between the two even taller Celts. They made a fine sight, and if he was not mistaken he could perhaps detect an intimacy about them. It was almost as though…

No, what a ridiculous notion! He dismissed it from his mind.

"They love each other."

What? Mathios locked eyes with his diminutive wife,

who did not back down. *When did she ever?* "What do you mean?"

"They love each other. As we do, except, there are three of them."

"You do not mean…? It is impossible. How might they…?"

He fell silent when his wife arched one elegant mahogany-hued brow at him. *Why not?* He was thinking exactly the same thing.

"We need not speak of it, but it is there." She leaned up on the tips of her toes to kiss his mouth. "You are staring, my husband. Have I grown a wart on the side of my nose?"

"You Celts are odd beings. Have I not always said it was so?"

"And you Vikings are much too sure of yourselves by far. Too inclined to believe that you are in charge and the world is yours for the taking." She smiled up at him, her delight and anticipation shining in her eyes. "Now, let me take Ronat whilst you assist the men in mooring the knarr. I look forward to learning how this first voyage has gone."

THE END

STORMY NIGHT PUBLICATIONS WOULD LIKE TO THANK YOU FOR YOUR INTEREST IN OUR BOOKS.

If you liked this book (or even if you didn't), we would really appreciate you leaving a review on the site where you purchased it. Reviews provide useful feedback for us and for our authors, and this feedback (both positive comments and constructive criticism) allows us to work even harder to make sure we provide the content our customers want to read.

If you would like to check out more books from Stormy Night Publications, if you want to learn more about our company, or if you would like to join our mailing list, please visit our website at:

www.stormynightpublications.com

Made in the USA
Middletown, DE
24 March 2020

87153979R00133